Pretend

A novel
Fine Line Series– Book 1

It's easier than the truth.

Jennifer Conklin

Cover Designed By: Aaron Trudell
Publishing Assistance/Editing By: Tempered Ink

Font Designer Creatype Studio, "Porcelain," 2019, via creatypestudio.co
Font Designer Impallari, "Kaushan Script," 2011, via impallari.com
Font Designer Khurasan, "Tahu!,"2020, via creativefabria.com
Illustrator Vlad Marko, "NYC Skyline Silhouette Vector," 2019, via istockphoto.com
Photographer: Clix Photography, Author photo, 2022
Photographer Katarzyna Bialasiewicz, "Girl with MD," 2016, via istockphoto.com

Author/Publisher: Conklin, Jennifer
First Edition: August 2023
Printed in the USA

jenniferconklinauthor.com
happydetours.com

ISBN: 979-8-9889850-0-6 (pbk)
ISBN: 979-8-9889850-1-3 (ebk)

To my mom.
Who always let me vent, rant, and rattle off stories to her...
LITERALLY for hours at a time,
and then said she loved every minute of it!
(Heart eyes!!)

Table of Contents

CHAPTER 1
What will I...

Kyle Whitmore

THERE WAS SO much blood. I wasn't even sure she was alive as I stood there frozen. Finding her took some time after I got to the park. It was an unusually muggy June night in New York City, and the streets were pitch dark. I could feel pressure on my chest. But was it from the summer heat or frantically searching for my brother's girlfriend?

The buzzing neighborhood and honking cars almost drowned out her small whimper as I approached the washrooms. I found her body slumped behind the building near a tree, scarlet streaking down her face. Hesitantly, I pushed tangled hair away as I called her name.

"Robin?" I asked quietly. When she didn't respond, panic welled inside me. I gently shook her as I repeated her name louder, "Robbie!"

As she groaned, I allowed myself a huge breath. Her pretty teenage features glanced up at me weakly. "Kyle." I helped her up, and we stumbled to the passenger side of my car. I buckled her in before running to the driver's seat. As I turned on the motor, she grabbed my hand.

"No hospital," she said. I looked at her in surprise.

"You need a doctor." I tried to keep my voice firm.

She tightened her grip. "Just get me to your house."

"Robin, you *need* to see a doctor," my tone grew desperate as she unbuckled. I gingerly moved her arm, careful of injuries, and guided the seatbelt back into place.

"Please don't take me to the hospital, Kyle. I'm begging you."

"Why?"

"I'm asking you to trust me," she whispered. Her intense stare had me swallowing dryly, the pain behind her eyes made my stomach hurt. I reached across and wiped the blood dripping from her nose, trying to make the right choice. Tears streamed down her cheeks, and I shifted the car into drive. I headed for my house, outside the city, against my better judgment.

My home. It was a depressing shade of beige with a black door. Very functional. No frills. The single-car garage was also plain and uninviting. Mom usually kept her vehicle there while the one I shared with my older brother Shane stayed in the driveway. The front entrance on the left was set back with a little covered porch and concrete stairs. Mom has a potted plant on the steps that I always forget to water, and it has already begun to wilt from the heat. Despite the place being drab, our yard bordered lush and beautiful green woods. The trees gave the illusion that our backyard was bigger than it was and provided privacy from the busy main road.

I snapped out of my driving trance as we arrived. The hour-and-a-half route had seemed eternal, but she slept on and off during the ride. Any bump on the highway roused her with a moan of pain, making me question my decision to bring her home. Once inside, she sat soundlessly on the couch while I gathered first-aid supplies.

The silence of the room prickled my skin. My heart pounded faster as I cleaned her face. Earlier, I realized she was bleeding from her nose and mouth, but now I saw the cut above her left eye, too. The pronounced swelling made her flinch every time I touched her, elevating my stress even more.

"Thank you," she muttered. "For not taking me to the hospital."

"I really think you should go."

"I'll be fine. I just need to rest for a few days. Is it okay if I crash here?"

"Of course, you can. But I—"

"I said no, Kyle," she winced.

I shook my head, dissatisfied. "Where does it hurt?"

"My ribs, mostly. They're bruised or maybe fractured. I'm not sure," she said calmly. However, I was reeling from this information. I never knew she could be this stubborn, I thought as my anger flared.

"We need. To go. To the Hospital." I was at my breaking point. Why had I even humored her this long?

"I'm not going! They can't do anything about broken ribs, and they'll heal. Eventually. They just need time."

"How do you know that? Have you injured them before?"

"Yeah, but it was a car accident. And they healed. On their own. With time," her tone snide.

"So, how did you hurt them tonight?" I asked cautiously, but she fell silent. Instead, she laid her head back on the couch, still holding the ice pack to her eye. Her lack of response made the hair on my arms stand. I thought of asking if she wanted to go upstairs to lie down in Shane's room, but I quickly dismissed the idea, unsure if she could make it up the stairs even with my help.

Shane is my older brother. They had been dating for around six months before he left for Portugal with Mom a couple of weeks ago. Shane got this huge opportunity to attend a soccer camp there, and they would be gone for the whole summer. Shane aspired to play professional soccer, or fútbol as they say in Europe, after graduation, so he couldn't pass this up.

Mom took advantage of transferring her work to the Lisbon office, always wanting to travel, and this was her chance. She asked me to watch everything here at home while they were away, and I was excited to have the summer to myself. Mom still had a neighbor check in on me every few days, even though I'm already seventeen, but other than that, I was free to do as I pleased.

Until Robbie called.

Robbie moved to town after winter break and was the new girl at our high school. She made an impression on anyone she met, being very pretty with a tomboy personality. Robin was kind and intelligent but guarded and reserved. I would also say she had an edge, but where it came from, I wasn't sure.

We didn't have classes together when she moved here, as she was a junior like Shane, and I was only a sophomore. She seemed nice, and she caught Shane's eye straight away. His quick wit, charm, and captain status easily won her over. I got to know her more as she would hang out at our house or go to Shane's games. I remember this one time when she–

"Kyle…" her voice startled me out of my thoughts.

"Yeah. I'm here." I blurted.

"I get you want to know what happened tonight so thank you for trusting me blindly. I know it doesn't feel right not knowing but I appreciate your patience."

"You're welcome, I think."

"And now I need a promise."

"A promise?"

"I am exhausted, and I need sleep. Promise me that while I'm sleeping, you won't call 911, the police, Shane, or your mom."

"But—"

"Please, Kyle. If you promise me this, I'll tell you everything." I stared at her, contemplating how to answer. "Promise me, Kyle!"

Her demand shook me from my trance.

"Okay. I promise," I answered hastily.

But did I mean what I said? I wanted to keep my vow and be a good friend, but I knew something terrible had happened, and she was in trouble. Plus, I had no idea if the person who did this was still looking for her or why she refused to get help.

This situation is so messed up, and I'm not sure I should be making stupid promises right now. What would Shane do?

What will I do?

Robin "Robbie" Fanning

Feeling somewhat reassured he wouldn't call the police or his family; I laid my head on the couch and closed my eyes. I tasted iron in my mouth, thick and heavy. Only a few hours ago, I was fighting for my life and had to get away from him fast. I sprinted out of the house, unsure of which way to go from the blood dripping in front of my view. I stumbled through dark alleys toward the park as my ribs screamed.

I stopped to catch my breath and looked down at myself. Under the dim streetlights, there was crimson everywhere. I wasn't quite sure what was mine and what was his. Tired from running and with my vision clouding, I needed to find a safer place to sit and rest. I saw the washrooms at the park and ran over to them, slinging myself behind a tree to remain covered by the shadows. I landed in a heap on the ground.

"Aagghh…" I winced in pain.

I scooted myself gingerly against the oak tree, taking a moment to assess the damage. I couldn't lift my arm without distress because of the throbbing in my ribs. I hoped they were only bruised, but I knew it was probably worse. My swelling left eye made it harder to see as the cut bled profusely.

I felt queasy and thought I might lose consciousness. I had to act quickly if I was leaving the city tonight. I reached for my phone in my back pocket, which I had hung onto with the tightest death grip while he...

Spots appeared in front of my eyes, and I knew it wouldn't be long before I passed out. I scanned my contacts and saw Kyle's name. I wanted to call my boyfriend, but Shane is overseas with his mother. He followed this huge opportunity to play soccer and would be gone the whole summer. Which didn't seem so long when he left two weeks ago, but now... I needed him.

Kyle would have to do.

I dialed his number. The phone only rang twice, but it seemed like forever.

"Robbie?" he asked, surprised.

"Kyle. I… um… need your help. I got hurt. Can you pick me up?"

"What happened? Where are you?" His tone alarmed.

"I'm in the city near the washrooms at Betsy Head Park. The corner of Strauss and Livonia. Can you come get me?"

"Yeah, but why are you in the city?"

"Please, Kyle. Can you get me or not?"

"Yeah. I'm leaving right now, but it's an hour-and-a-half drive without traffic. Are you safe?"

"Yes."

"Okay. Stay there. I'll be there as fast as I can."

Once I heard he was on his way, I hung up. I turned the phone off and tried to take out the battery. When I couldn't, I reached for a rock and smashed it to pieces. I stuffed the shards into my front right pocket, no evidence left behind.

Knowing Kyle would be here soon, I laid my head against the tree and closed my eyes. It must be well after nine o'clock since it was dark already. The air was thick and warm, and I felt myself fade.

Kyle is Shane's younger brother; we became friends when I started dating Shane. He was friendly and always seemed levelheaded, even though he would only be a junior this coming year. Shane and Kyle were born twelve months apart and similar in build. Both were tall, athletic, and very handsome. The girls at school went crazy, called them 'The Whitmore Twins' because of how close they were. It wasn't often that I saw a brother without a girl tagging along after one of them.

That's why when I arrived in mid-January, I was surprised Shane showed interest in me. He was this soccer phenomenon and the high school's only hope for notoriety in the area. He was on track to go professional and was treated like royalty. I assumed he wouldn't be interested in me since I'm not into sports. Well, organized sports, anyway. Not that I could get involved with him. He wasn't part of the plan.

I hated being the center of attention, and he was smack dabbed in the middle. I prefer to keep it low-key and simple, including my wardrobe: jeans, T-shirts, hoodies, and sneakers. Literally, every day. I don't like dressing up, not that I had anything formal to wear, or anywhere I could wear it. I was average height, lean, and I liked to run. It was something I could do alone. A quiet moment with myself to think, to escape. Shane also ran to maintain his speed, endurance, and stamina for soccer. And that's how it started. Running together. Being quiet and focused together.

I guess he was interested in different. Not flashy or high-maintenance or chasing him. In fact, I rebuffed him many, many times. But he wore me down, and I finally relented. I keep him at arm's length because I can't risk him getting to know the real me. My only goals were to stay under the radar, finish school, and graduate. Not getting involved with someone.

Then I went and messed up the plan again tonight. I was careless and got hurt. Now, I needed help and had to rely on someone else. On Kyle. I already struggled with trusting others; Shane included. Not that Shane wouldn't understand, but because he's not part of the plan. Also unplanned was my promise to tell Kyle everything. I'm not sure if I should make stupid promises right now. What should I do?

What will I do?

CHAPTER 2
And if...

Kyle

AS SHE LAID back again on the couch to rest, I moved over to the recliner next to the sofa. I sat there watching her sleep, contemplating what I should do next. I promised her I wouldn't call the police, but every fiber of my being screamed at me that I should. The urge to call my mom was strong. I almost wished she would contact me right then, deciding for me. Mom would know how to convince Robbie to get help since she wouldn't listen to me.

The sound of her voice repeating my name had me leaping out of the chair.

"I'm here," I said, startled.

"I'm sorry. I didn't mean to scare you."

"I must've dozed off."

"You didn't call anyone?" She asked, slowly attempting to sit upright.

"No," I said regretfully. I did exactly as she requested. Stupidly.

Relief washed over her face. "Thank you for keeping your promise. I really appreciate it. And I'll keep mine, too. I'll tell you everything soon."

"Okay, sure," I replied, still feeling conflicted. I leaned her head forward so she could drink the water placed beside her. She took a long sip, almost finishing the bottle in one go.

"You don't seem very comfortable and didn't sleep very long. Do you want to try going upstairs to lie down? I can help," I asked.

"That's probably a good idea. Although with all the pain, I doubt I'll be comfortable lying anywhere." The unease of my decision not to get her help flooded my mind again.

I moved a chair to the bedside once she was settled in Shane's room. I slouched, trying to find a restful position to fit my tall frame. As exhaustion took over our bodies, my mind still fired off doubts.

Was I doing the right thing?

Robbie

A heavy breath lingered beside me as I tried to open my eyes. It was hard to see with my left side swollen shut. As I lay awkwardly, I adjusted my body to get a better look. But as I moved, everything hurt, like screaming bloody murder hurt. That's when I realized I had made a sound. A loud, painful sound. It startled me to hear his low voice. I gathered my bearings, forgetting where I was.

"Robin? You, okay?"

"Yeah, I'm fine. I'm sorry. I didn't mean to wake you," I said groggily.

"It's okay. Did you sleep? Like at all?"

"I did. Ish. You?" I quipped.

"Sure. Ish," he returned the playful mood as we flashed each other a smile. "I'll grab us water and get you more ibuprofen. Be right back." And in a flash, he vanished from the room.

It gave me a minute to regroup. I reached up to wipe my watery eyes, recoiling from the pain of lifting my arm. My ribs throbbed. Fractured? Broken? At this point, it didn't matter. They hurt. And I couldn't move my left arm without major distress. Well, that's great. This revelation will upset him. I shook my head at the growing complexity of the whole situation and dreaded the inevitable question from Kyle at any moment: what happened?

When Kyle returned, he thought to bring me ice. I was so grateful, holding it to my swollen face. He sat in the chair and quietly sipped his water.

"You don't have to babysit me. I'm just going back to sleep after I finish my water. You should get some rest too. In your bed, because I know that chair can't be comfortable," I said.

"I'm good. I want to make sure you don't need anything."

"Kyle, you're next door. I can holler if I need you. So please get some rest in your own bed. I feel bad enough as it is for ruining your night."

"You didn't ruin my night," he said earnestly.

"Well, I'm sure it's not what you had planned."

"No, but I wouldn't say my night was ruined. Instead, I guess I would say that my night has been… surprising."

"Surprising?"

"Yeah. I guess that's the right word because I was surprised when you called me, surprised by all the… blood, and surprised you didn't want real help."

"And now?"

"Honestly?" he asked, looking at me for my answer. I nodded.

"Scared."

We sat there looking at each other silently. I knew what he meant because that's how I was feeling too. Scared that I had put Kyle in danger. Scared that my injuries would need real medical attention. Scared that I had to tell him what had happened.

"I am sorry about that." Grateful for Kyle's understanding.

He nodded and pulled up my covers. "I'm right next door."

I smiled at him as he left the room.

I lay there in the dark, trying to figure out what I should say to him when he finally wanted answers. I had promised, and he had been very patient with me, but that wouldn't last forever. As I drifted off to sleep, questions weighed heavily on my mind. What do I tell him? How much do I tell him?

And should I tell him who?

Kyle

I stood in the hall for what seemed like an hour. Just listening to her breathe. I could tell she was in a lot of pain but was trying not to show it. I remember doing the same thing two summers ago when I totally thrashed my bike and flew over the handlebars. I had road rash everywhere. My mom was so upset. I put on a brave face whenever she was around so she wouldn't worry as much.

Robin was doing that right now. I could tell. And what makes it worse is that I can't take her to the hospital to be checked out properly. I promised her. Why did I agree? I had no idea how many injuries she really had or if there was something worse like internal bleeding or broken bones or…

Ugh, I needed rest. If she needs anything, then I need to be fully recharged.

I reluctantly went into my room but left our bedroom doors open. I didn't even bother changing my clothes, flopping onto the bed. That was the last thing I remembered.

***

I woke to screams coming from Robin's room and flew up and out of the covers, running toward her.

"Robin!" I yelled. That's when I realized she was asleep and having a bad dream. I shook her gently, waking her up. I pushed the hair out of her face as she looked up at me with tears streaming down her cheeks. As a small sob escaped her lips, I held her in my arms and let her cry.

"I'm sorry," she said after her sobs slowed.

"There's nothing to apologize for. You were having a nightmare. It's out of your control."

"I know, but I'm still sorry—" she protested.

"No apologies. I don't understand the full story yet, but I can guess. I want to help. Please let me?"

"Well, I'm still sorr… I mean, I didn't mean to scare you again. I'm fine now; go back to your room and get some sleep."

"Oh, I'm not leaving. I'm staying right here. In this chair. And I'll hold your hand so that *you* can sleep."

"Kyle—" she started to protest.

"I'm telling. Not asking." She saw my resolve and relented.

I helped her readjust in bed, making her as comfortable as possible. I slid the chair back over, taking her hand in mine. She looked exhausted, defeated, and sad. My stomach turned. Whatever happened in her nightmare frightened her. Her wild eyes and guttural screams completely unnerved me.

I know she promised to tell me everything, but a tiny part of me didn't want to know either. I could see the damage he did to her on the outside, but what kind of toll was it taking on the inside? I'm trying to be strong for her, but I'm terrified, and the urge to call the police overwhelms me. Would Shane have handled this better if he were here instead?

I kept eye contact until she finally gave up, shutting her eyes. Her breathing slowed, becoming steadier and rhythmic. I scooted closer to the bed and laid my head on the edge, still holding her hand. At least I know I can do this. Hold her hand to keep the nightmares away. As for tomorrow? I had no idea what I should do tomorrow. Do I keep my promise, or do I break it?

And if I break my promise, will that break her?

CHAPTER 3

No...

Robbie

WHEN I WOKE up, I saw Kyle lying on the edge of the bed, holding my hand. He had kept the nightmares away, and I was grateful. I spotted a sliver of light peering through the bedroom window, but I wasn't sure what time it was. His loud snoring made me chuckle under my breath because he was in such a deep sleep, but I was glad. I tried to be still so he could rest longer. He couldn't be comfortable hunched on the side of the mattress.

"Hey," he said groggily.

"Hey. I didn't mean to wake you."

"I wasn't really sleeping."

"Well, your snoring would say otherwise." I snickered.

He grinned as he rubbed his neck. "Did you sleep too?"

"I did. Finally. Thank you for keeping the bad dreams away."

"You're welcome."

"So... I have a favor to ask," my voice trembled with trepidation.

"Sure. Anything."

"Can you help me to the bathroom? I'm desperate," I asked, embarrassed about the circumstance.

"Of course," he said, unaffected by my bodily functions. Kyle carefully helped me swing my legs over the side of the bed, giving me a minute to get used to being upright. He held onto me as I shuffled slowly to the bathroom so I wouldn't lose my balance. He hesitated at the doorway.

"I'll be okay on my own," I said quickly.

He slowly let me go. "Okay. I'll wait in the hall." I felt sheepish but, at the same time… thankful. "Hey, don't lock it in case you need me. Er, I mean, in case you need something."

I nodded and shut the door. I went straight to the toilet, my problem now an emergency. It took some finagling to get my pants down with one hand, but I did it. The bathroom was dark except for the light coming in through the small skylight, but I could still see without the overhead light on.

The room was functional. Beige, much like the entire house. No frills or colors except for the tray of vibrant makeup and perfumes in the vanity's corner. Kirstie had placed them there after I started dating Shane, so I could use them whenever I wanted. I felt bad that she went to all that trouble for me since I never wore the stuff.

When I finished, I tugged up my pants slowly, but the twisting motion made my ribs burn. I went over to the sink, flicking on the mirror lights. That's when I saw myself in the mirror. I gasped. Out loud. Louder than I expected.

Kyle immediately knocked on the door.

"Are you okay? Do you need me to come in?" he asked, alarmed.

"No, I'm fine," I answered abruptly.

I was transfixed by what I saw in the mirror.

My left eye was so inflamed that it completely closed shut and my mouth swollen. There was dried blood all over my face. My hair matted within my injuries, clumping together wildly. I looked like I had gone five rounds in a boxing ring. I was taken aback at how everything looked distorted. So, foreign. I knew it had to look bad, but I had no idea. To think this is what Kyle had been looking at since he brought me here. No wonder he hovered like a hawk.

Kyle knocked again. "Robin? Are you okay?"

"Yes," I said, quickly turning the water on and letting it run. "I'm washing my face." I hoped the noise would distract him.

"Can I come in?"

"I'm okay, really," I reassured.

"Still, can I?"

"Do you not believe me?"

"I do," he stuttered. "But I would feel better if I could… check on you."

I sighed with resignation. "Okay."

He opened the door so quickly that it made me jump. Kyle had a set of towels and a washcloth that he placed beside the sink. He immediately grabbed the cloth and wet it with warm water. Holding my chin, he moved my face toward him as he washed off the dried blood.

He was so focused, careful, and gentle. I looked into his eyes, tired but kind. His eyes. They reminded me of someone, but I couldn't put my finger on it right at that moment. He was being patient with me. Not pressuring me for details or pushing me to talk. What do I tell him when he finally asks? Because he is going to ask. Eventually. Can I lie to him?

Convincingly?

Kyle

I tried to be as gentle as possible, washing the dried blood off her face. It caked on her skin. Even though I knew it didn't feel great, she stayed still. The swelling and the bruises were more pronounced and looked painful.

Suddenly, she winced. "I'm sorry. I didn't mean to hurt you."

"You're not."

"I know you can't really use your arm, so I…"

"I appreciate the help," she answered softly. Just then, her stomach growled. She glanced up at me, embarrassed.

"I should have asked if you were hungry. Are you? Of course, you are. That's a stupid question," I rambled.

"I'm fine. You don't have to get anything."

"I'll make something because I'm starving too. What do you like? Well, I only know how to make a few things. So, it has to be one of those."

"And what meals are those?" Robin asked curiously.

"Well, I can make sandwiches. Wait, we don't have bread. I ran out the other day. I can cook spaghetti. Nope, scratch that. No sauce. I can make buttered noodles if you want or bacon and eggs."

"I'll take bacon and eggs. I've always loved bacon. It reminds me of… home."

"Okay. Done. I'll help you back to bed and bring it up."

"You do not have to do that."

"I know. I want to. Plus, it's for me too." I said honestly.

She smiled at me as I took her arm. Once she was back in bed, I rushed downstairs to start the food. I found some orange juice and took the last glass and some ibuprofen up to her room. She had her eyes closed, so I quietly left them on her nightstand.

As I headed out of the room, I looked back at her. She seemed peaceful now, but I couldn't shake the feeling that she was fighting a war… one I still knew nothing about.

And I was afraid.

Robbie

The smell of bacon roused me from my slumber. I've always loved the smell. It brought me back to Mom making breakfast on Saturday mornings. We couldn't afford bacon more than once a week, so it became our special treat. Our time to bond amidst the chaos.

My mother. How I loved her. A free spirit, unlike me in every way, even as a child. She sucked at adulting. Struggled with making schedules, keeping appointments, and managing daily life. Having a flighty and carefree mother was fun for a while. But always taking care of her wore on me. I knew I was her number one priority, so I settled for that. But when she met him…

"Breakfast is served." Kyle bounded into the room with a plate full of food. I smiled at the façade that everything was normal.

"Wow! It looks delicious. I didn't realize I was hungry until I smelled it all."

"Well, dig in. I hope that's enough because I'd like to say there was more downstairs, but I ate all the extras. Apparently, I really was starving. Sorry."

I chuckled. "It's fine." I took a big bite of bacon. He grinned at me, and suddenly, I knew who his eyes reminded me of… my mother. His eyes were kind, expressive, and so deep. Just like hers.

"How's the food?" His question interrupted my thoughts.

"Sooo… good. I was hungrier than I thought. You're a great cook," I mumbled with a mouthful. He grinned again as we emptied our plates.

While Kyle cleaned up downstairs, I sat on the side of the bed, my stomach fully satisfied. I hadn't realized how hungry I was or how much better I would feel once I ate. Then, I made the mistake of looking down at what I wore: dirty, ripped, and bloody.

My thoughts flashed to what happened, and immediately panic rose inside, as the memories of him hitting me flooded back. Between gasps of air, I knew I needed to wash away this nightmare. I needed to wash away reminders of him. But I had another problem to deal with.

No clothes.

CHAPTER 4

... I'd believe it too.

Kyle

SHE HAD EATEN everything on her plate as I rinsed the dishes in the kitchen sink. Robbie looking rested made me smile. I had kept the nightmares away long enough for her to sleep. I had been so scared and questioned my promise to her all night, but she seemed to have turned the corner.

As I reached the top of the stairs, I heard an odd sound coming from her room. When I entered, she sat on the side of the bed, extremely pale and hyperventilating. I rushed over and had her tilt her head.

"What happened?" I shouted above her gasps. "I'm calling 911," I said, reaching for my phone. She grabbed my arm and looked at me with wild eyes. I pulled my hand out of my pocket and tried to match my breathing with hers to help slow it down. I didn't know what I was doing, but I had to do something. She kept me locked in her gaze as we breathed in and out. Eventually, her breath normalized, and she could speak.

"Thank you."

"What happened?" I asked through an exasperated sigh.

"I don't know," she said with pain in her voice. "I think I was having a little panic attack."

"A little attack? I was freaking out, Robbie," I raised my voice.

"You didn't seem like you were freaking out."

"Well, I was. You scared me to death. Something is wrong, Robbie. We need to go to the hospital," I growled.

"I told you, no hospitals!"

"Why? Why can't we go to the hospital? Tell me, Robbie," I begged.

"Please, Kyle. I can't. I'm not ready to talk. Please."

I took a calming breath. "Robbie… we need help. Like, professional help."

"I'm feeling better. Really, I am."

"For now. But what if it happens again?"

"It won't. I just panicked when I saw the dried blood and dirt all over my clothes. It made me think about… but I'm fine now. And I'll feel better after I take a shower."

"Robbie, what we should do is—"

"Please, Kyle."

I rolled my eyes. What we should be doing is going to the hospital. But instead of saying that, I felt myself giving in to her again. A small, traitorous word escaped my lips.

"Okay."

Robbie

I felt terrible for avoiding the conversation again, but what I said was true. I needed a shower. I wanted to wash away all the hurt, pain, and memories.

"So, I have a minor problem," I started.

"What's that?" asked Kyle.

"I don't have any extra clothes. Can I borrow some? A pair of shorts and a T-shirt will work."

"Yeah, sure." He dug through his brother's dresser. "Shane doesn't really have anything here. He packed most of it. I'll go see if I have something," he said as he bolted out of the room.

I sat on the side of the bed waiting; every nerve in my body screamed in pain. Showering would not be easy, but I've already upset Kyle. I needed to show him I could do this on my own. I stood up quickly, for the first time without his aid, and wobbled. As I lost my balance, Kyle appeared out of nowhere, catching me.

"Whoa. I've got you."

"Thank you," I relented. We slowly made our way to the bathroom. As I was about to shut the door, he stopped it with his hand.

"Leave it unlocked. You're still unsteady, and I don't want you to fall."

"Okay," I answered, feeling a bit embarrassed at the thought of him having to come in to help me. The old hinges squeaked loudly while closing. When it snapped shut, I took a huge breath. I glanced in the mirror but turned away quickly. It's easier to pretend it hadn't happened if I don't have to look.

My ribs burned as I tried to undress, and my body ached everywhere. Having one functioning arm proved to be a harder challenge than I had expected. I pushed past the pain, biting my tongue with each twist to stifle my screams. I huffed in frustration when I realized this wouldn't work, and I had to abandon my hopes of showering. I jumped, hearing Kyle knocking.

"You alright? I don't hear the water running," he yelled through the door.

"Just a minute," I yelled back.

"Okay."

I got dressed, basically just pulling my pants back up. The pain was excruciating. I ground my teeth to muffle my sounds of anguish. As I opened the bathroom door, I blurted, "I decided I don't need a shower after all."

"Wait, what? Why?" he asked.

"I'm suddenly tired. I need to lay down again," I lied.

"Robbie, what's going on? Because a few minutes ago, you had to shower immediately, and now you don't want one?"

"Yeah. I changed my mind."

"What's going on?"

"I told you. I'm really tired," I said, frustrated.

"That's not the real reason. Tell me."

"I can't."

"Why?" he asked, mirroring my tone.

"Because I can't take my clothes off! Okay? I can't use my arm, and everything on my body hurts so much it makes me want to scream. So, I can't shower!" Tears pooled in the corner of my eyes. He stared at me in shock, but then his expression turned. Seeing him look at me like that, I felt helpless and defeated. "It's fine. I'll wash up a bit in the sink and—"

"I can help you undress. If you want," he interrupted, quickly clearing his throat. "I won't look. I promise."

His offer shocked me. "It's...uh... not just taking my clothes off. I can't lift my arms to wash my hair or body..." I trailed off.

His eyes darted side to side while a single breath quickened. "I can help you in the shower too." He cleared his throat again. "I'll wear swim trunks."

My mouth fell agape.

Unable to speak for the longest time, rumblings bubbling deep below the surface. My breathing hitched, "I uh... I mean... you don't have to do that," my mouth quivered at the exact moment tears streaked down my cheeks.

"It's okay," he said as he pulled me close. "It'll be okay."

I sobbed out, "Kyle..."

"Shhh… I'm here. I'm here," he comforted. I stood crying in his embrace as the flood of emotions I had kept in check until now erupted from me. I couldn't stop them. Sob after rolling sob tumbled from my lips. But he held me tighter.

My voice cracked, "I need a shower, Kyle. I need it! I have to wash this nightmare off me." When he stepped back from me, I could see his tear-stained shirt. He tilted my head up, wiping my cheeks with his thumbs. He looked at me with an unnerving intensity.

"Okay. Then that's what we'll do." I blinked hard, trying to see him through the tears. "I'll go get my swim trunks on and… and you'll leave your underwear on. Like a bikini. Okay?" I nodded. "Do you trust me, Robbie?" Trust. This wasn't something I did often or took very lightly. With anyone. But in that moment, I answered with swift confidence.

"Yes."

Kyle

I headed to my room, rifling through my dresser for swimwear. Anger swelled inside me, and I felt myself wanting to act on it. What did he do to her? The question repeated in my mind. I seethed at the thought of getting my hands on whoever he was because I wanted to strangle him.

I grabbed the first pair of trunks I found, putting them on as fast as possible. I didn't want to lose my nerve. The reality of what I had offered made my face flush. I can do this. It's just like the beach. Swim trunks. Bikinis. No problem. But there was a problem. It's not the beach. This is my brother's girlfriend, and I'm about to shower with her.

I shook the thoughts from my head. I'm helping her. He would understand.

I scoffed at that thought. Who was I kidding? No, he wouldn't. He would totally smash my face first and ask questions later.

My heart raced thinking about the shower, but the pain of her sobs as I held her sealed my resolve. It became clear that the damage on the outside was nothing compared to the hurt on the inside. I returned to the bathroom, seeing her standing there vulnerably. My neck burned, a flush creeping up my face with heat again. My nerves getting the best of me, I swallowed hard.

"Are you... still okay with this?" I asked slowly.

"Are you?" she questioned.

"Yes," I answered quickly, so I'd believe it too.

CHAPTER 5

So, how do we...

Robbie

HE WAS SERIOUS about helping me. I should be embarrassed, but I didn't feel that way. Like, at all. I wanted this shower. The memories scourged my soul and body, and I needed to wash it all away. And if I were being honest, I wanted to wash my entire old life away. And it started with this shower.

I needed to start healing, so I could get stronger. Shift my focus. The plan could no longer exclusively be about graduating and leaving. It had to be about 'him' now. I would never let him hurt me again. Ever.

"How do we do this?" I asked.

"Umm… I guess we start with your jeans and go from there," he stuttered.

"Okay. I think I can get them off on my own." I started to pull them down but immediately let out a grunt. He jumped in to help right away. As he did, his hand brushed my front pocket.

"What's this?" he questioned.

"Nothing." I tried to block his hand, but it was too late. He pulled out the smashed-up pieces of my phone.

"Who did this?"

"I did," I quickly replied.

"Why?"

"Because they can track it. If the battery is still inside, they can track it. Even if it's off. I couldn't get the battery out, so I smashed the whole damn thing."

"And you know this how?" he asked, perplexed.

"I don't know. I just do."

He noticed my irritation and dropped the subject. He threw the pieces into the small garbage can under the sink. I was relieved that it was finally gone. With his help, I wriggled out of my pants and watched as he placed them on the sink. Kyle's face was already beet red as I stood in my undies and blood-stained T-shirt. If he's this embarrassed now, wait till we're in the shower.

"How do you want me to remove your shirt? I mean, what will be the easiest, least painful way for you?"

"I guess we could cut it. That would probably be the easiest," I answered.

His eyes widened. "Okay." He reached into the drawer of the vanity and found a pair of small scissors that seemed sharp. Hopefully.

"I'll start on the left side since you can't lift that arm." As he cut, I heard the blades tugging through the material. He stepped behind me, pulling the cloth away from my body. I suddenly heard him gasp. "Robbie…" he spoke faintly. And I knew why. He saw it. The bruises. The scars. The new and the old. All my pain on full display. Now… I was embarrassed.

I could hear him take a deep breath before he continued. Stepping around to face me, Kyle tried to look me in the eyes, but I didn't want to see his pity. So, I looked away. It would crush me, and I hated feeling helpless. He quietly pulled off the rest of my shirt.

With my head still turned, I spoke, "Please keep the pants and shirt together. I need to put them in a plastic bag after the shower." His gaze bore a hole through me. I tried not to look at him, but my head involuntarily turned toward him anyway. What I saw in his eyes wasn't pity.

It was tenderness.

Kyle

Heat rose off me from the weight of her words, but I did everything in my power so she wouldn't see. As she had asked, I carefully placed her clothes on the sink, stepping into the shower to turn it on. My head spun from what I had seen... and heard.

There were so many bruises. More than I realized. Old scars littered her back as if they had been there a while. Images seared into my brain. This wasn't the first time she had been hurt or in pain. It turned my stomach.

I distracted myself by checking the water temperature and grabbing shower toiletries. Hanging our towels on the hook near the glass shower door, I felt my cheeks flush again. "You ready?"

"Mm-hmm," she nodded. I helped her into the shower and stepped in after. Facing me, she tilted her head back, letting the warm stream wash over her. I watched as the water loosened dried blood, streaking down her skin in a pinkish hue. I wasn't sure what she needed me to do, so I followed her cues. I trained my eyes on her face, knowing her underwear wouldn't hide much.

She opened her eyes and gave me a little smile. I smiled back.

"How can I help?" I asked nervously.

"If you could wash my hair, that would help." She turned around for me to lather up the soap. Her hair sat just below her shoulders. Not too long or short. It was honey-blonde for the most part, with dirty-blonde streaks on the underside. Considering the dried blood, it still felt soft to the touch.

As she faced me again, I pumped soap onto a washcloth and handed it to her. She gently cleaned her swollen face, moving down her neck to her body. I tried with every ounce of my willpower not to follow her hand as she washed her stomach, but it didn't work. When I finally peeled my eyes away, her gaze locked on mine. I blushed hard, but she didn't call me out on it.

"Could you wash my back and legs? It's way too painful to bend and reach," she asked shyly.

"Um… yeah. Sure." As she turned, I placed her hair to rest over her shoulder. The injuries were shocking. Some bruises merged into one giant discoloration, my soul seething as I gently touched her. I carefully scrubbed her bruise-covered back, bending on a knee to clean her legs. She turned around so I could reach her feet, lifting each foot for me to wash as I kept my eyes down. As I moved higher, my breath hitched.

I chastised my betraying body. Without meaning to, my eyes had darted to her wet beige underwear. I glanced away, trying to slow my breathing while thinking of anything other than this shower or her body. A difficult task. I closed my eyes as I stood, not opening them until safely face-to-face.

"I'm done. Thanks," she murmured.

I reached for my towel first, wrapping it quickly around my waist before getting hers. Carefully, I put the towel around her shoulders and helped her out of the shower. I was about to ask if she needed help to get dressed when I realized I had dropped them in Shane's room when she almost fell out of bed.

"Shit. I forgot your stuff. I'll be right back."

I ran to my room as if my life depended on it. Which it kind of did because I needed to get away from her and that shower. I quickly dressed, then grabbed the clothes I had dropped earlier near Shane's bed. As I picked them up, I scolded myself for not controlling my hormones. I had promised I wouldn't look and asked her if she trusted me.

And then, I broke that trust.

Robbie

As I stood alone in the bathroom shivering, my underwear soaked, and my hair dripping wet, I felt… relief. Not embarrassed, considering I took a shower with a boy. Not just any boy. My boyfriend's brother. Shane would be pissed regardless of the circumstances.

Kyle was gentle, and sharing such an intimate space, it was hard not to look at each other. He tried to be as respectful as possible, and I really appreciated it. I have asked so much of him since I got here, and he has helped me every single time. Without hesitation.

Although Shane and Kyle look different in many ways, they are similar in others. They're both very thoughtful, caring, and kind. I can credit Kirstie with that, raising them without any help. The brothers are tall, with similar jawlines, athletic, and muscular. Shane has dark hair with blue eyes, and Kyle has dirty-blond hair with hazel eyes. Shane looks like his mother since they have similar coloration, but Kyle must take after his dad.

Well, I assume that he did. Their dad left when he found out Kirstie was pregnant again so quickly after Shane. They haven't heard from him since. It was a sore subject. I never asked Shane anymore about it, and he never brought it up.

Kyle rushed in with a pile of clothes. "I wasn't sure what would work best. So, I brought a few things." I went through my choices, picking out shorts with a drawstring that I could tie, and grabbed a zippered hoodie. "I thought the hoodie might be the easiest to put on. You wouldn't have to lift your arm, and we can slide it on that side first," he reasoned.

"Yeah. It'll work perfectly. Thanks," I said, smiling. He had really thought about this.

He grinned back. "I guess we should get your shorts on first."

"Actually… I have another huge favor." I asked, a bit embarrassed again.

"What's the favor?"

"Could you, um… could you help me take my underwear off before I get dressed?" I spat out the words. His eyes went wide, mouth falling open. "I know. I'm sorry. I'm needy with all these uncomfortable requests. It's just that I, um… I mean, I need to, um…"

He took my hand, helping to stop rambling. "Robbie, you don't have to explain. I'll help you." I nodded.

"So, how do we do this part?"

CHAPTER 6

... I was.

Kyle

MY HEART POUNDED. I knew I said I would help, but now she'd be completely naked. Shane would absolutely freak out. I'm freaking out. And Mom, she would be so mad at me for not calling the police the second I found Robbie. And the fact that I brought her to our house instead of getting help, like proper help, would make her furious.

What the hell am I doing?

The shower had me reeling. Not just because of her injuries but the surprising fluttering in my stomach when I touched her. When she looked at me, like really looked at me, it was like she could see my soul. I've never had anyone see me like that. It was very jarring. Come to think of it, I'd never seen her look at Shane like that. But then again, I'd never really noticed her... before.

"We can start with shorts like you said, and I'll keep the towel covering me as much as possible."

"Yeah. That sounds good." I rolled my eyes at myself. *That sounds good?* I'm an idiot. I was freaking out at the phrase "as much as possible." I stepped behind her and drew a deep breath. I wanted to be a good friend, but my hormones were already screaming.

Reaching under the towel, I shimmied the wet material down her legs to her feet. I lifted each foot, slipping them free and replacing them with shorts. I pulled the shorts up, thankful that the towel still covered everything. I went around to the front to tie the shorts, preventing them from falling. When I looked at her, her sweet smile made my stomach flutter again.

My hands shook as I unclasped her bra after stepping behind her. She let the towel hang, holding it to her chest so I could slide the strap off her injured arm. The towel dropped to the floor as I slipped the other arm out. I let the beige bra fall to the floor in a heap on top of the towel. Heat reignited through my body.

I grabbed the zippered hoodie from the sink behind me and carefully draped it over her back. I gently slid the first arm in and then the next. She pulled the two sides together in front, covering herself. I walked around to the front of her and took the zipper to hook the clasp. My eyes followed the zipper all the way up her body. When I found her eyes, I hadn't realized I was holding my breath. I sucked in air and noticed how thick it felt. Thick with the scent of her.

And I was enamored.

Robbie

I needed to break the trance we were in, like immediately. "Thank you, Kyle. I really appreciate all your help. I mean it."

"You don't have to thank me," he said genuinely.

"No, I do. It was a big ask and an awkward situation I put you in, again. So, thank you!"

He smiled and nodded. "I'm going to change your sheets and… grab a plastic bag. There's a hairbrush in the drawer if you want. I mean, feel free to use anything. I'll be right back." He rushed out of the bathroom.

He left so quickly that he tripped over the towel still on the floor. He bent down and grabbed it, shaking the bra off, and then he was gone. It was obvious I made him uncomfortable with my requests, and felt the need to run away as fast as possible.

I turned to look in the mirror to assess the state of my hair. And my face. I felt better after the shower, even if I didn't look better. My face was still swollen. *And the bruising was coming in quite nicely*, I thought sarcastically. A pretty shade of dark purple with lovely magenta along the edges, I scoffed.

I tried brushing my hair, but everything in my body hurt. I groaned out loud just as Kyle walked back into the bathroom. He brought the plastic bag and carefully put my clothes inside, sealing it. Then, without a word, he took the brush from my hand and gently untangled my hair. As I watched him in the mirror, it reminded me of my mother. She would do the same thing after my bath. I missed her so much.

My heart ached, and when I finally snapped out of my reverie, our eyes locked onto each other in the mirror. And in that moment, everything felt… different. He quietly placed the brush on the sink and fished out a new toothbrush. He got it ready and handed it to me.

"I'm going to make us something to eat. I'll be back to help you down the stairs." And just like that, he was gone again.

***

A bit unsteady on the stairs, I traversed them well overall. Kyle helped me keep my balance, and I felt like I'd turned a corner. Everything still hurts. But it was manageable with lots and lots of ibuprofen; I slyly smirked. Kyle had made soup, and my swollen mouth was glad it was something easier to eat. The warm broth sliding down my throat felt satisfying. It had been a while since I had warm meals and company to enjoy them.

Kyle was attentive and ensured I didn't have to ask or want for anything. He's much like Shane in that department. Shane may be driven athletically, but he always doted on me. Even though I told him he didn't need to, it felt nice. It's been a while since I was taken care of, so when I met him, it made me even more drawn to Shane. Kyle was very similar, and it became apparent that it was all because of Kirstie. She raised two wonderful boys, and I felt fortunate that I got to know them both.

After dinner, we sat in the living room. Kyle put on a movie, but it was just background noise as we sat quietly together. From time to time, I would see him texting. I wanted to ask who he was texting, but I held my tongue. I wondered if he would break his promise, but as the evening wore on and no one came, I felt reassured.

As night fell, we went upstairs, and after a quick pit stop in the bathroom, I was back in bed with fresh, clean sheets. As soon as my head hit the pillow, I could feel my eyes getting heavy. He hesitated for a moment, as if he were going to say something. But instead, he turned out the light. I wanted to ask him what was up, but the darkness made my lids flutter.

Then, involuntarily, I closed my eyes.

Kyle

I left her door ajar to hear her if she needed me. I'm unsure why I hesitated at the edge of her bed. I'm not even sure what I was going to say. All I know is the emotion in the bathroom earlier was so palpable that it left me flustered. I shook off my thoughts and went to take my own shower.

I let the hot water run over my body. I didn't realize the tension I was holding in until I could finally relax. I closed my eyes when images of her popped into my head: bruises, blood, scars. My throat tightened.

After, I checked in on Robbie before heading to bed. She was sound asleep. I smiled as I lazily wandered to my room, ready to let slumber take over. In my dreamscape, I heard a scream. I looked around everywhere inside my hazy dream, but the screaming only got louder and louder. I was driven to cover my ears when I realized this wasn't my dream. It was Robbie.

I shot out of bed and ran to her room. Terrified screams permeated the air as I flipped on the light. I shook her awake, with her wild eyes and streaming tears. She clung to my chest and sobbed. I held her as tightly as I could.

Through her sobbing hiccups, she squeaked out, "I'm sorry."

"Don't be." Subconsciously, I wiped her dripping nose with my thumb. She blushed and turned her head quickly, wiping the rest with her hand.

"I'm really sorry this keeps happening."

"You've got to give it some time," I replied.

"I know. But I'm exhausted. And I'm making you exhausted."

"Don't worry about me. I'm fine," I assured her.

"I do worry."

"Don't. I'll stay until you fall asleep."

"No. No way. You're not sleeping all hunched over in that chair again. I won't allow it."

"You won't allow it?" I asked sarcastically.

"No."

"Well, it's not up to you," I smirked.

"Kyle…" she mocked.

"Robbie…" I mocked back. Then I had an idea. "Scooch over."

"What are you doing?" she asked, confused.

"Compromising. There's plenty of room in the bed for both of us. Plus, I think we're way past the awkward stage." She snickered.

We got comfortable, as much as possible, considering the situation. I turned out the light and leaned my head against the headboard. I felt her touch my hand, so I turned mine over, and we interlocked our fingers.

"Thank you, Kyle," she said, squeezing my hand.

I squeezed back. "You're welcome. Goodnight, Robbie."

"Goodnight, Kyle."

I lay there listening to her breath and hoped to keep the nightmares away. As her breathing slowed, her hand went slack. She was right. I was exhausted. I hadn't realized it due to the adrenaline rush earlier. I closed my eyes; the lack of sleep definitely catching up to me.

And I finally gave in.

Robbie

When I woke, Kyle was snoring again. The bags under his eyes darkened as time wore on, and I was to blame. I didn't dare move, knowing I'd wake him. Instead, I lay motionless, like a statue. From my frozen state, my mind was actively trying to figure out how much I should say to him about what happened. I needed to share more of the story with him before I lost my courage. He deserved at least that.

But where should I begin? Do I tell him all the sordid details? My visible scars and bruises already shocked him. I didn't want to make it worse for him or shock him into calling the police. He knew I fought back hard, but should I tell him it was my stepdad?

It startled me when Kyle flipped over, now face-to-face. I held my breath and watched him sleep soundly. I had put him through the wringer since he brought me here, and I felt guilty putting all this on him. But I had nowhere else to go, nobody else I could turn to.

"Hey. You, okay?" he whispered.

"Yeah. I'm fine. Go back to sleep," I whispered back.

"I'm good. Any nightmares this time?"

"No. I slept. Like, really slept. I just woke up, too."

"That's great. Can I get you anything? Make you anything?"

"You don't have to do that. Wait on me hand and foot."

"Well, it's easier than waiting on you knee and elbow." He laughed.

"That was. So cheesy," I teased back.

It was nice to hear him laugh. I haven't heard that since I've been here. But to be honest, I haven't really given him anything to laugh about. It's all been doom and gloom. He sat up, resting his back on the headboard as his expression turned grave. I knew the dreaded question was coming. "Robin? Can I ask you something?"

"Sure…" I said as blood drained from my face. The talk was imminent, but I wasn't entirely ready to answer.

"Can I ask what happened? I mean, I can figure out most of it... I think. Someone hurt you, and you said it was 'him.' And then you needed your clothes bagged, and they were... torn," he said carefully.

Heavy breaths escaped me as tears stung my eyes. I wrung my palms to settle their trembling. I didn't understand why it was so difficult for me to tell him. I could trust Kyle.

He took my hands. "You're safe now."

"I know..." I breathed. I pulled courage from the depths of my being. "It was my um... stepdad. He was drunk. High. Maybe both. And so angry with me. He kept asking me where 'his stuff' was that he knew my mother must've given me. But I didn't know what he was talking about.

"Furious, he slapped me. So, I hit him squarely in the jaw. But that just made him angry even more. He shoved me, and I tripped. I landed hard. That's when he started kicking and hitting me. He leaned down and punched me in the face. Stunned by the pain, I rolled onto my stomach, trying to get away. I could feel blood dripping from my nose and mouth. My vision blurred, and my face stung. That's when he turned me over onto my back again.

"I felt his weight on me, and felt his hands everywhere, and then... and then he tried to... but I fought him off with every ounce of strength I had left in me. I hit him with the hand weight that I finally reached. He was bleeding everywhere, writhing in pain. I crawled out from under him, but he was still breathing when I ran. At least I think he was. I didn't bother to—"

I heard a quiet sniffle from Kyle.

It brought me to the present, and I looked at his face. His lips quivered as tears hung in his eyes. I lifted my hand to touch his face. He held my palm to his cheek and wept quietly. All I could say was, "Shhh," over and over as my own tears fell, intensifying the intimate moment between us.

He looked at me with dark eyes, pained and angry.

"I swear, Robin. I'm going to find him. And I'm going to kill him," he choked.

I held my fingers to his lips. "Kyle, no. Don't ever say that. I don't want you anywhere near him." And I really meant it. I didn't want Kyle anywhere near him. And I definitely didn't want Kyle to kill him.

Because I was.

CHAPTER 7

And we...

Kyle

MY TEETH CLENCHED as my blood boiled. I seethed over what he did to her. With her fingers still pressed to my lips and eyes pleading... it broke my heart. How could anyone do this to another person? To her? I slowly took her hand and held it within mine. I didn't know what to say except "I'm sorry," but that felt lame. Then, before I thought of anything better, I heard myself say it.

"I'm sorry, Robbie. I truly am. Maybe if I... or if Shane had..." I said through gritted teeth.

"No. Neither one of you could have. I kept it hidden for a reason. So please, don't blame yourself. I mean it," she said sternly. Heat still emanated from me, and a lump formed in my throat. How did we all miss the signs? How did Shane? He knew her better than any of us.

"Thank you for telling me what happened. For trusting me. That couldn't have been easy for you to relive." She nodded.

I looked down at our hands still clasped. The urge to drive into the city to get this bastard was overwhelming, but I would have absolutely no way of finding him. Without Robbie. And she has been through enough. Calling the police flashed across my mind. I looked at Robbie, knowing if I broke my promise—

"What are you thinking?" she asked softly.

"Uh... I was thinking about making dinner. You hungry?"

"I could eat."

"Will you be okay if I go downstairs?"

"I'm fine. Really." I hesitated, body frozen in place. "Go. I'm hungry," she smiled reassuringly.

"Let me know when you're ready to head downstairs so I can help you."

"I will."

***

A while later, I heard the toilet flush and Robin hobbling down the stairs. I rushed to the stairwell to help.

"Robbie, I told you to call for me," I said, exasperated.

"I know, but I should do it myself," she said, determined.

"I get it, but… it hasn't been that long. Give yourself a break."

"I don't need a break. I need to—" she stopped mid-sentence.

"Need to what?"

"Nothing." She continued down the stairs, wincing at each step. I stood by to assist if needed, but she tapped my hand away. I'm learning very quickly about her stubborn streak. After we ate, I suggested she order some clothes online that would fit her better than mine. Although, if I'm being honest, I really liked seeing her in my hoodie.

"I can't. I don't have any money," she protested.

"No. I meant I'd buy them. You order them online, and I'll pay."

"I'm not letting you do that. You've done too much already."

"I want to," I said kindly.

"And I appreciate that, but no."

"Robbie…"

"Kyle, no," she said, annoyed.

"Why won't you let me?"

"Because," she shot back.

"That's not an answer."

"Because I don't like owing people. Okay? I'm a very independent and self-reliant person. I've had to be."

"It's okay to accept help sometimes."

"I did. I called you to help me when I was in the city," she snidely replied.

"Because you were dying," I said, irritated.

"That's a bit dramatic," she chided.

"Is it?" I asked, frustrated.

"Yes," she taunted.

I took a deep, calming breath. "I have no problem letting you borrow my clothes, but you need some of your own, too. Clothes that fit. So let me help you. It'll be a loan, and you can pay me back."

"Kyle…"

"Look, we'll only get a few things that you really need. Okay? Deal?" I asked, hopeful that she would go along with it.

"Fine. But it's a loan. I'm paying you back. All of it."

"Okay. I wouldn't have it any other way."

She rolled her eyes as I pushed the laptop over.

***

Later that evening, still perturbed at me for offering financial help, Robin sulked onto the back porch. The deck sat off the kitchen and held a pair of Adirondack chairs. I went out, sitting in the chair next to her. She squinted in my direction but didn't protest.

The sun shone brightly, and the heat on my skin felt comforting. When I looked over, she rested her head against the back with her eyes closed. The slight breeze blew tendrils of her hair from side to side, but she finally seemed calm, easing my stress as well.

I opened my music app and set the phone on the table between us, realizing I didn't know what type of songs she enjoyed. I clicked on my favorite list of alternative bands. Hopefully, she liked them. I noticed her skin turning a rosy pink from the sun as she sat quietly. I decided to lay my head back as well and close my eyes.

I let the sun wash over me, warming my skin and my soul. We relaxed on the porch, enjoying the sun's warmth, listening to tunes, and our breath floating through the breeze. It had been a very chaotic and stressful time since I brought her home, both of us still reeling from it all. So, finally taking a moment from the reality of this situation was needed. I know this respite won't last, but for now, I'm content.

And I was happy.

Robbie

As I sat with the sun's heat on my face, warming my skin... I could feel some of my stress melt away. My restlessness and annoyance finally dissipated to a state of calm.

And I was happy.

Happiness has been tough to come by these last couple of years. This was unexpected. I still felt terrible that I didn't tell him everything. But I gave him enough for now. It was all he could handle. It was all I could handle.

To see him cry, for me, cut deeply. The fact that he could be so open and vulnerable with his emotions and his heart in front of someone else was surprising. I've never known anyone willing to freely share the deepest pieces of their inner self with another. It shook me to my core.

***

Over the next few weeks, our days turned into nights... full of nightmares. We were exhausted, and I felt terrible putting him through sleepless evenings. I tried to stay awake as long as possible to allow him time to sleep. I basically woke him up once or twice a night. He always offered to stay, but I never let him. Begrudgingly, he returned to his room, but disagreed every time.

One late night, I slowly wandered around the room, trying to stay awake, when I heard a faint knock on the door. "Robin? Can I come in?" he asked quietly. He hesitated at the door, waiting for my answer.

"Yeah, sure."

He entered, took my hand, and pulled me along after him. We walked past the bathroom and into his room. He turned to me, still holding my hand. "Get in," he nodded his head over toward the bed.

I looked at him with surprise. "What?"

"I can hear you walking around his room every night. I know you're trying to stay awake, and I'm not sleeping because I'm worrying about you. You always make me leave, but I just lay here listening to you pace. So, I have a solution. You sleep in here with me. In my bed. Which is big enough for the both of us."

I stared at him.

"If you're in here, we keep your nightmares away, and I won't worry about you all night. Then we both can sleep." I still couldn't speak. "We can't keep doing this, Robbie—days and nights on end with no sleep. We're exhausted. This is my solution." He nodded toward the bed again.

"I... um..." I stuttered.

"Look, we try it for a few days and see if it helps. And if it doesn't, well then, no harm, no foul. We go back to walking and worrying," he smirked.

I smirked back. But he was right. I was tired. So. Very. Tired.

"Okay. We'll try it," I relented. He released my hand so I could move to the right of the bed and get in. I gingerly slid under the covers and turned to the side opposite my injuries. Kyle climbed in, rolling over onto his left, facing me.

He smiled. I smiled back.

"Goodnight, Robbie," he whispered sweetly.

"Goodnight, Kyle," I whispered back.

He closed his eyes, and I did the same.

And we slept.

CHAPTER 8
Wasn't...

Kyle

AS I SLOWLY woke, I heard an old familiar hum. I opened my eyes, focusing on the ceiling fan. I watched as it spun around and around, always having a calming and lulling effect on me. The blades cut a single streak of sunlight beaming into the room, making the light flash. As I stretched my stiff body, I felt refreshed, which surprised me since I had been utterly exhausted these last couple weeks, when suddenly my arm touched... her.

I snapped my head toward Robin, forgetting she was in my room. Sound asleep, I rolled to face her like when we went to bed. I wondered if she had moved at all last night. I smiled, glad she could finally get some rest after so long. Like real rest. All night.

As I watched, I couldn't resist brushing aside a strand of hair that had fallen over her still-swollen black eye. I tucked it behind her ear as her lids fluttered open. She seemed groggy at first. But when she finally focused, she looked deep into my eyes and smiled—her traffic-stopping smile.

"Hi," she said it so... so sexily.

"Hi back."

"Did you sleep?" she quietly asked.

"Yeah. And apparently, so did you."

"How can you tell?" she smiled.

"I can tell because of all the drool on my pillow," I snorted.

She reached up to touch the drool on her mouth, making her cheeks blush a dusty pink hue that made her face glow. I grinned ear-to-ear when I had to remind myself that this was MY. BROTHER'S. GIRLFRIEND.

"I'm so embarrassed…" I reached down to help her wipe the drool from her chin. I didn't mean to touch her; it happened before I could stop.

"Don't be. My solution worked. I'm a genius." I wiped my hand on the sheet. She giggled, eyes crinkling at the edges.

"Did you sleep? Be honest with me," she asked.

"I did. Honest."

She flashed that smile. "Good." And I felt that flutter. Again.

***

Later, as I stood under the stream of hot water in the shower, my thoughts wandered. Summer. Not anything I expected it to be this year. With both Shane and my mom gone, I expected it to be my summer to party. Have fun. Get into trouble as I wasted the days away.

But then she came in like a force of nature. Crash landing into my life. And it changed everything. I could feel her pull on me, like gravity, yanking me into her orbit. It was out of my control, and I couldn't stop it. But did I want to?

I lingered there, letting the water pound down on my neck and back, massaging the tension from my muscles. I smirked to myself, realizing I already knew my answer.

And the answer was "no."

Robbie

As summer waged on, our days turned into weeks, and we quickly fell into a routine. It felt natural and ingrained to be together, just the two of us. We spent our summer reading, talking, dancing, cooking, walking, watching movies, exercising, or a combination of all those things every single day. We were so fundamentally comfortable with each other now that it shocked me.

Besides my mother, I had never been this close to anyone. Even with Shane, I never felt an undeniable draw or longing to be near someone. But in his defense, I haven't spent every waking moment with him for weeks at a time. Well, to be honest, every non-waking moment too.

Because at night this summer, Kyle and I had been sleeping in the same bed. His bed. In his room. We would stay on our own sides until we fell asleep, and then… anything goes. Many mornings, I'd wake up draped over him or him over me. At first, it was a bit awkward, but then that became comfortable and a part of our routine too.

We were in our bubble. And I liked it.

For the first time since my mom passed, I felt content. And it was because of Kyle. I guess I could have gone back to Shane's room with all my nightmares gone, but I didn't. And he didn't ask me to go.

We had this ritual a few times a week; we'd make popcorn and watch movies while sitting together on the couch or porch. He'd tease me if I jumped at the scary scenes, or he'd annoy me by spoiling the ending. But he was sweet, too. During sad parts that made me cry, he comforted me. He'd put his arm around me and pulled me close. He never complained about my tears or my nose dripping onto his chest. Ever.

But tonight felt different. It's late August now, and the humidity is heavy. We decided to watch a movie in the air-conditioned house. We sat on the couch together in the living room like usual, but he seemed off. I noticed him watching me more than he was watching the movie. It wasn't awkward, but it was noticeable. I moved closer to him and laid my head on his shoulder. At first, his body stiffened, but then he relaxed into me too.

His closeness calmed me. And I craved it. I trusted him completely, and I felt safe with him. Lately, I—

"Hey. Earth to Robbie," his words interrupted my thoughts.

"Sorry. What did you say?" I asked, blinking heavily.

"I asked if you wanted to watch another movie."

"Is this one over?"

He snorted. "I guess you really liked it," he said sarcastically.

"Oops," I answered, feeling shy. "Sure, we can watch another movie."

"You okay?"

"Yeah. Just some stuff on my mind," I said coyly.

"Like, what stuff?"

"It's nothing. Let's watch the movie."

We both kept shifting positions on the couch as the next movie played. I could see him fidgeting with the remote instead of paying attention to the film, and I was busy watching him. The air filled with unspoken tension between us. But I didn't understand why.

We followed our usual nighttime routine, but that felt different too. Typically, we talked about the movies we had just watched or anything really, but he was eerily quiet. It made me nervous. As we got into bed, I rolled to my right side at the same time Kyle moved to his left, facing each other. Our eyes locked, bodies frozen in place.

He closed the gap between us and kissed me.

The kiss was gentle, warm, and tender. The unspoken tension melted away and was replaced by electricity coursing through my veins. And then, just as suddenly, he pulled back like my lips were on fire.

"I'm so sorry, Robbie. Please forgive me," he said regretfully.

"It's okay—" I started to reply.

"No, it's not. I should've asked you first."

"I just meant it's been a crazy summer, and sometimes emotions get the better of us."

"I promise I won't do that again," he said sincerely. I smiled awkwardly. He rolled away quickly, turning out the light. "Goodnight, Robbie."

I paused. "Goodnight, Kyle."

As I shifted onto my back, staring at the dark ceiling, I replayed his words. *I should've asked you first.* Is that the reason he seemed off tonight? Because he was going to ask to kiss me? And if he had asked me, what would I have said?

I closed my eyes tight, a buzzing still dancing on my lips. I smirked to myself, realizing I already knew my answer.

And the answer was "yes."

Kyle

A pit settled in my stomach as I woke. I kissed her last night. She trusted me, and I broke that trust. But I know why I did it. The end of summer was happening, and I felt the pressure of Shane's return. Everything would change again, and I wasn't ready to let her go.

The guilt stifled my environment; I needed to get out of the house. I left her a note and ran off as if I were being chased. I pushed hard. My muscles ached with each footfall that hit the pavement, trying to forget what I had done. I pushed harder. But it didn't matter. Because the more I tried forgetting her, the more the thoughts of Robin crept into my mind. Her smile, her mouth, her lips. Warm, soft, and sweet…

"Aagghh." I sprinted down the block. When I returned to the house, Robbie was up and working out in the garage gym. She looked over as I trotted in.

"Hey," she greeted.

"Hey."

"Have a good run?"

"Um, sure. I mean, yeah, I guess," I stuttered.

She simply nodded and went back to her exercise.

I decided to join her. We had been lifting weights together almost daily for her to get stronger. As she healed, the more intense our workouts became. She had the time to devote to the gym, and with her phone smashed, it became easier to avoid talking to Shane. She told him she broke her phone and couldn't afford a new one, so she would 'come over' to use mine. We kept our conversations with Mom and Shane short and sweet. I did the same with the neighbor Mom had paid to check in on me.

As we continued training, she was unusually quiet. She seemed more driven than normal, pushing herself to the brink. I gauged her mood carefully before I spoke. "Look at you. Killing it with the reps. But you don't have to push so hard, you know. You've got time. Take a break and rest."

"I'm tired of resting. That's all I've been doing this summer. I need to get all my strength back," she replied curtly.

"Well, you weren't resting. You were healing. There's a difference. And we still don't know how severe your injuries were on the inside because what I saw on the outside… it was bad."

"I need to take charge of my life. I can't wait anymore. I need to be strong."

"You can, but you don't have to push it. It's only been seven weeks since I brought you home. When Shane blew out his knee and tore his ACL, he lost most of his freshman year. It can take a long time to heal and regain strength."

"He had a tear and needed surgery. Mine are bruises that needed healing."

"Severe bruises, Robbie. Maybe even fractures and who knows what else?" I said, exasperated.

"Okay. Fine. I'll take a break. It's not worth arguing with you, "she growled.

"Were we arguing?" I asked, confused.

"It felt like it," she retorted.

"Because to me, it feels like you were just being stubborn. As usual," I snapped back.

"Stubborn as usual?"

"Yes!"

"You don't understand," she said, frustrated.

"Then help me understand."

"Just forget it! I'm going inside and taking a shower." She stomped out of the garage and slammed the door. I grunted. She's obviously upset about the kiss last night and had every right to be. Exasperated, I ran my fingers through my sweaty hair, wishing I hadn't kissed her.

But deep down, I knew that was a lie.

Robbie

He can be so infuriating. I banged around the shower, still fuming over my interrupted workout and being called stubborn. I'm not stubborn. He doesn't understand. I'm so mad I let myself believe I could be normal and enjoy regular teenage things this summer under the guise of healing. Instead, I should have been focusing on the plan. But I just keep getting distracted. First with Shane and now with Kyle. What was wrong with me?

I needed to refocus, which meant I couldn't sit around anymore. I had to be strong for what happened next. If that means pushing hard during my workouts, so be it. He had no right to call me out on it.

After showering, I changed into my last pair of clean shorts and a T-shirt. Returning downstairs, I stomped into the kitchen, where Kyle busily made lunch. I walked past him to the kitchen table, spotting newly cleaned clothes neatly stacked and folded. My cheeks flushed with heat. I'm such a jerk.

"How was your shower?" he asked.

I avoided his eyes as I mumbled. "Fine."

"I'm making us some lunch."

"I see that. Thank you. And, um… thanks for doing my laundry."

"Yeah, no problem. I was doing mine so—"

"Why do you put up with me? You've been supportive and helpful this whole summer, and I treated you like crap."

"We all have our bad days, Robbie. I could tell something was bothering you. I think I know what it is… but I figured you'd tell me when you were ready," he answered calmly.

"Yeah, you're right. We should talk. Can it wait till after lunch? I'm starved." I asked sheepishly.

"Yeah. It can wait."

Due to my grueling workout earlier, I scarfed down everything on my plate. I noticed Kyle picking at his meal, which was totally unlike him. He usually cleaned his plate and then got more. But instead, he dumped his unfinished food into the trash and went upstairs to shower. I knew it wouldn't be long before he returned, so I went out and got comfy on the back porch. The sun was hot, but my skin prickled from the slight afternoon breeze; it struck me oddly when my hands started trembling too. This was just a regular chat with Kyle. Right?

Wasn't it?

CHAPTER 9

And I could feel...

Kyle

I RAN SO fast up the stairs that I stumbled on the last two steps at the top. I caught myself on the wall but ended up stubbing my toe. As I hobbled to my room, I noticed I was sweating. Like profusely sweating. It was a warm summer day, but it wasn't that hot.

I showered quickly so I could get back to her. She wanted to talk, and I'm sure it was about the kiss. I rolled my eyes at myself. I shouldn't have done that, but it's too late now. All I could do was hope that she'd accept my apology.

"Hey. Sorry that I took so long," I breathed heavily.

She giggled. "It was like three minutes, Kyle."

I laughed nervously, still on edge. "So, what did you want to talk about?" I asked, balancing awkwardly on the arm of the Adirondack chair.

"Well... uh... I've been dreading this conversation, but..." she started.

"I'm sorry, Robbie. I really am."

"About what?" she seemed confused.

"The kiss. Isn't that what you wanted to talk about?"

"No. We talked about that last night. It's over and done with."

"Oh," I said regretfully. Her words stung.

"What I wanted to talk about is hard to share. I struggle to open up to people. It makes me extremely uncomfortable, but you make it look easy."

"It's not easy for any of us, Robin," I said honestly.

"Well, I've been trying to build the courage to tell you more about my life. About my mother and what happened before… that night in June. You asked me to help you understand, so I wanted to show you why I need to push myself. Also, I wanted to apologize for taking my frustration out on you earlier. You didn't deserve that, and I'm sorry."

"You don't have to apologize for anything. I'm here for you, Robin. With as much or as little as you want to tell me. Because I'm on your side for all of it. You can trust me."

And I meant that. I wanted her to know that she could still trust me.

"I know I can. That's why I want to tell you about my mother." She took a deep breath. "My mother was the kindest person I knew and trusting to a fault. I never knew my real dad, which was a good thing, I guess. My mom tried hard, but I still had to parent her rather than her parenting me.

"Sometimes it was annoying, but it's amazing what you can accept for the ones you love. Her taste in men was crap, but they didn't usually hang around long, so it never really mattered. She meant well and always hoped it would work out, but it never did. Until she met… him." A chill went down my spine when she mentioned "him," rage building from the depths of my soul.

"He differed from the rest. He had a good job and seemed sweet and doting. I thought it was working out since they were inseparable, and then they got married. He had a gruff personality, but it didn't seem out of character for him. But it got worse later. Their relationship had harsh ups and downs.

"When he was in a bad mood, we all knew it. Yelling. Smashing things. But he never laid a hand on us. Not then, anyway. She stayed because when he was in a good mood, we were all on top of the world. And for a while, it seemed like we could be happy. Be a family." She paused, biting her lip.

"Are you okay? I asked.

"Yeah. It's just hard to talk about her," her voice trembled.

"You don't have to do this," I said honestly.

"I want to. I want you to understand. Do you remember when I first got here, I mentioned I was in a car accident?"

"Yeah."

"It was about a year and a half ago. My mom was driving, and there was a terrible snowstorm. The roads were slick, and we crashed. I survived, but my mom… died. I ended up breaking my ribs and my left wrist. At first, when I got home, my stepdad mourned my mother too. But as the months passed, he became mean and always got drunk or high. Anything I said or did was like an imposition, and eventually, he told me to my face that he wished… that I had died too."

"I'm sorry, Robbie. He's a shitty person."

"It gets better because he'd knock me around whenever he was under the influence. He thought it was funny. So did the creeps that were at our house day and night. They made me uncomfortable, and I locked myself away in my room. I was barely sixteen. Then I found out he was selling off my mom's stuff to fund his drug habit, and he hocked all her jewelry. I decided to hide some pieces under the floorboards, including this special oval locket she loved with a songbird on it.

"She had our birthdays engraved on one side and my nickname on the other. She wore it the night of the accident, and I was determined he wouldn't get his hands on it. But then, one night, he was super trashed, and the men he had over gave me bad vibes, like seriously bad vibes. I had to split. Right then and there.

"I didn't have time to get the jewelry and left with the clothes on my back and the cash in my pocket. I knew when he sobered up; he would come for me. So, I left the city and bounced around a few little towns until I moved here. I cut my hair, forged paperwork, and enrolled at our high school in January."

"Where did you live all this time?" I asked with shock in my voice.

"Here and there. Once I started school, I could crash at friends' houses, making it easier." I couldn't wrap my head around what she said. Had she been homeless the whole time we knew her? How did we all not know?

"So, what happened at the end of June? How did he find you?" I asked.

"He didn't. It was my fault. I went back to my house to get my mother's jewelry. I thought I had waited long enough. The place seemed abandoned, so I went in. I had hidden it all down the crack in the floorboards and didn't have time to get them out when I split. Pulling up the old wood took me some time, then he came out of nowhere. He pulled my hair and threw me to the ground. As I scrambled to grab everything, he kicked me. I grabbed my stomach in pain, seeing him pull out the jewelry. I stood up to grab the locket from him, and that's when he slapped me. I was so mad that I hit him back and then... well, you know the rest."

"Robbie, none of this is your fault. None of it. Why didn't you tell me or Shane? He would've helped you. I would've helped you."

"He's a dangerous man, Kyle. By then, I had made so many mistakes that I didn't need to add any more to my list by involving either of you."

"What mistakes?" I interrupted.

"Well, first and foremost, not sticking to the plan I came here with, and then Shane, of course."

"What mistake did you make with Shane?" I asked, confused.

But hopeful.

Robbie

I was mad at myself for saying that out loud. It came out before I could stop it. I shouldn't have said the word 'mistake' to him. It took on a different connotation and was not what I wanted to convey. He awaited my answer, and I wasn't sure I had one. Not the answer I knew he desired.

"Mistake is not what I meant to say, Kyle."

"Then what did you mean, Robbie?" he huffed.

"I only meant that I made a mistake getting involved with him. Or with you, for that matter. The plan was to get away from my stepdad, finish high school, and get the hell out of here," I said, frustrated.

"Involved. With Shane and with me?"

"Yes."

"We're involved?"

"Yes, I mean, you're the only person who knows anything about my past. And that includes Shane."

"Why didn't you tell Shane when you were together?"

"Because… because I wanted to protect him," I said honestly.

"But not me," he said, hurt.

"No, I mean, yes. I wanted to protect you, too. But I needed your help, and you found out what happened… uugghh. You're twisting my words," I retorted.

"Am I?" he said sarcastically.

"Yes!" I was butchering what I was trying to say, messing this all up. "He wasn't part of my plan, and neither are you."

"The plan to get the hell out of here?" He used my words against me.

"Yes! I didn't mean to go out on a date with Shane or be his girlfriend. Any of it. He was supposed to be… a distraction," I yelled in frustration.

"A distraction. So, am I your distraction while Shane's away?" he accused.

"That's not fair," tears stung my eyes.

"Fair?" he scoffed, shaking his head in disbelief.

I was hurting him and making it worse. I bit my lip to stop myself from saying anything else. He walked away from me, and I should have just let him go. But instead, I reached for him. I slid my fingers down his arm and into his hand. He held my hand back, surprising me. He slowly turned toward me. I could see the pain on his face, and it killed me that I made him look like that.

"Kyle—" I croaked out sadly.

"Robin, I'm so confused. I'm confused about what I'm feeling. I'm confused about everything that happened. I'm confused about you. And I don't know what to do. Sometimes, I think—"

Suddenly, his phone began ringing. He quickly glanced at the screen. "It's my mom. I need to take this." I could only hear bits and pieces of the conversation. Kyle paced back and forth, making it difficult to eavesdrop. I finally heard him clearly say, "Yeah. Me too. See you soon," before hanging up. He stood there looking at his device, frozen in place.

When he didn't say anything, I softly called his name.

"Kyle?" That shook him from his trance.

"Uh, yeah. That was my mom. She said they'll be home sometime tomorrow," he replied blankly.

"Oh," was all I could manage to squeak out. He looked pained, both of us standing in silence.

His expression soon changed, as if he was on a mission. "So... we have the rest of today to prepare the house for them to come home. We need to make it look like you haven't been living here all summer, as if you've been here for a few days, at best. We'll move your stuff over to Shane's room and make it look lived in, and... Robbie? Did you hear me?"

"Um, yeah," I replied, dazed.

"It's time for us to return to reality. We can't pretend anymore; the sooner we realize that, the better. But if we stay focused, we can get it all done. I'll start downstairs, and you can start upstairs."

And just like that, he jogged into the house. I stood there stunned and alone on the back porch with my head spinning. I wasn't pretending. I hadn't been for a long time. My heart suddenly ached. And that's when I heard it.

Our bubble bursting.

Kyle

I don't know why I reacted that way, yet my stomach was in knots, and my head wouldn't stop pounding. I knew this day would come, and I had no right to feel this way. She's his girlfriend. Not mine, and he had done nothing wrong. She had done nothing wrong. I did.

I should be excited. I haven't seen my mom or Shane in over two months. But instead, all I felt was guilt and dread. I couldn't change anything that happened between Robin and me this summer or how we felt. Well, how I felt anyway, because I'm still unsure how she feels. But what I do know is that Shane's coming home. Coming home to her. And I had to face that reality.

But reality sucks.

I focused on cleaning the downstairs and making it presentable, but not clean. Mom wouldn't believe it otherwise. Robbie had quietly come in and gone upstairs without looking at me, and I couldn't blame her. I was harsh earlier, and I'd be surprised if she ever talked to me again. She was probably happy that Shane would be back and didn't have to deal with me anymore.

I ran upstairs to see if Robbie would accept my help. As I walked past the bathroom, I hesitated when memories flooded back. How I helped her in the shower, seeing her bruises and scars for the first time. Remembering how broken she was, literally and figuratively, had nearly broken me.

I shook off my recollection, which seemed so long ago. We shared so much this summer that it almost felt like I grieved for us. But I had to remind myself there was no 'us.' Not really. So why is there a pit forming in my stomach?

"Hey," I said tentatively.

"Hey," she replied.

"Do you need help?"

"No. I got this."

"Are you sure?"

"Yep. I'm good. I don't have much," she answered curtly.

She was mad, so I retreated to my room to see if she left anything behind. But she was right. She didn't have much.

***

As night fell, we took our turns in the bathroom as usual. She had gone first, so when I finished showering, it startled me to find her waiting in the hall.

"I think I'm going to sleep in Shane's room tonight," she said indifferently.

It caught me off guard. "Uh… you don't have to do that. You can stay."

"You were right. We can't pretend anymore. It's time to get back to reality."

"That's not what I meant," I said regretfully.

"Well, either way, it's time. You know it, I know it. It's for the best. I can't keep relying on you, so… goodnight, Kyle."

I watched her walk away from me and into Shane's room. My heart ached for her. Ached to tell her I didn't mean what I said. That I wasn't pretending. But I didn't. Instead, I went to my room and got into bed, which now felt empty and cold. Everything was shifting in my world.

And I could feel her orbit releasing me.

CHAPTER 10
But I'm...

Robbie

AS I LAY in Shane's bed, confusion washed over me in waves. I should be happy. My boyfriend is coming home tomorrow. Although he wasn't part of my original strategy, he had been a great distra... diversion to my plan.

Shane was caring and considerate and always made sure I was treated well. He held the door for me, pulled my chair out at restaurants, and returned my texts. Even when he was super busy with training. We only dated for six months before he left this summer. I knew our relationship couldn't go anywhere, so I didn't have to let him know the real me. He was leaving for Europe after graduation anyway, and I was leaving too. It would have been a perfect relationship. No expectations, no future.

Not that we really talked about what lay ahead. He was so focused on his goal of playing professional soccer overseas that I couldn't imagine that his dreams included me. And honestly, I couldn't imagine a future with either of the Whitmore brothers. I was leaving and not coming back. But then, why do I feel so conflicted?

I was forced to involve Kyle this summer because he answered my desperate call for help. He was the one who got stuck here with my problems, laid raw before him. I had to trust him because I needed him. We had a very intense start to the summer, but he was my friend. He apologized for the kiss, and it wasn't like he meant to kiss me. A lot of emotions swirled between us, and sometimes that can get confusing. Believe me, I know.

But despite everything, he's the only person I've ever opened up to like that. It was scary but wonderful at the same time. But what did that mean? At worst, it meant I had an emotional connection with Kyle that I didn't have with Shane. But that's okay. I'm leaving; I can't get invested with the Whitmore brothers any more than I already am.

I squeezed my eyes shut. I needed to get some sleep. Tomorrow would be a very long day, and I needed to be at the top of my game. My game of lying.

The pressure on my chest was back. I've lied so many times and to all of them before. Why am I feeling bad about it now? I lay there contemplating that question as a dull ache formed in my heart. It wasn't about lying. It was about my plan, and I was wavering. Should I stay or should I go?

All I had to do was stay focused, graduate, and leave town for good. One year. *That's all I had to do*, I berated myself. So much for keeping my head in the game. But deep down, I knew I couldn't blame my head.

I blamed my heart.

Kyle

Light streamed through my window, reflecting off the mirror above my dresser. *Great. It's morning,* I thought pensively. Time for reality. I got up sluggishly from the lack of sleep. I tried to listen to see if Robbie was awake and stood at my door for what seemed like forever. When I thought it was safe, I stepped out into the hall. As soon as I did, there she was. She had stepped out of Shane's room precisely as I did.

"Hey," I said with a gravelly morning voice.

"Hey," she replied quietly.

"Um... you can have the bathroom first," I said.

"No, that's okay. You go first. I'm taking a shower, so I'll be a while," she said pointedly, walking back to Shane's room.

"Okay, I'll be quick then," I called after her, but she didn't acknowledge me. I rushed into the bathroom. *That went well.* I rolled my eyes. *This was going to be a great day.* My thoughts dripped with sarcasm.

Later, when she finally came downstairs, she sat by the kitchen island. I grabbed her a drink from the fridge, pushing a glass of orange juice her way.

"Thanks," she said quietly.

"Sure. Want some breakfast?"

"I can make it," she said, getting up.

"Nah, I got it. Really," I threw bacon into the frying pan.

"So, I guess we should talk then?"

"Yeah." My words echoed with a touch of dread and guilt. I was up half the night wondering exactly what we'd say to Mom and Shane because we had to get our stories straight.

As if reading my mind, Robbie spoke. "We need to discuss what we'll say to your family. Then I'll call Sarah to see if I can crash on her couch or something," she said nonchalantly.

"What? Why would you do that?" I asked, surprised.

"Talk to your mom and Shane?"

"No, to Sarah."

"I'll need a place to stay, Kyle."

"Yeah, I know. You'll stay here," I answered, still confused.

"Kyle, I can sleep on her couch as easily as yours."

"You're not sleeping on a couch anywhere. You'll take my room, and I'll move into Shane's with him," I said.

"What are you talking about?"

"I'm going to talk to my mom about you staying here. Permanently. You're not going to be homeless again, Robbie. Not if I can do something about it," I said sternly.

"No. I am not kicking you out of your room. No."

"It's not up to you. It's my room. My choice."

"Well, it doesn't matter. Your mom will never go for it," she said, annoyed.

"She will."

"She won't because I'm dating Shane," she snapped.

A pang of jealousy stirred inside me. "She'll let you. I promise. Plus, Shane will be on my side and help convince her too."

"I am not turning your life upside down any more than I already have."

"And I'm not having you couch surf when we have a bed here for you."

"Shane won't share a room, and there's no bed for you," she huffed.

"There's an old twin bed in the attic from our old bunk beds. I'll use that."

"Absolutely not," she retorted.

"Robbie. It'll be fine. She'll say yes, and Shane will be hyped."

"Just Shane?"

"I mean, yeah. And my mom, and… me," I conceded.

She shook her head. "Then I'll take the small twin bed."

"Nope. Can't."

"Why not?" She asked, irritated.

"Two queens won't fit in Shane's room. It's the only way both beds can fit."

"I don't want to take your room from you, Kyle. It's your room…"

"And I'm offering it to you. I want to do this. Plus, you deserve your own space. Your own bed. Finally," I said sincerely.

"And you shouldn't have that?" she protested.

"Nah, I'm a guy. We don't need our own space. Can't take care of it, anyway. Shane and I throw everything under the bed when we clean, and it smells. We're all slobs," I cracked, which made her grin.

"Kyle..." she tried pleading.

"Robbie..." I cracked. She smiled at me again and then sighed. "It'll be fine. I promise," I reassured her.

"Shane will not like sharing a room."

"Yeah. Well. He'll like the tradeoff. To have his girlfriend living here in the room next door. He'll be totally stoked," I said, with an edge of pain in my tone.

"Kyle..."

"No more protesting. It's a done deal."

"Kyle..." she said louder.

"Really, Robbie. I mean it. It's all going to work out."

"No, Kyle, the bacon. It's burning!" she yelled.

"Oh. Shit!" I shouted as I threw the pan into the sink.

We both laughed for the first time in days, able to sit and enjoy each other's company without anything getting in the way.

And it made me smile.

Robbie

It felt good to laugh. Relax and not worry about anything except for the here and now. For once. And it made me smile. Minus the small, annoying feeling teetering on the edge of my mind, making me feel like… I don't know. It's hard to explain, even to myself. But it lingered there on the ready to either make me angry or cry at any moment. I had never felt so emotional in my life.

And then there's Kyle, messing with my emotions without even knowing. He is one of the most compassionate souls I've ever met. I didn't know people had the capacity to be that selfless because I hadn't experienced that before. But here he is. Giving up his room and his bed. Easily handing over his comfort and privacy. He was so confident that his mom would go along with his plan. All for me. His brother's girlfriend. These boys were screwing up my psyche.

And now, his mom and Shane would be home soon. Kyle and I still had to get our stories straight and figure out what to say to both. So why was my stomach in knots? Because I should be used to all the lying.

But I'm not.

CHAPTER 11

...was definitely different.

Kyle

I PACED, WRINGING my hands, and already sweating. *Aagghh,* I screamed in my head. They would be home any minute. Why was I nervous? It's just Mom and Shane. *Oh,* I thought, rolling my eyes, *I know exactly why I'm nervous.*

Maybe it's because I showered with his girlfriend. Or maybe because I kissed his girlfriend. Or maybe because I slept with his girlfriend. Take your pick. It won't matter to him that we did, in fact, sleep. But Shane won't hear that part.

I'm screwed. Even if I don't tell him all the little details of what happened, I still know them. And I can't lie for shit. He's going to see right through me. Robin and I decided that we would keep our story simple. Make it easy to remember so that we, mainly me, don't mess it up. Her stepdad lost the house, and then he split. She had nowhere to go and asked if she could crash here for a few days. That's it. Short. Simple. Easy to remember and easy to lie.

I looked over at Robin, who seemed oddly calm. But also, strangely absent. Her mind was obviously elsewhere as she sat on the couch, staring off into the distance. In fact, I had to look closely to make sure she was still breathing.

"You okay?" I asked her. She didn't answer. "Robbie?"

"Huh? Yeah," she said unconvincingly.

Oh, crap. She's not okay. I needed her to stick to the story. I don't think I could lie on the fly all by myself. I'd start by adding details, making the tale much more convoluted. I went over and sat next to her and took her hand in mine. She clung to it as if she didn't want to let go. It surprised me, but I liked it. I squeezed her hand back.

"We got this. Everything will be fine. I promise." I said, but my confidence waned if I was being honest. Then I heard the doorknob turn. I jumped off the couch, dropping her hand as if I had just been bitten.

I stuttered out, "Hi. Welcome back!"

"Oh, my sweetie!!" Mom fawned. "Look at you! You've grown so much! Did you get taller? Have you been eating? How did it go?" She pulled me into a huge bear hug. She squeezed me so hard I could barely catch my breath.

"Mom, I can't breathe," I croaked out.

"Oh, honey. I'm sorry. I just missed you so much! I wanted to—" but then she paused suddenly.

"Robbie? I didn't see you there. How nice of you to come over to welcome us home," Mom said sincerely and strode over to hug Robin. Robin hugged her back, although a bit tentatively.

"Hello, Ms. Whitmore. Welcome back," Robin said.

"I've told you before, call me Kirstie, sweetie," said Mom.

"Welcome back, Kirstie," Robin corrected.

Then Shane walked in. "Hey there, little bro!" he said, coming over to greet me when he stopped dead in his tracks.

"Babe?! I didn't know you'd be here too. Man, you are a sight for sore eyes!" he gushed. He ran over, picked her up, and spun her around. As he placed her down, he kissed her. Like, full-on kissed her. I tried to look anywhere except them, but my eyes wouldn't allow it. I stood there trying with every ounce of my willpower not to pull them apart. I wouldn't be able to do this lying thing.

"Shane, say 'hi' to your brother too!" Mom scolded.

"Oh yeah. Hey bro!" He stepped away from Robbie to hug me. He gripped my shoulders as we pulled apart from our "bro" hug. "Sorry. Got distracted by my gal. You know how it is," he smirked, winking at me. Little did he know.

I did.

Robbie

I've never felt so out of my element in my life. I tried to be excited they were home, but knew I had to lie to them. But isn't that what I've been doing all along? Even before summer, so why am I having a crisis of consciousness now? We had our story; I just needed to stick to it.

But that's the problem. It's now painfully obvious I'm not good at sticking to my plans. Especially now that I have involved not one but both Whitmore brothers in my life.

"Babe, why didn't you tell me you would be here?" Shane's question interrupted my thoughts.

"I wanted to surprise you," I answered honestly.

"Well, I am thrilled," he said seductively, pulling me into another deep kiss. I pushed him back, a bit embarrassed.

"Shane. Not in front of everybody," I protested.

"Oh, better idea. Let's go up to my room." He grabbed my hand and pulled me toward the stairs.

At the same time, both Kyle and I yelled. "No!" Shane looked at us with a shocked expression at our unified refusal.

"What's going on?" Shane asked.

I froze. Kyle froze.

I stammered out, "I didn't want to do this the second you both walked in, but I, I need to… I—"

"Mom, we need to talk to you. There's a little situation," said Kyle.

"Okay…" Kirstie replied tentatively.

"Here, sit down, Mom. Have some water." Kyle poured her a glass. I sat too, nervously sipping my drink.

His mom started rambling. "Oh, my gosh. This isn't good, is it? What happened? Did something break? Are you in trouble? How bad is it? How much will it cost—"

"Mom. Stop. What's this 'little' situation you both have?" Shane asked. I finally got my wits about me because it was time for me to do what I did best.

Lie.

"It's a problem I have. Kyle was nice enough to offer a solution, but we need to talk to your mom about it first," I said reassuringly. I went over to hold Shane's hand. I could feel Kyle's eyes on me the whole time.

"So, what's this problem… and solution?" Kirstie questioned, looking between us.

I sputtered, "My stepdad split and didn't tell me the house was in foreclosure. I'm eighteen, so I don't need a guardian, but what I do need is—"

"I thought she could stay here," Kyle interjected.

"Here?" Kirstie said, surprised.

"Yeah. I thought I could give up my room since it's smaller and move the twin bed into Shane's room. Then she can take my old room," Kyle said confidently. Kirstie looked like she was processing. Shane too, as he stared at Kyle intently.

"Live here?" Kirstie finally questioned.

"Yes," Kyle said.

"For how long?" she asked.

Kyle hesitated. "Till she graduates."

"My, that's a big commitment. I don't mean any offense, Robbie," Kirstie said as nicely as she could.

"None taken. I get it. It's a huge ask, and I wouldn't have even suggested it, but Kyle insisted," I said, embarrassed.

"That's very nice of you, Kyle, to give up your room. But what brought about this huge act of chivalry? Not that I'm questioning your integrity, but I mean, Robbie is your brother's girlfriend. Not yours," Kirstie said.

"I know," I answered wistfully. "But she had to crash here the last few days because she had nowhere else to go. She's basically homeless, Mom. Homeless. And we have two extra beds in the attic sitting there doing nothing. So, I offered her a solution. And just so you know, she said 'no' to the idea, like so many times. But I insisted we speak to you despite her better judgment."

Kyle turned to Shane. "Come on, bro. Help me out. You'll have your girlfriend living right here in the house. It's a win-win!"

Mom interjected. "Oh no! This is definitely not a win-win. There will be a lot of discussions about boundaries and severe consequences if any funny business is had, and so on and so forth."

"You're considering this?" I asked, shocked.

"Of course. Believe me, I've known my fair share of shitty men, and I'm not going to have you homeless," she said earnestly.

I looked at Kyle with surprise. He smiled. "I told you she would consider it." Everything built up to this moment all summer, and I could feel the tears streaming down my cheeks.

"Oh, sweetie. Did you think I would say no? Hug her, Shane. She needs a hug," she chided. Shane pulled me to his chest as I looked over at Kyle. His eyes, always kind, now seemed conflicted. The pressure on my chest came back.

And along with it, the ache.

Kyle

As I looked at Robbie, I couldn't help the feelings bubbling up inside. I wanted to be the one to hug her and wipe away her tears. I wanted to tell her I knew it would all work out, just as I promised. But I shook away my thoughts.

"Thank you, Mom. I mean that. Thank you for saying yes."

"Of course. I'm proud of you for offering your room to help someone out. You're such a good boy," Mom gushed.

"Let me take your bags up to your room."

"Thank you, Kyle. That's so nice of you," Mom smiled.

"Hey Shane, do you want to come up so we can get the twin bed out of the attic? And then Robbie can get her things out of your room since… that's where she's been staying," I said, lying my ass off.

"Sure. Be right up. I want a few more minutes here with my new live-in girlfriend," he said eagerly.

"Okay. Okay. You mean a friend who happens to be a girl who lives down the hall. And don't get used to this alone time, son. I'll be watching you like a hawk," Mom warned.

"Yeah, yeah, yeah," he mumbled, distracted. I walked over to grab Mom's bags and started up the stairs. I could hear Shane whispering to Robbie how much he liked the fact that she had been sleeping in his bed.

I told myself not to look over, but that's precisely what I did. Shane pulled her onto his lap and nuzzled her neck. She looked up at me, catching my eye. I felt a jolt that rattled me. I quickly turned and continued up the stairs. Mom followed behind, chirping about, "What a good friend I was to Robbie," and that, "I'm such a good brother to Shane." Blah, blah, blah. I hated lying to them. But they both seemed to buy it. Which is good, I guess, since I'm horrible at lying to myself. Especially when it came to her.

When Shane finally headed up, we got the twin bed from the attic and set it up. We realized just how tight the fit would be in his room, and both grimaced. Shane didn't say anything, but I could tell he regretted being so agreeable.

Robbie kept herself busy gathering clothes and other items from Shane's dresser and moving them back into my room. Again. Had it only been a day since she was fully entrenched in my room in every way? Her water and a book on the nightstand, her clothes in my top dresser drawer, and her sneakers at the end of the bed. Last night without her made me restless.

I was so used to her sleeping beside me, feeling her shift, hearing her breath, and being close to her that last night felt like an eternity. I rubbed my face. I had to let this summer go. I can't do this to myself. She's his girlfriend, and he's back now. So, I needed to step away. It's the right thing to do. But could I do the right thing?

At that moment, I wasn't sure.

Robbie

They had only been home for a little while, yet I already felt so out of place in this house. Before, it felt like my sanctuary. My safe place. My home. But now?

I moved my clothes and stuff back into Kyle's room, pretending it was for the first time. It felt so duplicitous. But that was me. Always lying to everyone about everything. Even Kyle wasn't safe from my machinations and lies. He just didn't know it. But I continued the farce without skipping a beat.

"That's it? That's all your stuff?" Shane questioned.

"I don't need much. You know me. Jeans and a t-shirt kind of gal," I smiled.

Shane smiled back and pulled me into a big hug. "I'm glad to be home. And I'm even happier that you'll be living here too."

I squeaked, "Me too."

Standing in Shane's embrace, I slid my arms around his back. He held me tighter, and I tucked my head into his chest. His heady cologne set off familiar feelings of our time before summer. Wonderful memories, which only made this moment even more complicated.

I grabbed my stuff and went over to Kyle's room. He was making a pile of clothes on the bed as I entered. It's weird that I suddenly felt so self-conscious around him. Just a few days ago, I was comfortable enough to be near him that I had been the big spoon in bed. Which at the time felt absolutely… normal. Having my face nuzzled into his neck, my body pressed against his, listening to him breathe. I shook away my thoughts and put my clothes on the dresser.

"Hey."

"Hey, back," answered Kyle.

"Can I help?"

"Sure. Do you need help putting your stuff away in here again? I mean…" he realized his mistake.

"No, I'm good." He looked at me with such intensity that I could feel the weight of the surrounding air, my breathing getting faster.

"How's it going in here?" Kirstie asked, startling us from our moment.

"Good, Mom. We're almost done," Kyle said.

"Oh, that's great. And what about you, Robbie? Need anything?"

"No, that's okay. Thank you again for your generosity. I really appreciate it. And I promise to help around the house, cook, and clean to help earn my keep. I don't expect this to be a free ride."

"Oh, sweetie. You're too nice. You don't have to earn anything. I'm glad we can all help," she said, smiling.

I smiled back. "Well, either way, I want to do my part in this family so the burden on you is lessened."

"It's not a burden at all! And I'm sending a big FU to your stepfather for abandoning you. Shame on him. We're lucky to have you. Plus, it'll be nice having another female in the house." Kirstie hugged me, then headed down the hall to Shane's room. I reached out to help carry some of Kyle's stuff when he placed his hand on mine.

"Are you really doing okay?"

"Yeah. I'm fine. Why?" I asked, trying to be convincing.

"I know it's been a bit overwhelming. Having them home."

He knew me well. "It's definitely different," I lamented.

"Yeah," he mumbled under his breath.

Kyle snatched his hand off mine as his mom strolled by, popping her head back in. She announced that she was making dinner, and I took that as my cue to earn my keep.

"I'll help," I said enthusiastically.

"Great. Thank you, Robbie," she replied warmly. She yelled from the hall, addressing both boys. "Finish the rooms up here, make the beds, and get some laundry going. Then, meet us downstairs to set the table. Get a move on. You've got lots to do!" Kirstie turned to head downstairs. I looked over at Kyle, and we smirked at each other as I followed her.

Yeah, having them at home was definitely different.

CHAPTER 12

Goodbye.

Kyle

AFTER FINISHING CHORES upstairs, Shane and I headed down to set the table as Mom directed. Mom and Robbie busily prepared dinner as Shane placed silverware and I retrieved the water pitcher from the fridge. As I did, I brushed Robbie. She instinctively reached out and touched me, then pulled her hand away immediately when she realized what she had done.

We sat down to have our first meal all together. Who knew we had this much food lurking in the kitchen? Because Robbie and I did NOT eat like this all summer. Robbie must have thought I was such a terrible cook but never complained. Not once. During dinner, the conversation revolved around their trip to Portugal. It sounded beautiful there, and when I found out they were going, I was a bit envious of Shane's opportunity. But now, after spending the summer with Robbie, I wouldn't change a thing.

"So, the beaches were amazing. My bunkmates and I would head to the Tagus River near the Sea of Straw every Sunday. And the food. I've never tasted anything so good in my life!" Shane said enthusiastically.

"Hey, I take exception to that," Mom teased. "Seriously, he's right. It was amazing. Remember that restaurant by the water, Último Porto?" Mom asked.

"It had the best seafood. So fresh. Mom and I tried to meet up there every couple of weeks," Shane reminisced.

"Kyle, if you ever visit, you have got to go to Panorâmico de Monsanto. It was so cool. You could see all of Lisbon from one spot. It was incredible."

"Did the scouts like what they saw from you?" I asked.

"It looks really good," Shane answered excitedly. "They said if I keep training at this elite level and continue making the growth they saw from me this summer, they felt confident I'd get a spot on a professional team next year," he said, floating on air.

"That's fantastic, Shane. It's everything you ever dreamed of," Robbie praised, shooting him a small smile.

"Thanks, babe." Shane leaned over and pecked her on the lips.

I was happy for him. This had been his lifelong dream as far as I can remember. He was always driven, even as a kid. I think he felt some self-induced pressure to be a provider for Mom and for me from our dad splitting. Like he needed to be the 'man' of the house and take care of all of us someday. For him, that was through sports. He was naturally gifted, but he also worked his ass off. I had no doubt that he would make it.

As fate would have it, Mom's work also had offices in Lisbon. Her regular post was in NYC at L'Oreal, and when they allowed her the opportunity to transfer for the summer, she couldn't pass it up. Mom hesitated at first, not wanting to leave me, but I reassured her I would be fine. I looked forward to having the summer all to myself. Get to do what I wanted when I wanted.

I was reliable and responsible. I never really gave her a reason not to trust me. Shane was the outgoing, center-of-attention guy. I preferred doing my own thing and staying out of the limelight. Mom had made sure the neighbors checked in on me, and of course, we called or texted each other when times and schedules lined up overseas.

As the dinner convo switched to school, I could see the reservation on Robin's face. It started in five days. Shane was excited to return and show off where he'd been and what he had done all summer. Plus, he would be the big man on campus. A senior. He was stoked, to say the least.

Robbie continued to be stoic throughout the rest of the meal. I don't think she shared his enthusiasm for returning to school or the clout of being a senior like he did. Shane and my mom overlooked the stress radiating off Robbie as the conversation rattled on and on. They didn't notice what she was going through. But I did.

***

The last five days flew by like a blur. We head back to school tomorrow, which was a myriad of stresses piling onto our lives. Having Mom and Shane at home had taken some getting used to. We all tried to get a new routine going in the house, but it wasn't easy. Especially for Robbie and me.

Shane went back to his usual training. Only needing a couple of days to shake off jet lag before returning to his strict regimen. Robbie tried to go with him on a few runs but felt guilty that she held him up. She wasn't as fast, and it was still uncomfortable for her to run full-on because of the… "incident."

She had confided in me about how she felt, and I let her since she couldn't talk to either of them about why she had rib pain. Shane and my mom only knew the lie we told them as the truth. That her stepdad left, and she had nowhere to stay. They didn't know he had hurt her, and that I had spent the summer helping her pick up the pieces.

Mom startled me out of my thoughts.

"Okay, everyone. Stop procrastinating. You all need to be up at the crack of dawn tomorrow, and it'll be a huge shock to your system. I can't miss my bus to the city tomorrow morning, so I won't be around. You'll need to ensure you're all up and out the door on time. Boys, remember to figure out how to share the car again. And speaking of which, what are the driving arrangements? Can someone take Robbie to school and back? What's the plan?"

"I'm training in the morning. I'll run to school and shower there. Can you take Robbie?" Shane asked me.

"Yeah. I got it. Does that work for you, Robbie?" I asked, looking at her.

"Yeah, that works," Robbie answered reflexively.

"And what about coming home from school?" Mom asked us both.

I interjected, "Mom, we got this. Shane and I will figure it out. Don't worry!"

"Yeah, Mom. Don't worry. We got this," Shane echoed. Then Shane looked over at Robbie, grinning from ear to ear. "Trust me, she's hard to forget."

I looked over at Robbie too, when he said that.

Yes, she was.

Robbie

I had dreaded the first day of school for a while now. It amplified after Shane and his mom came home. I'm not exactly sure if I was ready to go back yet. I was fine with Kyle when it was just the two of us. But adjusting to being around Shane and his mom was much harder. Tomorrow, I would be in an entire high school with hundreds of people. I shuddered, thinking about it. I wasn't sure I could handle all the people: the social interactions, the gossip, and all the lies I had to spin.

Then, there's Sarah. My only female friend in this town. She was far less receptive than I had hoped when I reached out last week to "catch up." I thought I could slip back into the tentative friendship we started the previous year, but she focused on how I ghosted her this summer. I mean, I couldn't blame her. I had to start weaving my web of lies about why, but I wasn't sure how long I could keep up this act.

I told her I had broken my phone and that my stepdad had split and left to live with a friend out of town for a while this summer. I don't think she believed me. She mentioned she thought she saw me walking near the park about a month ago. But I told her she was wrong, even though she was right.

I remembered that particularly bad and frustrating day. I needed to get away from the house I had been relegated to all summer and even considered making plans to run. To spare everyone from my past. But I knew Kyle well enough that he would've followed. So, I came back.

The three of us got ready for bed, jockeying for our turn in the shared bathroom. I was the last one in, and when I finished, I stepped out into the hallway. It shocked me to see both Shane and Kyle waiting.

"Night, babe! Sorry, I can't ride to school with you tomorrow morning, but I'll meet you at the front door. Then we can walk into the auditorium together for the opening assembly," he said sweetly.

"No problem. You've got to get your training in. I understand. I'll see you at the assembly. Sleep well," I said.

"You too, babe!" he said. Then he leaned down and kissed me full on the lips. His hand snaked behind my back as he deepened our embrace.

Kyle cleared his throat.

Shane pulled back from me and scolded him. "Dude? Some privacy?"

"Dude, you'll see her tomorrow. She lives here." Kyle snapped. Shane grumbled but quickly pecked my lips and went into his bedroom. Kyle and I were left standing in the hall, staring at each other. After a few awkward seconds, he spoke.

"I just wanted to say I know tomorrow will be overwhelming with all the people and the crowds. I know you have Shane now, but if you need to... you can call me. I'll be there."

I blinked heavily as I reached up and hugged him around the neck. He held me close. It was only a few moments, but that embrace spoke volumes. I had needed him this summer, and I trusted him implicitly. But he deserved his life back. And even though it pained me, it was time for me to let him go. We shared so much of ourselves with each other, and for that, I'm grateful.

Thank you, Kyle.

Goodbye.

Kyle

Holding her this time felt different. It felt like goodbye. My stomach twisted into knots. I pulled away and instinctively reached to touch her face, but she stepped back quickly.

"Goodnight, Kyle." She went into her room and shut the door. I returned to my room and climbed into bed. I could hear Shane's heavy breathing, indicating that he was already falling asleep. Unfortunately, that wouldn't be the same for me as I lay there staring at the ceiling.

So many thoughts and feelings went through my head. Knowing I needed to let her go, but wanting to be with her right now. But I needed to do the right thing. Shane's her boyfriend and my brother. My family. Who had no idea the pain that was inflicted on her or what happened between us. He didn't deserve my dishonesty, and it certainly wasn't his fault that he was gone this summer. But he's back now. And even though it pained me, it was time for me to let her go. We shared so much of ourselves with each other, and for that, I'm grateful.

Thank you, Robbie.

Goodbye.

CHAPTER 13

Again.

Robbie

I GROGGILY OPENED my eyes to the sound of my alarm. I had only fallen asleep a couple of hours ago. I was so restless and anxious I couldn't sleep. And now it's morning. The first day of my senior year. Ugh. I felt like death warmed over; not the mood I needed for today.

I threw on jeans and a T-shirt and headed downstairs, hearing Kyle in the kitchen rattling around. *He's up early*, I thought. Glad someone got some rest.

"Morning. I made you a cup of coffee to-go and grabbed you a banana, but that's all we have time for," he said.

"That's great. Thanks. Sorry, I got up late. I didn't sleep well," I said groggily.

"Yeah, guess that's going around. I didn't sleep either, so I gave up and came down here."

"Oh, I'm sorry. Is Shane gone already?"

"Yeah. About fifteen minutes ago. Mom too. We should get going. I need to make sure you get to school. Mom's orders."

"Right. Mom," I said somewhat sarcastically. I followed him out to the car. The ride wasn't long, but the ease we usually had diminished and felt strained. I couldn't help but feel a loss over it. Not to mention my stomach hurt. It always did whenever I was nervous.

Plus, I still had to see Sarah. Who made it clear she really didn't want to see me. And I couldn't blame her. But I knew Shane would be there. That brought me some comfort about heading to school. I'm glad he could be a buffer.

Pulling into the school parking lot brought me back to reality. I can't believe I'm back already. My stomach gurgled.

"Thanks for the ride. I appreciate it."

"Of course. Do you want me to walk you in?"

"No. I got it. I'm meeting Shane, and hopefully Sarah, if she isn't still mad at me." He nodded his head but looked a bit sad. I didn't mean to make him feel that way, but it was time that I did things on my own. I had become so dependent on him. I needed to take care of myself. As we got out of the car, a couple of his buddies, who were with his best friend, Brody, yelled over to him. He greeted them back. They wanted him to join them, and that's when he looked at me.

C'mon Robbie, do the right thing, I scolded myself.

"Have a good first day," I said as I shut the car door. I walked toward the school entrance without looking back. Leaving him standing there.

"You too," he said sadly. His words felt like a punch in the gut, my stomach churning. Out of the corner of my eye, I could see him turn and walk over to Brody and their friends. I refocused on the school entrance. The tan bricks around the front door reflected how I felt. Depressing and dull, like the ache deep inside me.

I felt my breathing get ragged, but then I saw Shane. He waited for me at the front entrance, like he said he would. I smiled. I forgot how dependable he was. Despite his heavy training schedule in the spring, he always made time for me. Funny how two months away from each other makes your memory falter.

I took a couple of deep, calming breaths, trying to stave off a full-blown panic attack as I saw Shane grinning while I walked toward him. I should have been happy to see him. I wanted to be happy to see him. But all I felt was regret. Regret about leaving Kyle behind despite having old stirrings of my time with Shane swirling in my stomach.

As I approached, Shane took my hand and placed a peck on my lips.

"Hi, babe!"

"Hi," I greeted, taking his hand. He led me into the auditorium. The red velvet carpet and stage curtains made the room dark and claustrophobic. I stuck close to Shane as the seats filled. My breathing seemed heavier again, and I squeezed his hand. He smiled at me, continuing on to get us some spots for the new school year message.

Once we had our seats, I looked around for Sarah. She was a senior, too. So, she would be in our section. But as I searched, I found Kyle, who looked right in my direction. We shared an awkward glance, but I turned away quickly. Thankfully, the junior seating was on the other side of the auditorium.

Then… I saw Sarah. I waved shyly as she approached.

"Hey," I said tentatively.

"Hey," she responded with an edge to her voice.

"Do you want to sit with us?" I asked, unsure.

"I guess," she groaned. I slid over so she could get into our row. She leaned over to Shane and tapped him on the shoulder.

"Hey there, stranger," she said, super friendly.

"Hey there, Sarah. Good to see ya.' It's been a while," he answered as he hugged her. Sarah lingered in his embrace a few seconds too long, Shane politely peeling her arms from around him.

"Yeah, it has, you world traveler! At least you had a good reason to ghost me this summer. Unlike some other people, whom I won't name, but who can be so selfish and rude!" Her snotty remark to me didn't land well. Already on edge, my anger exploded, and I didn't even realize it had. Until it did.

"Okay. Sarah! I get it! I'm a terrible friend. Selfish and rude. I told you I was sorry so many times. What more do you want from me? I'm sorry I didn't talk to you this summer while my whole life imploded. Pile it on, Sarah. If you can't—"

"Whoa, babe. Take it down a notch. The whole auditorium is looking at you," Shane interrupted as he glanced around. I followed his gaze around the room, so embarrassed because he was right. The hall was silent, and they were all looking at me with various expressions of shock.

"Geez, Robbie. I was just joking. Lighten up!" Sarah scolded.

"You're making a scene," Shane chastised me. I sat, angry and frustrated.

I can't do this, I screamed inside my head.

I tried to control my breathing, but I could feel myself losing it. I jumped when I heard a buzz on the new phone Kirstie had given me for school. Looking down, I spotted a text from Kyle.

> **Take deep breaths robbie**
> **Tilt your head and take deep breaths**
> **In out in out**
> *Sent 7:07AM*

I did as he said, and before long, the air settled peacefully in my lungs. I lifted my head and looked over at the junior section. Kyle stared right at me. He smiled, and I smiled back, still taking slow, deep breaths. I glanced back at Shane, who was busy chatting with friends while Sarah hung all over him. Neither one had any inkling I had been struggling today.

But Kyle did. From across the room. He did.

I sat numbly, zoning out at the stage while waiting for the principal to speak. I only needed to get through this welcome message without causing any more "scenes," as Shane put it. Day one. Plan blown to hell. One year. That's all I had to stay under the radar. I hated being the center of attention, but my huge outburst proved otherwise. Planned or not.

It was definitely going to be a long year.

Kyle

I didn't know what else to do but text her. I could tell she had started hyperventilating from the embarrassment. But I also knew she wouldn't want to draw more attention to herself than she already had.

After the assembly, I tried to check in on her but saw Shane guiding her through the crowd toward the senior halls. I wouldn't see her now for most of the day, which I guess was a good thing. I mean, I'm supposed to be moving on.

***

Near the end of the day, I finally spotted Robbie in the hall and ran to her before I could stop myself. "Hey. How are you? How's the day going? Are you feeling better?" I nervously blurted out.

"Whoa, that's a lot of questions. Fine. It sucks. And sure," she answered sarcastically, biting the corner of her lip.

"First days always suck." I tried to reassure her.

"Yeah, well. You didn't scream and make a scene in front of the entire school and then hear about it the rest of the day. Including the teachers. So... that was fun."

"Sorry. That does suck. So... I guess realizing my fly was open for half of my classes isn't so bad after all," I joked, trying to lighten the mood. It worked.

"Thank you. I needed that. It's... easy with you. You know when to push me, when to back off, and when to make me laugh. Shane practically shamed me, and Sarah, well... I offended her. They don't understand me," she lamented.

"I do," I said honestly, although I probably shouldn't have.

Her eyes snapped up to mine.

"I know." We stood silently until the class bell rang, shaking us from our trance. She exhaled, "I better get to class. I don't need to add being late to my long list of fuckups today."

I smiled at her words. "Okay. Meet you at the car at three?"

"Yeah. I'll be the one drawing a crowd of teenagers hoping for another dramatic scene before the end of the day," she said, annoyed.

My smile widened. "Okay. I'll look for you and your crowd of fans."

She rolled her eyes, and as she walked away, she yelled over her shoulder, "Don't be late to class."

"I won't," I yelled back.

I watched her walk down the hall until she was out of sight. *I guess letting her go doesn't stick*, I chided myself. Because I knew it when—

Then the final bell rang.

I looked up at the clock. *Perfect*, I thought, shaking my head. I dragged my late self to my next class.

***

At dinner, Mom asked us how the first day went. Shane went on and on about how wonderful and exciting being a senior is, how everyone was blah… blah… blah… his summer trip abroad and that he can blah… blah… blah. It never ended. Robbie and I sat silently eating. When Mom finally turned her attention to us, we had already finished.

"So, how was your day, Robbie? Does it feel good to be a senior, too?"

"Oh yeah. It was great," she said. Her words dripped with sarcasm.

Shane chuckled, moving his food around with a fork. "She started a fight with Sarah in the middle of opening assembly—"

I interrupted, "Oh, Mom… I forgot to mention what happened to me today. It was so embarrassing. My fly was down for over half the day, and no one told me. Not even Brody. He thought it was hilarious and took a picture. So that was super awesome."

It shut Shane up long enough for Mom to shift her attention to my embarrassing story. I continued, launching into my day, schedule, and ice hockey tryouts later in the fall. Anything I could do to keep the focus off Robbie.

She shot me a small smile of appreciation. Robbie escaped the table, washing the dishes in the sink. Mom nudged Shane to help, so I continued rambling.

After supper, I headed out onto the porch to wind down. As I lazily watched the sunset, Robbie stepped out and asked to join me.

"Thanks… for distracting your mom."

"Sure, it wouldn't be great to relive it. Did you patch things up with Sarah?"

"Well, kinda. I apologized again, and then she said, 'You didn't have to bite my head off and embarrass me in front of the whole damn school.' So, I guess that's patched," she mocked.

"I'm sorry. Did everything else go okay?"

"I guess. I signed up for a photography class elective. So, I think that will be fun. Maybe sometime we could go—"

She jumped when Shane burst out onto the porch.

"There you are, babe. I was looking for you. Did you see there's a school mixer Friday night?" Shane said, out of breath. Then he looked over at me. "Kyle, you going?"

"Absolutely not," I answered confidently. Shane rolled his eyes, shifting his focus to Robbie.

"You want to go, right, Robbie? I mean, we have to. We're seniors, it's our last year, and it'll be a blast!"

"Shane, I…" she hesitated.

"Come on, babe. Please? It won't be fun without you," he pushed.

"It's just, a lot of people…" she tried to explain.

"I know, right?! It'll be awesome! So, it's settled. Max is planning the senior-only after-party; it's gonna' be amazing." He pecked her on the lips before running back into the house.

She looked stunned.

I didn't like how Shane inferred he might go without her if she didn't give him the answer he wanted. I would never have even considered that.

"What happened? My head is spinning," she asked.

"I'm not sure, but he seems to think you said yes about the mixer."

"Did I say yes?" she asked, confused. I looked at her and shrugged. Her face shifted to a mix of pain, worry, and anxiety all at once. Damn it, Shane. Why do you have to make everything about you? I took a deep breath, knowing what I had to do.

I walked into the house and called out my brother's name.

"What?" Shane yelled out from across the room, annoyed.

"I changed my mind. I'm going to the mixer."

"Okay," he answered sarcastically. I watched with disdain as he disappeared up the stairs. I bit the inside of my cheek, stewing over how he had decided for them both without any regard for what she wanted. But I was angrier that he didn't notice her anxiety about the dance. Because I noticed.

I sighed loudly. It only took one day to undo the promise I made to myself. Despite saying I would do the right thing and let her go, I did the opposite. The force of Robin's gravity pulled me back into her orbit.

Again.

CHAPTER 14

...does that make me?

Robbie

FRIDAY APPROACHED, AND I dreaded it. All those people in a tiny, cramped gym. But Shane was so excited about the mixer that I didn't want to spoil his senior year fun. I'll just suck it up and go. It's only a few hours, and then the after-party at Max's will be less crowded and a bit easier. *I can do this!*

Going meant needing to call Sarah. I had to borrow a nice top for the party because my T-shirts wouldn't cut it. I only bought a few items when Kyle offered to purchase my clothes at the beginning of summer. First, I didn't need much, and second, I hated owing people. I had stuck to the basics but still had to pay him back. I told him I'd start tutoring in the after-school program to earn money, but that wouldn't begin until mid-October. Kyle said he didn't mind waiting, and I believed him, but I minded.

Sarah remained upset about my outburst on the first day, but things got better between us as the week went on. She had forgiven me somewhat and replied to texts. Hoping she would say yes, I asked to come over and borrow a shirt for the mixer. She jumped at the chance. If there was one thing I knew about Sarah, she loved fashion. There wasn't always an opportunity for special events in this sleepy town. She took any opening she could to dress up and or dress others.

Shane dropped me off on his way to Max's to finalize the after-party plans. Walking up the front path to Sarah's house brought back memories of the fun times I had spent there last spring. Sarah had taken pity on the new girl at school. We weren't best friends, but we were friends. I took that as a win.

It was a little blue home with a very pretty, white-covered porch holding a couple of chairs and a table with some flowers. A small light fixture lit the way in the middle of the ceiling. I walked up to the yellow front door. Like lemon yellow. It wouldn't be my first choice for an entryway color, but it did seem like sunshine in a big open sky. Glad the house was happy to see me. Let's hope Sarah felt the same.

As I was about to knock, the door swung open, and I jumped.

"Hey Robbie," Sarah greeted me cheerfully.

"Uh… Hi Sarah," I stuttered. Her mood swings were all over. I guess this one liked me.

"Come on in. Let's get you looking like a girl for once instead of being a raggedy ol' tomboy."

And there it was. That's the mood I'm used to.

After rifling through her closet and trying on a thousand shirts, I finally settled on an eggplant-colored silk top with cold shoulder cutouts. It was dressy enough for the party but casual enough to wear with my cuffed jeans. It was perfect. It wasn't Sarah's first choice or what she "envisioned" for me, but she relented and let me borrow it.

With that out of the way, she wanted to do a little girl talk. Which was code for gossip. Well, it's more of an interrogation about my living arrangements. Ever since Shane told everyone at school I lived at his house, I had become quite the celebrity… and a pariah. All the two-faced popular girls desired to get on my good side for the juicy details. Then they would rant about me unmercifully behind my back. It was brutal.

"So… what's it like living with the Whitmore twins?" she asked.

"It's good. They're very nice."

"That's it? That's all you're giving me?" she chastised.

"There's nothing more to share. I just live there now."

"Do you stay in Shane's room?" She winked, waggling her eyebrows.

"No, of course not. Kyle gave up his space and moved in with Shane."

"Kyle? Why did he give up his room?" She asked, surprised.

I stammered, "Well... um... his room is smaller, so it made sense that he bunks with Shane since, obviously, I couldn't."

"And their mom is fine that you live there with your boyfriend?"

"It's not like that. There are rules and consequences," I answered, annoyed. Rules that I was thankful for at this point.

"But I'm sure there are ways around that," she goaded.

"Hey, I'm sorry, Sarah. I have to go," I replied quickly, trying to flee.

"C'mon. You've got to give me more than that," she begged. But instead, I grabbed the shirt and walked toward her bedroom door.

"Thanks for the help. See you at the mixer." I retreated as fast as I could. Once outside, I realized I hadn't texted Shane. I decided to start walking and call him on the way. When Shane didn't answer, I let out an audible groan.

I dialed Kyle's number, and as it rang, I thought to myself...

Please don't pick up.

Please don't pick up.

Kyle

I had almost finished my English assignment when my phone's vibration startled me. A quick glance showed Robin's name at the top of the screen. I raised a brow, wondering what she'd be calling about. I swiped the device into my hand and answered.

"Robbie?" I asked, concerned.

"Hi, Kyle. I'm sorry to bother you. I tried calling Shane, but he's not…"

"Why? What's going on?"

"I'm at Sarah's… well, I'm near Sarah's house. Can you pick me up?"

"Yeah. Where are you exactly?"

"I'm on the corner of Crescent and Aldrin."

"Everything okay?" I asked.

"Yeah. I borrowed a shirt for the mixer. Shane said he would pick me up at Sarah's, but I can't reach him."

"Okay. I'm on my way." I hung up. *Where the hell was Shane?* It's so typical of him to get caught up in whatever he's doing and shirk his responsibilities.

It only took me about ten minutes to get to her. I borrowed Mom's car, and as I pulled up to the corner, I spotted Robbie standing under a streetlight. Suddenly, the memory of that night in June flooded back; it made my stomach turn. Images of all the blood, her blood, invaded my brain. Seeing her unharmed, my muscles relaxed. I threw the car into park, hopping out.

"You okay?" I asked anxiously.

"Yeah. I'm fine."

"Are you sure?"

"I just… needed a ride. That's all. Are you okay?" She raised a brow.

"Um… yeah. It was… when you called me out of the blue, I remembered… never mind."

"Oh, I'm really sorry. I didn't think of… that. I didn't mean to scare you."

"It's all right. I'm glad you're okay." We walked over to the car and got in.

"Was Kirstie mad about you borrowing the car?" she asked.

"No. Not at all," I smiled.

"Okay. Good," she smiled back. We drove the rest of the way home in uncomfortable silence. I wanted to say more but decided I shouldn't.

As we pulled into the driveway, her phone rang. It was Shane. I heard her tell him that she got a ride home with me. I didn't want to intrude or say something like, "Where the hell was he?" or, "Why didn't he answer her call?" So, I went into the house. She followed me inside a few minutes later.

"That was Shane. He's on his way home," she announced.

"Where the hell was he? Why didn't he answer your call?" Oops.

"He was at Max's house setting up for the senior after-party. He didn't hear the phone." Furious, I bit my tongue and said nothing more.

Mom interjected, "Oh, that sounds like such fun. I know you'll have a great time! Robbie, were you able to find a shirt you liked at Sarah's?"

"Yeah," Robbie held up the shirt wadded in her hand.

"Honey, you're getting it all wrinkled. Hang it in the bathroom so the steam from the showers smooths it out."

"I'll do that right now since I'm headed to bed. Goodnight, everyone."

"Okay, sweetie. Goodnight! Sleep well," Mom said. Robin quickly ascended the stairs, avoiding any further conversations with Kristie about the mixer.

"I have to finish my English homework, so I'm heading up too."

"Okay, honey. Goodnight!" Mom hugged me.

"Goodnight." I embraced her back before running up after Robbie.

As I lingered near her door, she spoke.

"Kyle?" I meandered into her room. "I'm sorry you had to come pick me up… again. And I'm sorry that it brought up bad memories for you. I didn't mean for that to happen. I really did try to call Shane first," she apologized. I stepped closer and placed my hands on her arms as I looked her in the eyes.

"You do not have to apologize. You can always call me Robbie. For anything. Any time. Anywhere. You know that, right?"

"I do," she answered wistfully.

I stepped closer, and she didn't stop me. My breathing quickened as I lifted my hand and touched her cheek. Her lips parted when she let her breath out. I stroked her face along her jaw to her mouth as she blinked slowly.

As I was about to move my thumb along her lips, I heard Shane enter through the front door downstairs. I pulled away from Robbie hastily and rushed to my room.

What the hell was I doing?

Robbie

I tapped the off button on my annoying phone alarm. It's Friday. Mixer day. And I didn't want to go! I rolled over, refusing to get out of bed. I just wanted to stay here. I was only going because Shane was so excited.

Shane. Poor Shane.

I felt so guilty about what happened between Kyle and me last night that I jumped into bed after Kyle sprinted from my room. When Shane popped in to say goodnight to me, I feigned being asleep, so I didn't have to face him.

What the hell was I doing?

As the school day dragged on, I felt even more anxious. Not to mention Kyle actively avoiding me. At all costs. To be honest, I was relieved. I couldn't seem to control my emotions around him. Shane was the opposite. He was so pumped by the dance and after-party that he couldn't stop talking about it. He kept blabbering about all the plans Max had for the party and… blah, blah, blah. I would smile and nod.

Finally, the last school bell rang for the day, and I could go home to decompress. I had to psyche myself up for the parties. I didn't want to disappoint Shane. He was reveling in his senior status, and I'd be the party pooper. Shane didn't have practice because of the mixer, so he drove Kyle and me home. It was uncomfortable, to say the least; I felt my neck hair standing on end from Kyle's eyes behind me.

***

After dinner with Kirstie, I reluctantly went upstairs to get ready. I threw on my faded cuffed jeans, the top I borrowed from Sarah, and slip-on shoes. I left my hair down instead of my everyday ponytail and tucked some strands behind my ear on one side. I didn't usually put on makeup, but Kirstie wanted pictures. I thought I should try to make an effort. I mean, she did work at L'Oréal.

I heard a knock on the bathroom door. "You ready, babe?" Shane asked.

"Just finishing up my makeup," I said, stepping into the doorway.

"You're wearing jeans?"

"Yeah. The mixer's casual, isn't it?"

"I just thought you might wear something else since you wear that daily, but it's not a big deal," he remarked.

Feeling a little embarrassed, "Do they not look good?"

"They're fine. Really. Is that the top you borrowed from Sarah?"

"Yeah. She picked it out."

"It's nice. I haven't seen you in that color before. Sarah has good taste."

"Yeah, she does," I said, defeated.

"Well... when you're done, come on downstairs. But you don't have to rush. Still waiting on Kyle, too."

"Okay." I looked in the mirror, second-guessing my outfit. Clearly, Shane wasn't sure if it was the right choice. But I had nothing else to wear. It's either jeans or workout shorts. Plus, it's too late to do anything about it now. I continued putting on makeup haphazardly. I was a fish out of water with the stuff. I tried to wipe away some rogue mascara with my thumb.

"Whoa!" Kyle stopped in front of the doorway. "You look so... great! I mean, you always look great, but I mean, you certainly look... a different great. I'm sorry. I'm rambling. I'll shut up now."

"It's okay, and thanks." I grinned. "The jeans look all right?"

"Yeah. You always look great in jeans. Why?"

"Shane was surprised I was wearing them to the mixer. That's all." It was hard to hide the disappointment in my tone.

"He doesn't know what he's talking about. Just ignore him. I do. Trust me when I say you look absolutely..."

"Great?" I joked. He shook his head, laughing.

"Yeah. Great!" We both smiled at each other.

"I'll see you downstairs."

"Okay," I replied, still grinning.

After the awkwardness between us today, it was nice to joke around with Kyle like we used to in the summertime. I missed it.

As I descended the stairs, I could hear everyone talking in the living room. Once I was in view, silence filled the air. The group swung their heads around to look at me. I felt my cheeks flush. Not only was I already anxious about tonight, but now I was self-conscious too.

"Oh, my goodness. You look wonderful!" Kirstie said, nudging Shane. "Doesn't she?"

"Yes. You look wonderful!" he echoed. Kirstie rolled her eyes.

Grinning ear-to-ear, Kyle said, "If you ask me, I think she looks great!"

We both started laughing.

"What?" Shane asked, confused, glancing between us. "What's so funny?"

Kyle and I glanced at each other again.

"Nothing. It just struck me funny," I remarked.

After a million pictures, we said goodbye to Kirstie and hopped into the car. Shane swiveled his head toward Kyle in the back seat as we headed to school. "So, do you have a date for the mixer?"

"When would I've had time to get a date, Shane?" Kyle asked.

"All summer, bro. You can't tell me you didn't hang out with any girls," he accused. I stiffened, wondering how Kyle would answer.

"Um, right? Yeah. I mean… there was this one girl I hung out with. But… she's not from around here."

"That sucks," Shane said, dropping the subject.

I heard Kyle mumble under his breath behind me. "Yeah. It does suck."

When we got to school, the parking lot was packed. There were so many people. The mixer was for all years, and it looked like everyone came. Kyle exited the back seat and opened the door for me. He held it until I got out. As I moved around the front of the car, he gently caught my arm.

"Just remember to take deep breaths if you feel overwhelmed. Okay?"

"I will," I said quietly before walking over to Shane.

Shane took my hand, and we headed inside. I glanced back at Kyle, who watched me go. A knot formed in my stomach, just like on the first day of school. Was I anxious, or was it guilt?

Either way, it was déjà vu all over again.

Kyle

I watched her walk away, holding my brother's hand. She turned her head back, sadness in her eyes. I wasn't entirely sure if the look was about going into a dance full of people or me. I hoped it was the latter.

As I strolled toward the school, Brody trotted up to me, jacked up and ready to party. Little did he know, he freed me from her gravity. "Are you ready, man?" He asked, eager to check out all the girls. But I already knew who I'd be looking for.

The gym was packed! There was barely any breathing space, and I knew that wouldn't bode well for Robbie. I immediately searched for her, and when I finally found her, she was pressed to Shane's side with a death grip on his hand.

He seemed at ease and totally in his element, unaware of the stress emanating from Robin. Her wide eyes told a different story. It would only get more crowded and louder as the night went on. I'd have to make sure that I—

Suddenly, I felt two hands cover my eyes from behind.

"Guess who?" she chirped.

"Hello, Sarah," I said unceremoniously.

"Oh, you party pooper. You were supposed to guess," she pouted.

"I did. I guessed you."

She looked at me pointedly. "So… I was wondering…" she started.

Oh, man. I knew where this was heading. She's smart, but she is the school gossip. She constantly annoyed someone by inserting herself into their business. It's a massive turn-off for me. She had these cute little freckles and red hair that fit her fiery personality, but I didn't like her that way. Knowing her most of my life, I've never thought of her as anything more than a friend.

At one point growing up, Shane had a little crush. But only because she fawned over him like the other girls at school. Once he saw Robbie though, his attention became totally captivated. I don't think Sarah liked that very much. It seemed odd when she befriended Robbie, and they started hanging out.

"…if you would save a dance for me later," Sarah finished asking.

"Uh… yeah. Sure. That would be cool," I said reflexively.

She beamed. "Okay. Cool," she said, skirting over toward the punch table.

As the party wore on, my friends got out on the dance floor and mingled with girls. Brody hung back to try to get me involved. He noticed I was highly distracted and not quite myself. He wasn't wrong. I had been keeping an eye on a miserable-looking Robin. I wanted to go over and ensure she was all right, but she had Shane. I had to keep reminding myself of that.

"Hey, did you hear me?" Brody asked.

"What?"

"I said, Kira's checking you out. You should totally go over and talk to her."

"Nah, she's not checking me out," I replied, uninterested.

"Yes, she is," Brody said more emphatically. "Dude, she just looked at you again." He shoved me forward. "Get over there."

"Brody…" I protested.

"Get your ass over there!" He shoved me forward through the crowd of teenagers. I finally relented and made my way.

"Hi."

"Hi, Kyle," Kira replied, smiling.

"Having a good time?" I asked, trying to make small talk.

"Yeah. You?"

"I guess."

"Not your scene?"

"Not really," I said, being too honest.

"So… how was your summer? Do anything fun or exciting?" Kira asked, trying to engage in conversation.

Summer. Of course, my mind wandered straight to Robbie. How it always felt so easy to talk to her, and I could barely speak three words to Kira. Robin and I would chat for hours. And we did. It felt natural.

I shook off my thoughts. I needed to at least try to stay in the moment. Kira deserved that. "Nope. It was just a normal summer." I lied. "Yours?"

"Well, mine *was* fun and exciting! I stayed at my aunt and uncle's ranch in Montana. It was so beautiful there, and I rode horses every day. It was awesome!" Kira said excitedly.

"Oh, wow. That sounds cool," I replied honestly.

Intimidated by Kira's willingness to share so easily, I wavered when she asked me to dance. I looked at Brody, who egged me on. I took her hand and walked onto the very crowded dance floor. As we slowly swayed, I tried to be present with Kira. Unfortunately, the song reminded me of how Robbie and I would dance together over the summer.

Some nights, we cranked the tunes and danced in the middle of the living room floor… like no one was watching us, kind of dancing. Then, when a slow song came on, I'd take her hand and pull her close. Robin would rest her head on my chest as we slowly swayed. The thrum of the music in sync with my heart. In those moments, there was nowhere else I ever wanted to be.

I shook myself out of my reverie and smiled down at Kira. As we continued dancing, I tried to covertly scan the crowd. That's when I saw Sarah, shooting daggers in my direction.

Oh shit.

I had promised her a dance, and now she looked pissed. She turned with a huff and walked away. I'm in so much trouble. Sarah was never one to hold back how she felt at any given moment, and I just gave her a ton of ammunition to unload on me. I rolled my eyes at the thought.

I searched the crowd again, and that was when I spotted her. There was panic in her eyes, chest heaving. She was gulping air, and I knew she was about to have a full-blown panic attack if I didn't do something about it.

I turned to Kira suddenly. "Thanks so much for the dance. I really enjoyed it," I tried to sound sincere, pulling away quickly.

"Yeah. Same," I heard her say as I vanished into the crowd. I moved through the sea of students toward Robbie. Where was Shane? He was nowhere to be seen. When I approached, I slid my hand down Robbie's arm into her hand. I pulled her through the dance floor as she grasped onto me like I was a lifeboat.

We went past the punch table and into the hallway. I saw the back door of the school and pulled her outside. Her panic got louder as I pushed the doors open. I spun her toward the brick wall as she placed both hands against it. She tilted her head down as I coached her to breathe. In. Out. In. Out. She tried her best to slow her breathing, matching my words.

When her breathing returned to normal, she leaned against the cool door that had slammed shut after we came outside. I pulled my cell phone out and tapped out a message.

"Who are you texting?" she asked.

"Shane. I'm telling him you're not feeling well and that I'm taking you home. I also told him to find a ride to Max's party." She stood there without saying a word. With the text sent, I took her hand and walked to the car. Although we rode in complete silence, the air between us was palpable.

When we got back, Mom was sound asleep on the couch. Robbie headed upstairs as I put a blanket over her. After turning off the TV, I slowly climbed the stairs. But Robbie was already in her room with the door shut. I lingered for a moment before going to my room. As soon as I sat on the bed, I heard my phone buzz. Shane finally replied.

Okay thanks bro tell her I hope she feels better
Sent 9:13PM

That's it? He's not coming home to check on her? I was so frustrated with him. I tugged at my shirt, throwing it on the floor. I kicked off my shoes when I heard a quiet knock on the door. I turned around to see Robbie standing in the doorway in her tank top and shorts that she wore to bed.

My stomach flipped, heart racing. I stood there looking at her. I felt everything in that moment. I wanted her gravity to pull me in and never let me go, and that's when I decided I'm not holding back this time.

Not anymore.

Robbie

My stomach flipped, heart racing. I stood there looking at him. I felt everything in that moment. This person that I had come to trust and to rely on. Need. And that's when I decided I'm not holding back this time.

Not anymore.

And before I knew what I was doing, I crossed the room into his arms, kissing him. His hands slid up my back and held me so tightly that I could feel his heartbeat in my chest. I was drowning and clung to him as if he were my life raft. I moaned, allowing him access to my mouth, to my tongue. His hand moved up to caress my neck as he deepened the kiss.

Our breathing grew ragged but in sync with each other. Bliss compared to the breaths of panic that had filled my lungs earlier. We continued as our hands roamed, everything we felt culminating in this moment. Every nerve ending in my body was on fire and screaming for more. His body responded to our closeness and his kiss, desperate and intense.

Abruptly, I opened my eyes, which totally broke the spell. I realized what was happening and pulled back slightly. When I looked at him, our bodies were still entangled, his gaze dark.

"I only meant to say thank you," I said, breathless.

"You're welcome," he replied, breathless.

Thrown off by the intensity of what had just happened, I stepped away from him. He let me go as I slowly backed up across the room. I turned and sprinted down the hall.

Still breathing heavily, I shut the door to my room and stood against it. Partly to catch my breath and partly to keep me from returning to him. Stunned and overwhelmed, tears slid down my cheeks. My emotions swirled as my skin tingled from his touch. I was so conflicted about my actions. The old familiar pressure on my chest and the ache in my heart rose to the surface.

And now, I am completely involved with not one, but both Whitmore brothers. Cheating on one of them while leading on the other. What kind of person does that?

And what kind of person does that make me?

CHAPTER 15
Well, that's...

Kyle

QUESTIONS SWIRLED INSIDE my brain. Now what? What did this mean? Because this time she kissed me. It was a full-on make-out session, and one of the hottest things I've ever done. I legit saw stars, and our bodies hummed. She fit perfectly against me, and her mouth... damn. Her mouth. I was dizzy from the thrill. The fact that she initiated made the whole moment perfect.

Until she ran off.

I wanted to go after her. Tell her everything I've been feeling. Tell her to leave Shane. Deep down, I knew I shouldn't do any of that. He's my brother, and I'm betraying him. I felt awful, but the more I tried to forget her, the deeper I fell.

The way we kissed felt like souls finding their other half. Fire consumed me as her flames lapped at my heart. Our mouths and hands explored scorched skin, driving me insane. I wanted this, and I wanted her. But did she feel the same? She had responded to the kiss, but when she had pulled away from me, her eyes sank my heart. And now I'm worried this fire will burn me.

***

In the morning, I decided to go for an endlessly long run. I needed to clear my head and avoid Shane. And Robbie. I had this feeling in the pit of my stomach that she would regret what happened between us, and I wasn't ready to give up how last night made me feel. Not yet.

Shane was still in bed when I left, so I wouldn't have to share this run with him. Not that he would be up this early after getting home at three-thirty A.M. I knew the exact time because I couldn't sleep because of that kiss. Apparently, he partied hard and passed out on top of the sheets, fully clothed.

As my house came into view, it snapped me out of my inner dialogue. I hadn't realized I had run my lap and was already almost home. As I approached, I saw Mom grabbing the paper at the end of the driveway.

"Morning, Mom!" I greeted, as chipper as possible.

"Hey there, kiddo. I'm surprised you went running. I figured after the big party, you'd be sleeping in like the rest," Mom said, smiling.

"I've got hockey tryouts soon. I'm trying to get back into shape," I said, which was basically true.

"Well, aren't you dedicated. I thought Shane was, but I guess both my sons are." I smiled at her. "Did you have fun at the mixer last night?" Mom asked.

"Yeah. I did." I answered evasively.

"Any cute girls there?" Mom asked.

I'm terrible at lying to my mom. Because what I really wanted to tell her was… yes. There's a cute girl in my life, and I'm really into her. That I kissed her last night and literally saw fireworks… but instead, I lied the best I could.

"Yeah. I danced with Kira. Remember her? She's the pretty brunette from my summer swim classes in middle school. Her dad owns the dealership."

"Oh, she's adorable. So…? Details!" she grilled.

"There's not much to say. She asked me to dance, and I danced with her."

"Oohh… very progressive. Asking a boy to dance. I like that. Was it a slow song?" She continued her interrogation.

"Yes, Mom," I answered, rolling my eyes. My head pounded.

"And…?" Mom pried.

"And that's it."

"Oh, come on. There's got to be more to the story," she pressed.

"Nope. That's it."

"Did you get her number?"

"Well… I was going to, but Robbie wasn't feeling well, so I took her home. She told Shane to go to the after-party without her. She didn't want him to miss it because of her."

"Is she alright?" Mom asked, worried.

"Oh yeah. She got overheated, I think. It made her a little lightheaded. I'm sure she's fine."

"Oh, poor thing. Now that I think of it, she looked a bit pale yesterday. You're such a good friend to her and your brother," Mom gushed. I swallowed the guilty lump of lies in my throat.

"I need to take a shower. I stink from the run," I said, trying to escape.

"Okay, sweetie. I'll start some breakfast." I smiled and ran into the house.

I crept up the stairs, hoping I wouldn't bump into Shane or Robbie. Their bedroom doors were shut, but the bathroom door was wide open. I couldn't believe my luck. As I rushed through, Shane prayed to the porcelain throne.

I should have known I wasn't that lucky.

Robbie

I willed my body to get out of this safe and comfortable bed. To face the day. To face Shane and Kyle. But I wasn't ready. I pulled the covers over my head. I forced my eyes to close so I could fall back asleep when I heard a muffled noise. Moving the sheets down, slowly training my ears to the sound. I stepped out of bed and shuffled to my door, hearing two yelling voices in the hallway. Oh, no. How would I explain what happened?

I opened my door quietly, peeking out while waiting for the onslaught of Shane's anger. But instead, he was on the floor in front of the toilet, arms draped over the sides. Kyle stood next to him.

"Are you okay?" I asked Shane carefully.

"Do I look okay? Like I told Kyle—"

"You mean hollered at..." Kyle snapped.

"I just want some fucking privacy," Shane roared.

"Then don't leave the damn door open."

"Fuck off, Kyle."

"Fine with me. I was trying to help, but I won't make that mistake again." Kyle stormed past me back to his room. Suddenly, Shane made a retching noise, and I slowly retreated before shutting the door.

I could hear Kyle banging around, mumbling angrily. I decided it was probably best I leave him alone. But my feet moved toward him anyway.

"Did you tell him what happened? Is that why he's mad?" I whispered.

"No. Of course, I didn't. I went in there to see if he needed help. My mistake," he said, frustrated and angry.

"Is he sick or drunk?" I asked stupidly.

"What do you think? Huge party last night, remember?" he answered curtly.

"Right. Sorry. Dumb question." He rummaged through the closet looking for clothes. "So... did you go for a run?"

"What gave it away? My running shorts, running sneakers, or maybe being covered in sweat from... running?" his voice mocked. I took the hint and turned to leave. He grabbed my hand. "Don't go. I'm sorry. Shane put me in the worst mood. I didn't mean to take it out on you. Please don't go."

I looked down at our clasped hands. He didn't let go, and neither did I. He pulled me toward him, unintentionally making me step closer. I was afraid to look up at his handsome face. Afraid I'd get lost in his eyes and kiss him again.

I sighed loudly. "We should probably talk."

"Yeah. Probably."

"Later today," I insisted.

"Okay." He let go, returning to rummage for something to wear. Sullen, I ambled back to my room.

I knew I should have stayed in bed this morning like I wanted to. The day hadn't even started, and I was already emotionally exhausted. And now we had to talk about last night. What am I going to say to him? That I had temporary insanity? That I might have feelings for him? Or should I do what I do best?

Lie.

Kyle

So, that went well. Every time I felt guilty for screwing Shane over, he did something to make me not regret it. He's so self-absorbed and infuriating. I should tell him about the kiss. I should tell him that while he was away, I fell for his girl, and I kissed her.

And then she kissed me.

But I won't. Because it wasn't just about me. It's about Robin too. It's about protecting her from the pain of her past and the demons that still haunted her.

I would never do that to her.

During the summer, I saw her when she was most vulnerable. When she had to rely on my help, even though she didn't want to. How she had to bare her soul. She trusted me then, and she can trust me now. Always.

Finally, Shane staggered back into our room and climbed into his bed without even a glance in my direction, which was fine by me. I didn't feel like interacting with him again. Truthfully, I wished I could go back to bed too so I could avoid the inevitable talk with Robbie.

Instead, I went into the bathroom to shower. The hot water running over me felt good after my long run. Unfortunately, as soon as I closed my eyes, all I saw was her. The summer, the school dance, and our kiss flashed before me. Sometimes, I'm overwhelmed by the intensity of my attraction to her. I held my suppressed feelings in for so very long. They rose to the surface and spilled over last night in the form of our all-consuming kiss.

The "talk" loomed over my head, my stress levels rising. What am I going to say to her? That I'm sorry we kissed? Because I'm not sorry. I wanted to kiss her. I want to kiss her still. And I know that makes me a shitty brother, but I can't help how I feel.

But that's not what I'm stressed about the most. I'm worried about how she felt. About me. I had no delusions of grandeur that she would suddenly tell me she was leaving Shane and wanted to be with me instead. But I wondered if she would admit she had feelings for me. And that was the reason why she kissed me last night.

After my shower, I went to my room and dressed as quietly as possible. I didn't want to wake the beast. I crept out and headed downstairs, where I found Mom and Robbie setting breakfast out on the table. I leaned against the door frame, watching them in the kitchen. I finally felt my stress melt away just by being around her. I loved seeing them together. It was a beautiful scene. These two women. The most important women to me in this whole world.

A grin stayed plastered on my face when Robbie noticed me, happening to glance my way. She smiled back. One of her traffic-stopping smiles, and I couldn't get my heart not to skip a beat over. It was hers now, and I had no control. Despite my guilty conscience, I decided I wouldn't deny my feelings for her any longer.

Well, that's definitely going to complicate things.

CHAPTER 16

...a bad habit.

Robbie

WE ALL SAT down for breakfast except for Shane. He nursed his hangover. I noticed Kyle seemed to be in a better mood after he entered the kitchen. I wish his positive vibe would rub off on me because I wasn't looking forward to our "talk" later.

Kirstie unexpectedly received a call from her friend, who wanted to catch up and hear about her adventures in Lisbon. I told her I'd clean up so she could chat. She appeared very appreciative, stepping out on the porch to take it.

Kyle and I cleared the table before washing the dishes. I washed the plates and utensils while he dried them. It felt like summer all over again when we cleaned the kitchen every night as part of our usual evening chores. It was nice to be back in that routine, even if only for a moment.

"Kyle..." I stated coyly.

"You don't have to say it. I know what you're going to say. And you're right. It's not fair to him. He doesn't deserve it, even when he's acting like an ass. Especially since he has no idea what happened to you in June or between us this summer. It's not a fair fight," he said.

"Fight?" I asked, surprised.

"Yeah. It's not a fair fight for your heart if he doesn't know the full story."

"You're telling him?" I couldn't help my nervous tone.

"No. But let me be clear… I'm not giving up. So, when you're ready, just say the word. And I'm yours," he said confidently. He put the last dish away and walked out onto the porch.

I stood there in shock, my mouth hanging open. What just happened? I was supposed to end this and stop whatever was happening between us. I'm leaving, and Kyle knew this, but apparently it didn't deter him.

And it's all my fault.

***

Over the next six weeks, the space between Kyle and me widened much to his chagrin. Kyle didn't tell Shane about the kiss, and Shane never suspected, but the chasm still lingered. I had distra… diverted my attention for far too long.

I allowed myself to stray and needed to pivot. Kyle had put the ball in my court, but I can't think about that right now. So, I just avoided him. His annoyance regarding that became apparent. However, I could only handle one brother at a time.

Shane and I had been struggling to get back to some type of normalcy since he came home. And it wasn't getting any better. I knew Shane felt me pulling away, but he never brought it up. We tried to find a comfortable rhythm as we had before summer, but that was proving easier said than done. And I knew the reason why. Or the reason "who."

School had become a mundane task. I was so uncomfortable in the large hallway crowds that I would avoid them at all costs. I made any excuse to hide out in the library or the darkroom of my photography class. At least there, I had a respite from the hordes of teenagers for a while.

As I developed my pictures, I realized my subject matter was bleak and dark. Pictures of dead autumn leaves, trash discarded on the ground, and Kirstie's now very dead plant on the front porch. I'm not quite sure this was what the teacher had in mind when she assigned the class the topic, "How we see the world." I scoffed. Just another example of all the baggage I carried.

I signed up to tutor peers after school, but that only paid so much. I still owed Kyle for the clothes he bought me this summer. So, when I saw a flyer to work concessions at sporting events, I jumped at the chance. Shane was pleased that I would be at all his games. I was pleased that I didn't have to be in the crowded stands.

Sports were in full swing as the fall air took on a chill, and the leaves turned into a gorgeous array of rich tones. Every weekend, I worked concessions. If I continued at this pace, I should be able to pay off Kyle in no time. When I took breaks, I'd make my way over to the fence to catch Shane's games. He was a striker, and he was fantastic. I didn't know much about soccer before dating Shane, but he ensured I got a crash course this past spring.

His excitement about the game was contagious. It amazed me how he made me feel like I was on the field with him as he shared stories of his goals. Going professional had always been his dream. So, when the opportunity came for him to go to Lisbon and attend that huge scouting soccer camp, he couldn't pass it up. I was honestly so happy for him. Little did I know his absence this summer would change everything.

The school buzzed again as Homecoming rolled around the corner. There were planning committees and grand gesture proposals from people all over the school. The students floated on a high. I, on the other hand, dreaded it. Another large crowd. Another chance for a complete panic attack. Another chance to draw attention to myself. Something I could not afford to do.

As Sarah and I trolled the halls before the start of school, she endlessly droned on about how she hadn't been asked to Homecoming. I reassured her to give it time. Then, to make matters worse, she heard Kyle had asked Kira, and it made her incensed. She didn't realize it was her own doing.

Shane found out about Kyle dancing with Kira at the mixer from Sarah, so Shane harassed Kyle until he finally asked Kira out. They went on a couple dates, but it wasn't serious, according to Kyle. Shane tried to badger him into a double date with us, but he resisted. Eventually, Kyle felt pressured to ask Kira to Homecoming when he heard that Shane had romantically proposed to me. Kyle was not thrilled. About either one.

Not that Kira wasn't beautiful. She was gorgeous. Long, flowing brown hair, deep amber eyes, and her skin tanned a tawny shade. She was absolutely stunning, and many guys (and girls) noticed. She would be perfect for Kyle if he would give her a chance.

So, basically, Sarah pushed them together inadvertently when she put the idea into Shane's head. I smirked a little that she hadn't realized the part she played. Sarah continued griping when I felt a tap on my shoulder. They spoke my name, but it took a moment for me to register who it was.

"Hi, Robbie. Hi, Sarah," Kira greeted us nervously.

"Hi," Sarah snipped.

"Hey, Kira. How's it going?" I asked with trepidation.

"Actually, I was wondering if we could talk."

"Me?" I tried not to appear too shocked.

"Just for a minute, if you have time."

"Um… sure, I guess. Classes are starting soon," I said, my throat dry.

"I know. It won't take long."

"Fine, I can take a hint when I'm not wanted." Sarah pouted and left. Kira looked around, checking if anyone would see or hear us. My stomach lurched. This couldn't be good. Questions invaded my brain. Did she find out about Kyle and me? If so, how did she find out? More importantly, would she tell Shane?

"What did you want to talk about?" I asked cautiously.

"So, Kyle let it slip the other day that Brody likes Sarah, and he wanted to ask her to Homecoming. Do you think she would say yes?"

"That's what you wanted to ask?"

"Yeah, because I know she has high standards, so just in case, I'd like to warn Brody before he asks. He may seem like a chill guy, but he's really into her. I know it would break his heart."

Oh, ugh. Kira's super sweet, too? Awesome. Just rub how perfect she is for Kyle right in my face, I thought, annoyed.

"I think Sarah would say yes." *I know she'll say yes.* "Is Brody sure he wants to ask her? I mean, she's not really... chill."

"Oh, yeah. He talks about her all the time. He likes her being spicy. Just the way he likes his food." She giggled.

"Well, if he likes spicy, then he struck gold." I grinned.

"Thanks, Robbie. I can't wait to tell Brody. I don't know why I was so nervous to talk to you. I guess it's because Kyle always talks about you and how great you are." I practically choked on her words. The bell rang, saving me. I had never been happier to get to class than I was at that exact moment.

"Gotta' go. See ya." I hastily rushed away.

***

"Hold still..." Sarah snapped.

"I'm trying," I said, frustrated.

"You're not," she snipped again.

I rolled my eyes and tried not to move. Sarah was helping me... again, as I needed a dress for the Homecoming dance. Shane had asked me a few weeks ago. He was charming about it but seemed nervous. That wasn't like Shane. He's very confident and knew what he wanted. But my aloofness these last few weeks took a toll on his ego.

He asked if I could watch the sunset on the porch with him. Although this wasn't out of character, this time seemed different. He had a single rose and got down on one knee. Then he asked me. I had to stifle a laugh. But when I realized he was trying to be romantic and sincere, I also kneeled on my knees and said yes. This was the Shane I remembered before summer, and I didn't want to disappoint him by saying no.

Sarah had insisted on coming into the changing room with me at the boutique as I tried on the dresses. It was so embarrassing. Sarah didn't understand my uneasiness with her being in there or the fact that I wouldn't take my T-shirt off to change. But that's Sarah for you. It's always about her.

I was already irritated that Kirstie offered to buy everything. My job as a tutor after school had just started, and I couldn't afford one yet. I was embarrassed, but Shane said I should accept the gift. I know he was being helpful. However, I hated owing this family even more. I felt obligated to them, but I needed to be able to cut all ties when the time was right.

Sarah didn't like my taste in dresses because they weren't strapless or low back, but I knew they weren't my style. Plus, I couldn't wear anything like that with my scars. Not that I was vain, but she would ask questions, and I didn't have it in me today to spin a web. It was bad enough that Kyle already saw them. But Shane hadn't, so I sure as hell wouldn't let Sarah see.

Sarah had been constantly hot and cold since summer. Well, ever really. It was hard to read her, but she was the closest thing I had to a proper female friend. So, I just rolled with it. It's not like we would be lifelong friends. I was leaving at graduation.

Sarah was unbearable when she discovered Kyle had asked Kira to Homecoming. She was livid. Sarah raged around her bedroom, yelling, "*I asked him to dance with me first at the mixer… Kira's sweet act… The Whitmore twins sucked… blah, blah, blah!*" I feigned interest and let her vent. I really liked Kira; I wasn't sure why Sarah didn't. Maybe in a different world, Kira and I could have been friends. Best friends even, but that wasn't possible now.

"There. All zipped up. What do you think?" Sarah interrupted my thoughts.

"About what?" I asked, confused.

"The dress?" she huffed.

"Oh, sorry. Yes. Wow! It looks great," I answered honestly. The style she picked looked fitting on me, and the navy-blue color was more to my liking. I've never been so dressed up before, like ever.

"I know, right?! I'm awesome at this. Maybe I'll be a personal shopper after high school," she said arrogantly.

"Yeah. That would be cool. You'd be great at it," I agreed. "Are you trying anything on?"

"Nah. I already got mine. Even though it sucks that a lowly junior had to ask me to go to Homecoming. But it doesn't mean I can't knock his socks off."

"Well, I'm sure Brody will love whatever you wear. He really likes you."

"No, he doesn't. He only asked because Kyle felt guilty and told him to ask me." I looked at her, confused.

"What do you mean, Kyle felt guilty?"

"Well, you're not the only one that wants to date a Whitmore twin," she said, her tone mocking.

"You want to date Kyle?"

"No, I want to date Shane, but I would have settled for Kyle. Except you and that bitch Kira beat me to it. Like vultures circling their prey and then sinking your talons into them!" she snarled. I stared at her in shock. Noticing my expression, she seemed to realize that wasn't something to admit out loud. "I'm sorry, Robbie. That didn't come out right," Sarah tried apologizing.

"No. I think that came out exactly the way you wanted it to." I grabbed my clothes with the unpurchased dress still on, heading into the dressing room next to us. Sarah banged on the door, begging me to open it so she could explain. I didn't have the mental capacity to listen.

"Go home, Sarah."

"Robbie, please…"

"I said go home, Sarah!" I yelled.

"Fine. Whatever. I don't know why you're mad at me. It shouldn't be that big of a surprise. Every girl at that school wants a Whitmore twin. At least you've got one. And if I'm really being honest, you technically have both brothers. Because not only do you live with them, but they follow you around like little puppies. And then there's me, who can't even get one. So… whatever, Robbie. Be mad at me. I don't care. I'm out of here!" she screamed. I heard her grab her stuff and storm out.

UGH! I snatched up the dress and bought it with Kirstie's credit card, which pissed me off even more since Shane had already purchased the tickets. They insisted on helping me regardless of my protesting. *Aagghhh! Now I owed all three of them*, I thought, frustrated. I grabbed the shopping bag and stormed out of the store. Walking down Skyline Drive toward home, I was fuming. Mad at the world. Mad at Sarah.

Stomping across the street, I looked up at the sky to see darkening clouds. I picked up my pace, but lugging this huge dress bag slowed me down. Stewing about our fight, I heard gravel crunch violently beneath my feet. Sarah made me so exasperated.

But was Sarah the one I was mad at? Because if I were being honest, deep down, I knew the truth. Even if I didn't want to admit that she was right.

I did have both Whitmore twins.

Kyle

As I looked over at Kira in the passenger seat, I tried to be upbeat about heading out for dress shopping. I mean, she was sweet, beautiful, and we got along. But I wasn't sure why she needed me for this. She said I could get my jacket and tie while we were there, so I relented.

Here I was, driving down Skyline Drive to the only dress store miles away. Typical of our little town. In the presence of the girl I invited to Homecoming, wishing it was the girl going with my brother.

This was so messed up. I ought to come clean and tell Shane about the kiss and how I felt. This was so unfair to Kira, too. But I wouldn't. I'm absolutely hopeless. Sometimes I wish I could—

"Hey, isn't that Robbie?" Kira pointed out the window.

I jerked my head and saw a girl carrying a giant dress bag on the side of the road. "Yeah. I think so." I pulled over and quickly jumped out. I jogged back a few yards, calling out her name. "Robin?"

When she looked, I could see the grimace on her face. "Oh, great. Just what I need," she said, annoyed. She turned around and started walking away.

"Robbie? Wait. What's going on?" I asked, catching up.

"Nothing! I'm walking home. Can I just do that without being interrogated?"

"Let me give you a ride. It's cold, and it's supposed to rain."

"No! I'm not cold, and it's not raining." Just then, as if on cue, raindrops fell. She looked up as water trickled onto her face. Robin glared at me with a mix of fury and resignation.

I carefully took the dress bag from her, and she reluctantly followed me. As we got closer, she stopped in her tracks and spun her head to look at me.

"Is that Kira in the car?" she asked.

"Yes."

"You're on a date!?" she exclaimed.

"No, we're going shopping for Homecoming."

"Forget it. I'm not crashing your date," she growled as her anger flared.

"It's not a date," I repeated.

"I'll walk." She tried to grab the bag out of my hands.

"Stop being stubborn!"

"I'm not stubborn," she snapped back.

I cocked my head. "Seriously? Get in, Robbie. Let me take you home."

"Don't tell me what to do."

"Well, I'm not leaving until you do," I smirked.

Anger flashed across her face. "Now who's being stubborn?"

"I learn from the best."

She gave me a dirty look but got into the back. She scooted to the middle as I placed the dress beside her. I returned to the driver's seat as Kira greeted Robbie sweetly. "Hi, Robbie. I thought that was you."

"Yep, it's me," Robbie answered snidely.

"Is that your dress for homecoming?" Kira asked.

"Yep, heard you're getting yours."

"Yeah, and then Kyle can get his jacket and tie, too. Two birds, one stone," Kira said pleasantly.

"Cool, cool, cool," Robbie answered coldly.

"So, you walked all the way to the dress store? It's very far," Kira asked.

"No. I went with Sarah."

"Where's Sarah now?" I asked, brows furrowing as I glanced at Robbie through the internal rear-view mirror.

"I don't want to talk about it." Robbie gave me the "look," so I dropped it.

We pulled into the driveway at home as rain poured. I jumped out to get her dress and met her on the porch. In that short distance, we were soaked. As I opened the front door, Robbie stopped me.

"I've got it. Kira's waiting for you," Robbie whispered sadly. The pain lingering in her voice made me reach out to brush a wet strand of hair from her face. I pulled my hand back swiftly, hoping Kira didn't see.

I handed her the dress. "You okay?" She nodded as she went inside.

I stood there for a second, trying to gather my bearings. Being around her always makes me flustered. It was still pouring. So hopefully, Kira hadn't seen what happened. I walked to the car hesitantly, causing the rain to soak me even more. I got in, running my fingers through my wet hair to get it out of my face.

"Sorry about interrupting the dress shopping," I said earnestly.

"It's fine. Is she okay? Because it seemed like she was mad or maybe sad. I couldn't tell for sure."

"She's upset about the whole Sarah situation. I was just making sure that she was okay."

"I saw."

"Kira…" I said nervously.

"It's okay. You guys are close. I understand. It's a good thing. I hear the rumors at school: her stepdad split, she was basically homeless, and her mom died. It's a lot of tragedy for one person. So, I think it's great that your family took her in and are giving her a loving—"

Before I knew what I was doing, I leaned over and kissed her. When I pulled away from the kiss, she looked intently into my eyes.

"Sorry," I said instinctively.

"Don't be. I liked it. And I like you," she said, smiling.

I returned the smile. "I like you too."

I reversed the car out of the driveway, heading back to the dress shop. We rode quietly, letting the weighted air settle between us. It shocked me that I said "I liked her" so naturally. But it shocked me even more that I kissed her. Because asking her to Homecoming was basically peer pressure. So why did I keep complicating things?

It's becoming a bad habit.

CHAPTER 17

My heart…

Robbie

IT TOOK SOME time and a lot of groveling on my part before Sarah would speak to me. I'm not exactly sure why I was the one apologizing, but Sarah seemed to think it was necessary. She explained that she only stated facts about everyone in school wanting the Whitmore brothers. So, I shouldn't have been that surprised. I took the blame rather than the mental exhaustion and conceded that I had overreacted, making her gloat.

Sarah and I were "friends" again, and she returned to her old self. She offered to come over and help me get ready for Homecoming. I knew she only did it because she wasn't sure I could do it without her. Full honesty, I wasn't either. So, I said yes. Once again, a floundering fish when it came to dressing up for special events.

We got ready here at the Whitmore's house. Brody planned on meeting her here, and Kira's mom would bring Kira later for pictures. Unfortunately, Sarah's mother couldn't make it, so Kirstie promised to send photos. She had warned us that she was taking a ton. Like paparazzi-level pics, so I knew Sarah's mom would have plenty.

"Wow, Sarah. You look fantastic," I said.

"I know. Right? The twi… I mean, all the boys will be jealous." I let the comment slide, knowing which boys she had been referring to.

"And of course, you would look effortlessly and ridiculously hot. No one can ever compete with you," she said snidely.

"I'm not trying to compete," I whispered.

"I know. It's so annoying," she snipped.

I turned away from her and rolled my eyes.

Her dress was an emerald-green satin, which looked stunning with her red hair. It was strapless but with a heart-shaped neckline. It had a tight bodice and flared to just above her knees. My dress was a simple navy-blue wrap with a full back and a bit of a plunging V-neck in the front. It had this little tie around the waist and ruffled chiffon on the short sleeves and at the bottom of the dress around mid-thigh. Sarah let me borrow a silver drop necklace that accentuated the V-neck.

"Are you girls ready?" Kirstie yelled upstairs.

"Yes, we'll be right down!" I called back. We rushed to put our shoes on because we were running behind. Yet another thing I borrowed from Sarah. Thankfully, we were the same size. She brought these cute, short, nude wedges for me, and wore some sparkly, silver, strappy high heels. The straps wrapped up her ankle, making her look like a celebrity ballerina. Just the way she liked it, I chuckled to myself.

"Babe?" Shane was the one to yell up now.

"We're coming," I answered back.

"I'll go first," said Sarah.

"Sure," I relented. She had this idea we should descend the staircase for maximum impact for our dress unveiling. Whatever.

As I followed Sarah out of the bedroom, my stomach started hurting. Here we go again. Another dance. Another nervous stomach. I held onto the railing at the top like my hand was made of superglue. As Sarah reached the bottom step, I heard Brody speak.

"Holy crap, Sarah. You look hot!"

"Oh, Sarah. You look wonderful!" Kirstie exclaimed. I could hear Shane and Kyle complimenting her, too. I ripped my hand away with all my might. As I descended, everyone turned toward me. I clenched my stomach muscles to quiet the churning. Kirstie audibly gasped and clasped her hands to her mouth. Both Shane and Kyle stared at me with their mouths agape.

"Exquisite!" Kirstie fawned. "I mean, you took my breath away." She crossed the room and hugged me.

"Thank you, Kristie," I said, slightly embarrassed. Shane and Kyle both stood frozen in time.

"Shane! Snap out of it," she scolded.

"Uh, sorry. I was… speechless. You look fantastic!" Shane said.

I smiled. "Thank you." He pulled me in for a hug and pecked my lips. I glanced at Kyle, who was about to say something, when the doorbell rang.

"Oh, that must be Kira," Kirstie chirped excitedly. She opened the door and let Kira and her mom into the house. "Oh, my goodness. Aren't you lovely, Kira," Kirstie gushed.

"Thank you, Ms. Whitmore," Kira said politely. Then Kirstie elbowed Kyle.

"Uh. Hi. I mean, you look amazing!" Kyle stuttered before hugging Kira.

Kira really did. She wore a peach halter dress, the bodice ruched. The fabric hung down just above her knees. The peach against her tawny skin… well, she could pass as a Greek goddess.

After introductions and pleasantries, the boys presented us with little wrist corsages. I was surprised at first since corsages hadn't crossed my mind. I mean, I knew that's the normal thing to do for a formal dance. But I've never been to one, and I'm certainly not a typical teenager either.

The flowers were beautiful. Mine held white roses, and Kyle had gotten Kira peach to match her dress. Sarah huffed when she saw that hers were bright red. Brody tried to defend his choice, that it was because she's spicy. But all Sarah could focus on was that it clashed with her hair. Kira and I looked at each other with unspoken regret. I mean, I did tell her to warn Brody about his selection of jalapeño.

After all the photos were taken, which felt like hours, Sarah finally announced it was time to leave. She didn't want us to be late. We said our goodbyes before heading out the door. I turned to reach for my purse on the hall table when I saw Kyle holding it. He leaned in close to my ear as he handed it over to me.

"What I wanted to say earlier was that you look stunningly... great!" I giggled. His eyes held me for a second, sending chills down my spine. I turned and hurried out the door to Kirstie's car.

We were taking her car because she had third-row seating. Brody and Sarah were in the very back row, with Kira and Kyle in row two. Shane drove, so I sat in front. The hairs on my neck stood, my mind knowing Kyle's eyes were on me. I wanted to return the gaze, but I trained my eyes on the road in front of me. *Just look forward, Robbie.* I snickered at my choice of words, knowing deep down that a future wasn't possible until I dealt with my past.

Oh, the irony.

Kyle

We headed out of town to the hotel for Homecoming. Being that far out, it was a bit of a drive. I couldn't help but want to be anywhere but here. It was hard not to be anxious and confused again. Since the last dance, my life has been a mix of avoidance and peer pressure to date. But as Homecoming neared, I felt compelled to ask Kira to go with me.

Not that I didn't like her. I did. She was funny, kind, and beautiful as well. But she wasn't Robbie. Then, watching Robbie descend the stairs, all my feelings bubbled back to the surface. While I struggled to hide them, I don't think anyone noticed.

I needed to focus on Kira. She deserved my full attention. As Shane stopped at a traffic light, I saw him reach up and touch Robbie's cheek. She turned toward him and smiled. The exchange was a small stab to my heart. My body stiffened, feeling hot and claustrophobic.

Kira touched my hand, stopping my spiral. "You okay?"

"Yeah. Fine. Why?" I asked back.

"You seemed lost in your thoughts."

"No, I'm good. Really."

"Okay," she smiled. I turned toward my window and closed my eyes. This was going to be a long night.

We piled out at the hotel parking lot filled with teenagers dressed to the hilt. Sarah led the charge into the dance, highlighting the night's itinerary of activities and pictures. We all nodded, knowing it was easier to agree with her. I took Kira's hand as we walked in, and she squeezed it in appreciation.

Signs in the lobby directed us to the large room down the hall where the dance was being held. The ballroom was enormous, with huge sparkly chandeliers. Gold and silver décor sparkled on the wall, looking gaudy, in my opinion. However, all the girls "oohed" and "ahhed" at how beautiful everything looked.

Our school colors of red and black were well-represented on the dining and buffet tables. There was even a photo booth where you could hold up silly signs and masks while taking pictures. I only knew because it was all Sarah talked about on the long ride here.

After checking in, Kira and I went straight toward the refreshments. I needed to get space away from our group. I saw Shane and Robbie head in the opposite direction to greet their senior friends. I tried not to watch her, but it was pointless. I convinced myself that I was helping since she still struggled with crowds, but I knew that was a lie. She had Shane. Unfortunately, that didn't comfort me at all.

"Yo, Kyle! Over here. Got us a table," Brody yelled. I signaled back to him and grabbed two cups of punch. Kira and I crossed the room, sitting beside him and Sarah. Kira took a sip of her punch as I engaged her in conversation.

"So… tell me more about your trip to Montana. Do you go every summer?" I asked. I had always meant to inquire when we went out, but it never came up.

"Mostly. The last three years or so. I hope to move out that way someday or, at the very least, go to school somewhere near my uncle's ranch. I'd love to do something related to horses or about the environment and ranching. I don't know yet. I have a couple of years to decide," she answered excitedly.

"Wow. I'm not sure what I'm doing tomorrow, and your entire future is planned out."

"Well, not quite. But if I'm going to work for the next fifty years, it better be something I love. Right?"

"Right." She was confident, with aspirations and dreams that she wanted to pursue. I liked that. We talked all the way through dinner, getting to know each other even more. She was interesting and intelligent. She told me she was one-half Native American Crow and that her ancestors settled in southeastern Montana. Her uncle ran the family ranch just outside Laurel, like his father and their father before him.

But Kira's dad was the black sheep of the family and went to college in New York City. He met Kira's mom, and they ended up staying in the area. My family wasn't quite as interesting. Mom was young when she got knocked up twice in the span of a year and a half, and my dad split when he found out he was having another kid. The end.

After dinner, I realized I hadn't asked Kira to dance yet, and she was too kind to mention it or be upset by my oversight. "I'm sorry, Kira. I should have asked sooner. Would you like to dance?"

"Yes, I would," she answered with a huge grin.

We made our way to the floor, and I put my hands on her hips as she wrapped hers around my shoulders. It was a little awkward at first, but after two slow songs in a row, we warmed up to each other. Some party jams started playing, so we swung about. We had a lot of fun laughing together. It felt nice. I really enjoyed myself until I happened to look across the room. My mistake.

Shane spun Robbie around the ballroom. The girl of my dreams smiling and laughing, too. She seemed to be enjoying herself, but it made me miss our time together last summer. My stomach twisted sharply when the realization hit me like a ton of bricks, that she could be happy without me. That someone else could be the one to dance with her, make her smile, make her laugh... it suddenly became too much to bear.

Abruptly, I walked Kira back to the table and told her I needed to use the restroom. When I finished, instead of heading back toward the ballroom, I turned in the opposite direction and went right out the hotel's side door. I needed air.

Once outside, I walked into the shadows toward a grove of trees. I sat on an iron bench, tilting my head toward the stars. A cool breeze whipped over my face. I took a deep breath of fresh air to clear my mind of her.

But it never worked.

Robbie

As I sat down to rest after dancing with Shane, my thoughts roamed to Kyle and Kira. They were really having fun together on the dance floor; a twinge of jealousy twisted inside my soul. I had no right to feel this way. I was with Shane, and he was with Kira. That's just how it was. With leaving in eight months, I needed to take my heart off the table.

But of course, my body never listened. My lungs turned heavy, the room feeling small and claustrophobic. I needed air. I told Shane I was going to the restroom but headed out the hotel's side door instead. I stood in the dark, looking up at the stars while breathing in the cool night. I placed my hand on my throat, willing air to enter my lungs. To slow my breathing and the beating of my heart. As I strode toward the bench by the grove, I jumped.

"You startled me," I said, surprised to see Kyle.

"Sorry. You okay?"

"Getting some fresh air. That's all."

"Me too." He stood up. "Are you having fun? It looked like you were," I asked as he lingered closer.

"Kinda. You?" he said.

"Kinda." I couldn't help but notice the distance between us diminishing.

"I meant what I said earlier tonight. You really do look stunning. Mom was right except for one thing. You took all our breath away."

"Well, Kira looks beautiful tonight, too!" I tried to deflect.

"Yeah. She really does. Kind, sweet, and a good person… but she's not you."

"Kyle…" I whispered.

"Robin, I can't help it. I think about you always. I honestly tried to keep my distance, but every time I do, there you are. As a matter of fact, I walked out to get space from you, and then…" He waved his arms, indicating my presence before taking another step closer. "I don't know how to stop. The truth is I want to kiss you so much right now that it hurts."

"You can't," I said worriedly.

"I know." He took me in his arms, and we slowly swayed back and forth to the music in the distance. He rested his head on mine as I melted into his chest. "I miss this. I miss us," he whispered. I wanted to say it too but knew I couldn't.

"Kyle… you know better than anyone that I'm not staying. That's always been the plan…" I mumbled wistfully. I could feel his heavy breath on my neck.

"Then I'll go with you, Robbie. Take me with you! We can go anywhere. Or we can find him together. I know you're searching for him, and I can help—"

"No! He's dangerous."

"I know he is. I saw firsthand when I found you covered in blood and bruises. The fact that he did that to his own stepdaughter is disgusting. So yes, Robbie! I'm aware of how dangerous he is."

"We're not having this conversation," I snapped.

"Why not?" he asked, upset.

"Because we're not. That's it!" Anger rose in me, spoiling the moment.

"Why are you always so stubborn?" he hissed.

"This is not me being stubborn, Kyle. It's me protecting you. Shane. Kirstie."

"I can protect all of us. Everything I know gives me an advantage. Shane's clueless." Panicking, I knew I had to make him let me go. For good this time.

"And that's how it should be, Kyle. If I could take back calling you that night in June, I would. If I could take back everything that happened between us, I would. Don't you get it? I lie. That's what I do to get what I need. And that includes lying to you. Because, you know what? I regret this summer. I regret getting involved with you and not ending this sooner. This isn't up for discussion. It's over. We're over!"

I stormed off, hoping I had made my point. I briefly glanced back, watching the heartbreak within his pained expression. I turned away, practically running to the hotel. I told him the truth. I did have regrets. A lot of them. But not regrets about us. I regretted putting him in danger. I regretted having to lie to him. But mostly, I regretted hurting him.

Again.

Kyle

Regrets. I stood there repeating that over and over. She said she had lied to me and that she regretted it all. That she regretted the summer and getting involved. The pain in my chest forced me to sit down. I sat on the bench for an eternity before hearing a faint sound in the distance. When I finally focused, I realized someone was calling my name.

"Yo, Kyle. Where the hell have you been? I was looking for you everywhere. What are you doing?" Brody asked, annoyed.

"Sorry. I needed some air. I wasn't feeling well," I lied.

"Ahh, gotcha. Drank too much. Why didn't you share with me?" he teased.

"I… uh… pre-gamed."

"Well, I was about to declare you dead and take over your hot little date with Kira," he smirked.

"And what about Sarah?"

"I can handle both. Trust me!" He slapped me on the back, roaring.

"I wouldn't trust you as far as I could throw you," I joked.

"Well, lucky for me, that's not far."

I laughed, trying to mask the pain swelling in my heart.

We headed back to the hotel, where I needed to make an apology of all apologies to Kira. As I entered the ballroom, I immediately spotted Robbie and Shane embraced in a slow dance. I couldn't catch a break. I turned away and made a beeline straight to Kira, who still sat at the table chatting with Sarah.

"It's about damn time you showed up, asshole," Sarah scolded harshly.

"I know," I replied ruefully.

I turned to my date. "I'm really sorry, Kira."

Sarah jumped in, berating me again. "You should be. We all thought you ditched her. That's a crappy thing to do, Kyle. Trust me. I know from my experience with you." *Glad she wasn't worried my disappearance meant they would find my dead body behind the hotel.* Looks like she still held the mixer against me.

"Sarah, could you give us a minute?" I asked as nicely as I could muster.

Kira interjected. "Sarah, it's alright. Why don't you dance with Brody? I've got this covered."

"Fine. But if you ask me—"

"I didn't," both Kira and I interrupted Sarah with the same phrase at the same time. We looked at each other and laughed.

"Whatever!" Sarah snapped sarcastically. She stormed off, dragging poor Brody behind her onto the dance floor.

Nervously, I looked Kira directly in her pretty face. "I'm sorry. I wasn't feeling well and needed air. I went outside and didn't realize I had been out there for so long." Which was kind of true. But had I shifted into balancing moods and lying as easily as Robbie? My heart sank at the thought of her name, emotions humming in an uneasy whiplash.

"Yeah. Brody told me he thought you probably drank too much before the dance and was outside getting sick," she said.

"Nah. He jokes. It's not something I would do. I agreed with him to try to save face. I didn't drink tonight. Sometimes, it's easier to go along with him. Honestly Kira, this whole night I've been feeling off. It's complicated, but I think I just needed to…"

"It's okay," she interjected. She tilted her head, a kindness in her gaze. It only made the guilt that coursed through my veins feel heavier.

"It's not. I'm genuinely sorry that I left you here alone for so long. But I'm back now, and if you aren't upset with me, I'd like to ask you to dance with me, if you are still willing."

"Yeah. I still want to. That would be nice," she smiled up at me. I took her hand, and we walked to the dance floor. As I held her close, it felt… nice. It felt right to be with her, to talk to her, to laugh and dance with her. Ask her about her future, desires, and dreams. She was uncomplicated, sweet, and obviously very forgiving. Maybe to a fault.

But most importantly, she was single. I didn't have to feel guilty to be with her, and I didn't have to sneak around to be with her. I didn't have to lie to be with her. I think I could convince myself that she would be the better choice for me. The easy choice. Maybe even the right choice. But unfortunately, my head wasn't calling the shots.

My heart was.

CHAPTER 18

I was...

Robbie

I HAD THE house to myself again, which had been a rarity in the past, but especially these last few weeks. Shane's training, Kyle's hockey practices, and Kirstie working late in the city thanks to the upcoming holidays created the perfect opportunity to finally be alone. It was wonderful and a much-needed break. From everyone.

It had been a little over a month since Homecoming. The tension between Kyle and me bled over into other parts of my life. I couldn't focus, my grades slipped, and Shane and I continued to be out of sync. It also didn't help that I had front-row seats to the Kyle-and-Kira dating game. The two looked happier than ever together. I mean, technically I did what I wanted to do. I pushed him away. And the horrible tirade I had unleashed on him at Homecoming apparently did the trick.

Trying to make the most of my increased time alone, I funneled as much of that energy as possible into the gym we had in the garage. Unsurprisingly, like all my other plans, that fell apart too. Adding insult to literal injury, I pulled a muscle in my back that had my ribs screaming in pain whenever I used any of the weights. Not wanting to curtail my workouts, I pushed through until the screams rising inside me forced me to stop. An exasperated sigh escaped my body. I did my best to stretch out what I could.

My frustration grew into anger at how completely off-course I had become since I first came to this town. I had become delusional thinking that I could be an average teen and lie low. Instead, I was fully entrenched in high school drama that had circumvented every aspect of my life. I barely recognized myself anymore; everything had changed.

Before my brain could catch up with what my feet were doing, I grabbed my jacket and backpack and headed quickly out the door. I walked down the street like I was on a mission. I ended up at the bus station and bought a ticket to the city. I'm not sure why or what I planned to do once I got there, but I knew I had to do something.

As the bus rolled out of the station, I could already feel the heaviness in my chest. My anxiety built the whole ride, and I scolded myself for feeling this way. Putting my earbuds in, I tried to soothe my nerves with music and positive thoughts. I'm only going into the city. That's it. There was nothing to worry about. Everything would work out. I wish it had calmed my anxiety, but my pounding heart betrayed me. None of it really helped.

When the bus pulled into the terminal, sweat graced my body. A flood of fear wavered back and forth like the tides. As I stepped off the bus into the Port Authority Bus Terminal, my breath became faster and shallower. I couldn't believe I was chickening out.

The memory of that night in June was still too strong. I started hyperventilating in the middle of an archway. My neck flushed as my eyes threatened to release tears. I rushed to the bathroom, hiding my face inside my hood, and locked myself in a stall to slow my breathing privately.

I practiced breathing techniques I had learned from videos online over the past couple of months. It seemed like a whole lot of nonsense, but I prayed it helped. I pressed my forehead to the cool metal door, taking slow breaths and blowing them out. When I finally emerged, I went straight back to the bus terminal ticket booth like a coward.

I bought another ticket home. I was so disappointed in myself. I needed to get my shit together. I knew I had to if I wanted to survive. If he… no, *when* "he" figured out where I was, he'd kill me. He promised me that. And he doesn't like loose ends.

I was thankful that there weren't many people on the bus as it left the city. I leaned against the window and watched the city lights dim in the distance as we continued our way… home. A mix of joy and guilt always filled my heart whenever I thought or said that word. Before, I had given up on having a proper space after my mom died. The mixed emotions I had now always surprised me. In a good and bad way.

The repetitive sounds of the bus wheels against the pavement below me had a calming and lulling, hypnotic effect. Allowing me to exist in a state between consciousness and unconsciousness. I cautiously ruminated over the events that had happened to me that night in June. My brain walked me through all my mistakes and how unprepared I was.

A chill trickled down my spine when I unexpectedly remembered the entirety of the threat he bellowed at me. We had been struggling on the floor. I was trying to get out from under him and was able to pull my knee up right into his groin to stop his assault. With fury and pain, he spat—

"I'll kill you, just like I did your mother!"

He killed her? Wait. It wasn't an accident. The realization snapped me back to attention, head bumping against the glass window. The shock was like a bolt of lightning through my mind. He had killed her. It was all too much to bear. I reflexively reached for my phone. I gasped, barely able to breathe, let alone talk, as the phone rang and rang and…

"Hello?" an annoyed voice finally answered. Kyle's annoyed voice.

"Kyle," I whispered through gasps of air.

"Robbie?"

"Ky…" It was too difficult to get air into my lungs. I gasped loudly.

"Robbie?!" I couldn't answer. "Okay. Take deep breaths. Come on. Breathe with me. In. Out. In. And out. That's it. Now, tilt your head down. Keep breathing. In. And out. You can do it." Kyle coached me through my panic.

I tried focusing on his voice, following his steps. In. Out. In. And out. Just like he said. I heard his words through my gasps. I kept following his soothing tone and slowly gained control of my body. I had drawn some attention from a couple of the bus riders. I put the phone to my chest, quickly assuring them I was fine and feeling much better. As the passengers returned to their seats, I finally allowed the building tears to fall from my eyes.

"Robbie?"

"I'm here," I croaked.

"What the hell's going on? Where are you?"

"I'm fine now. I'm on a bus headed back from the city."

"What? Why did you go there? What happened?"

I was still catching my breath and couldn't eek any words out.

"Did you see him? Did he hurt you?" he asked, alarmed.

"No, but I went to the city to see him. I think. I don't know. It was so sudden… I'm not completely sure what my plan was. But it doesn't matter. I chickened out and got back on the bus."

"Why would you do that? Why didn't you take me? Or, I mean, take Shane?" he asked incredulously.

"Kyle, I remember everything he said to me that night in June."

"I do, too. He said he would kill you," he huffed.

"But that's not all he said. While on the bus, I remembered everything. That's why I couldn't… that's why I couldn't breathe." I sobbed quietly, unable to hold back the discomfort in my chest.

"What did he say?"

"He said he'd kill me, just like he did my mother. He killed my mom, Kyle. It wasn't an accident. I was supposed to die in that wreck too, and I messed up his plans. He killed her. He killed my mother. He killed her…" I wept softly.

"Shh, shh, shh, Robbie. I'm here, baby. I'm here. I got you," he comforted me over the phone. The quiet sobs kept coming. "Shh. Shh. It's going to be okay. What time does your bus get in?"

"Nine," I squeaked. My voice sounded so small.

"Okay. I'll meet you in the bus station waiting room?"

"Okay."

As I hung up, my mind screamed at me. I should have said no to Kyle. I should have stopped dragging him back into my chaos. But I didn't. I needed him, and that had trumped all my common sense. Because my head wasn't calling the shots.

My heart was.

Kyle

At the rink, I raced out of the weight room and jumped into the showers. I threw on clean shorts, a t-shirt, and my favorite zippered hoodie, the one she wore after our shower together. I grabbed my gym bag and ran to my car.

As I parked in the bus station parking lot, I checked the time. It was 8:45 P.M. and dark outside. There were only a few vacant cars settled underneath the lights. I still parked near the back left of the lot anyway, away from everything. It was odd that more travelers weren't at the station, even on a Monday. Thanksgiving was right around the corner. The city bustled through the night in mid-November as it geared up for the holidays. People were always coming and going this time of year.

The place was lit up inside. I could see a few people milling about. It was an old red-brick building with a nice archway over the front door. You couldn't see the bus area due to the fencing, but you could hear the buses traveling through.

I glanced at the clock again. She would be there soon, and my stomach immediately twisted with excitement and… guilt. My body shuddered when I thought about how I almost didn't answer her call tonight. This past month has been brutal since the fallout of our conversation at Homecoming. We avoided each other constantly, making it noticeable and awkward to the others. We had hardly spoken a dozen words, so I hesitated when I saw her name on my phone. I wasn't sure if I had it in me to talk to her.

I got out of my car and walked in. My skin prickled with the realization that her stepdad was much more dangerous than I ever thought. He had graduated from threatening her to hurting her and was now a confessed murderer. It alarmed me. This was way beyond what I could handle, and we needed to get the police involved. We couldn't wait any longer. But it wouldn't be easy to convince her.

I paced around the terminal, watching the hands of the clock slowly tick by. I heard an announcement over the loudspeaker that the next bus would arrive shortly, but it felt like forever. My fingers anxiously tapped the phone in my pocket, just waiting. Waiting to see her in person. I knew we had talked on the phone, but I wouldn't be satisfied until I finally saw her.

I scanned the crowd of departing passengers when my eyes landed on her. I audibly breathed a massive sigh of relief. Her eyes were red and swollen. She looked devastated. It broke my heart to see her hurt by "him" again. Anger bubbled deep down inside me.

I pushed the feeling away as I strode over and pulled Robbie into a hug. She melted into my chest and held me tight. I felt my body relax into hers. I hadn't realized I was tense and nervous until I felt the ease of my burning muscles. I didn't let go as she quietly sobbed. My heart raced when she finally looked up at me with her sad but beautiful face. Her eyes held mine as a powerful energy coursed between us. It was insane.

"I'm glad you're safe," I whispered.

"I'm glad you're here," she whispered back.

As if her gravity pulled me to her, I leaned down. She stretched up to meet our lips. At first, it was a slow and gentle kiss. I breathed out, our open mouths intertwining in a dance. It didn't matter who led; all I needed was to fill my presence with her. Avoiding her had been pointless. As our embrace intensified, I held her tighter. Our tongues entangled each other, getting lost in a passionate intimacy.

My body was on the fritz from being so close to her. A flood of mixed emotions washed over me. I had lied to myself these last few weeks. That I had moved on with Kira. That I could forget how Robbie made me feel. As I kissed her, I knew this was what I wanted all along. She was what I wanted all along.

We pulled apart from each other. I silently reached for her hand, and she placed hers in mine. Like vines, our fingers intertwined. I led her out of the bus station to the car. Neither one of us spoke or cared if anyone saw. I didn't want to let go as I opened the passenger car door. But reluctantly, I had to. Holding the door instead, I found myself locked into her gaze. Resisting her was futile.

I stepped forward, and once again, she met me halfway. I bent my head down, cupping her face in my hands as I kissed her again. I gradually reached down, wrapping my arms around her waist so I could pull her against me. I didn't want any space between us. She wrapped her arms around my neck and kissed me deeply. Her closeness drove me wild.

I walked her backward until I leaned into her body against the car. She moaned, parting her lips. A deep growl rumbled through my throat. My hands slid further down her body, and I slipped them into the back pockets of her jeans and squeezed. I lifted her off the ground, settling her body above my waist as I held her against the car. I preferred her ragged breath in my mouth here, safe with me, over a panicked Robin far from my embrace. Maybe this time, she would choose to stay? Choose me?

Her fingertips wove through my hair as she tilted her head and pulled me closer. She kissed me hard, driving up her hips. I gently bit her bottom lip to try to hide my own moan that dared to escape. She smirked. I was desperate for her. I shifted my hold to her thighs as I pressed her into the car. She threw her head back to take a deep breath, so I took advantage of the moment to trail my mouth down her neck.

My body reacted to her every movement as she slid her hand to my chest, going lower and nudging me away from how I pinned her. As she reached my shorts, I found her mouth again and kissed her. When she slipped two fingers into my waistband, I gasped. I pulled back, eyes glazed over with lust as I tried to catch my breath.

"Does he kiss you like this?"

"No."

"Good."

I kissed her again with a passion that I had never felt before. My body burned aflame as every nerve ending tingled from her touch. She consumed every part of me, and I hers. Her own form responded fervently. She clung to me, and I traveled kisses down her throat, down her chest, and to the top of her breasts. My hands moved over her entire body. I was frantic.

I knew I had hit my breaking point when she slid her hands lower. I peeled myself away from her with every ounce of strength I had left. I placed my palms on the car, on either side of her head. We both stared at each other, panting heavily. My eyes darted down to her swollen lips, but I closed them so I couldn't see them. I couldn't believe I had fallen under her spell. I had to stop.

"We should head home," I growled through gritted teeth. I looked at her, and she nodded in agreement. I moved my hands away from the car, and she entered the front seat. I shut the door quickly before I changed my mind.

After I got in, I looked in the rearview mirror to run my fingers through my hair several times. My lips still tingled, but I ignored them as I started the car. I didn't dare look over at Robin. I feared that I would pull my key out of the ignition and kiss her again.

As I drove home, the streetlights danced on the hood of the car. I couldn't stop thinking about what had happened between us. My mind spiraled with confusion and guilt, while my heart was overwhelmed with joy. And my stomach? It was in knots. Knowing I would have to face my mom, Shane, and pretend that I didn't just have my mouth and hands all over Robin's body. My willpower was waning, and next time I didn't know if I would have the strength to deny anything happening between us.

I took a couple of breaths to calm my lust-filled body. I had to be ready to lie my ass off as soon as we walked in. Pretending and lying. It's a fine line and a delicate balance.

And I hated them both.

Robbie

What did I do? I would have screamed in the car if I could have done so without scaring Kyle. What I should've done was jump out, run as far as I could, and never look back. This damn heart of mine was making everything so complicated. It just kept pulling things deeper into my stupid drama.

I inwardly kicked myself for dialing Kyle's number, but it was so automatic that I couldn't stop. How would I look at Shane or his mother after what just happened? That reality hit me hard. Almost as hard as Kyle had kissed me.

With that thought, my spine went rigid. I sat straight and pulled the visor down to inspect my face in the mirror. I looked like I had been making out, and my eyes were still puffy from the bus. I tried smoothing my hair, wiping my eyes, and pinching my cheeks so I wouldn't appear disheveled. It didn't help.

After we pulled into the driveway, I leapt out of the car and ran toward the front door. As I threw it open, Shane and his mom swung their heads toward me from the couch.

"There you are! We were wondering where you went," Kirstie said.

"I've been texting you," Shane huffed.

"You have?" Honestly, I hadn't noticed.

"Yeah, like for an hour or so."

"Oh. Well, my phone—" I jolted when Kyle walked through the doorway. "Uh, as I was saying… my phone died when I was in town. I couldn't call you—"

"And I was heading home from the gym when I spotted her near the corner store," Kyle interjected. "Thankfully, I stopped to ask if she needed a ride because… apparently, her phone died. And here we are."

Shane jumped up, heading toward me as he addressed Kyle. "Wow, bro. Always in the right place at the right time." He enveloped me in a hug, kissing me full on my mouth. I flinched imperceptibly.

"What does that mean?" Kyle asked, aggravated.

Shane defensively held up his hands. "Whoa. Take it easy, man. I was just stating facts. You helped her out this summer, then again at the mixer, and now tonight. I was curious, that's all. You always seem to be in the right place at the right time."

"Hey, I missed you tonight," I said quickly, needing to distract him. I squeezed Shane into another embrace.

"I missed you too, babe! Let's go upstairs and you can show me how much." He waggled his brows before kissing me again.

"Okay, okay. Not in front of the Mom. And leave the door open!" Kirstie exclaimed. I grabbed Shane's hand and pulled him toward the stairs.

"Yeah. Yeah. Yeah," Shane teased.

"I mean it, Shane," Kirstie responded.

We had to move past Kyle, who glared at me. The disgust I saw on his face made my throat feel like it was closing. It felt like a stab in the heart, but I forced myself to walk past him up the stairs. Shane grinned as I took his hand and dragged him into my room.

"Oh, I like this assertive girlfriend," Shane teased.

I threw my backpack down. "I need to use the bathroom. I'll be right back," I stated, practically running to the hall.

"I'll be waiting," he said gleefully.

I went into the bathroom, tears already stinging my eyes. Shane didn't deserve this. Kyle didn't deserve this. And I didn't deserve either of them. What was I doing?

I scrubbed my face clean and splashed it with cold water to help with the puffiness under my eyes. I quickly brushed my teeth and gargled some mouthwash. My stomach churned after having kissed both brothers in one night. Feeling melancholy, I hunched back into my room.

"There you are," Shane said suggestively.

"Here I am." My tone fell flat.

"Come here, babe," he said, patting the bed. I slowly lingered over and sat on the side.

"Come closer," he said, gently tugging my arm to lie down.

"I'm sorry, Shane. I'm not feeling very well. My stomach is a mess."

"Oh, I'm sorry. Can I get you anything?" His sweet and concerned tone made me feel ashamed as he shifted closer to me.

"I'm good. Thanks. But is it okay if we only snuggle?"

"Of course." He took my face in his hands. "I really did miss you tonight. Well, I miss you all the time." *Ugh. He's killing me,* I thought. "I'm glad Kyle was able to help you out again. And that he gave you a ride home tonight. But you know you can call me too, right?

"I mean, if your phone isn't dead, you can call me. Maybe I can get you a portable charger so that doesn't happen again? Because I don't like that you were stranded in town at night by yourself and couldn't reach me." Jealousy floated through his tone.

"You don't have to do that, Shane," I squirmed with guilt.

"I know. But I want to." He leaned in and kissed me.

At first, he was hesitant and slow before adding more pressure to my mouth. He slid his fingers down from my face and caressed my neck with one of his warm, strong hands. His tongue raked across my lips when his eyes opened wide, and he pulled back. "Sorry. Got carried away. I know you said you weren't feeling well."

He scooched back onto the bed, and I crawled beside him as he lay his arm around my shoulder. He pulled me toward his chest, and I felt his heart pounding. I placed my palm against him, but my heart didn't feel the same as his did. Because I didn't feel the same as he did. And lying in his arms at that very moment felt so cruel.

I was cruel.

CHAPTER 19

...how to stop.

Kyle

I OPENED MY eyes as my phone alarm blared. I lay there for a few minutes and stared at the ceiling before feeling around for my device. After silencing the alarm, I finally willed myself to sit up on the side of the bed. I was still processing last night's events.

I had gone from feeling happy to rotten in under an hour. When I saw Shane and Robbie go up to her room together, after what had happened between us at the bus station—it was more than I could handle. I thought we were on the same page, but I guess I was just her distraction again.

Frustrated and angry from the events of last night, I flopped down on the couch next to Mom and laid my head on her shoulder.

"Long day?" Mom had asked.

"Yeah. Long day," I replied quietly.

She laid her head against mine, and we sat there until her movie ended. I wished I could tell her more. Tell her about Robbie and me. But I couldn't disappoint her. I didn't want to be another one of the "rotten men in her life."

I reluctantly dragged myself upstairs. I tried not to look in her room as I passed, since the door was wide open, but that was hopeless. They were asleep in each other's arms. I felt such jealousy at that moment, it nearly rocked me off my feet. I slinked to my room as Mom came up the stairs so she wouldn't see me watching them.

With just the hallway light shining into my room, I hurriedly kicked off my shoes and jumped into bed. Mom was waking Shane, and I didn't want to see him when he entered. I closed my eyes and tucked my head slightly under the covers to block the light. After taking a huge breath, I froze.

I could still smell Robbie on me, and my body reacted viscerally. I wanted to get up and rip my clothes off. I needed to stop the assault on my nose, but I heard Shane approaching. Instead, I held my breath. I wondered how long I could. Not long enough.

My morning alarm went off again, pulling me to the present. After I silenced it for good, I worked on my motivation to get up and out of bed. I finally shuffled out into the hall toward the bathroom when I saw Robbie heading back into her room, dripping wet, in only a towel. *She literally wants to kill me. I'm not sure how much more I could take,* I grimaced.

Once showered and dressed, I darted down to the kitchen. I ran right into Robbie. She had made coffee, and a couple of fruit cups sat on the counter.

"This is for you," she spoke as she handed me the coffee and fruit.

"Thanks." It was all I could muster.

"We should probably head to school," she said quickly.

"Yeah," I grumbled. Once in the car, the silence was deafening. As I parked, I couldn't wait to make my escape. That's when she said my name.

"Kyle?" I turned to her slowly, still unsure how to answer the question I knew was coming. "Can we please talk about what happened last night?"

"There's nothing to talk about, Robbie," I said coldly, dismissing her.

"There is, Kyle. I'm so sorry…" And there it was.

She was sorry about last night.

Sorry about the kiss.

And before I could stop it, I snapped.

"You know what, Robbie? I'm done. You're sorry. I'm sorry. We're all sorry. It doesn't change the fact that you're with Shane. But I've got to tell you, the way you kissed me at the bus station makes that fact confusing. I've made it very clear how I feel about you. That I want to be with *you.*"

I paused, lips pressed into a thin line. I stared into her eyes as my brows furrowed before glancing down. I felt an unease in my chest as my tone turned sullen. "But it's obvious that you don't feel the same. Especially when you kiss me one moment and then take him to your room the next. It kills me to see you with him. Kills me, Robbie. I can't keep doing this to Shane, Kira, and myself. I'm lying to everyone. I want space from you." I desperately begged, "And I know I answered your call yesterday, and that's on me. But moving forward, I need space. From you. Can you do that? Because I need you to do that."

"Yes," she whispered, her lips quivering. Tears filled her eyes and threatened to overflow. I wanted to grab her, hold her, and tell her I didn't mean any of it. But I knew I couldn't. I needed to stay strong. I needed to because whenever I'm around her...

I jumped out of the car and hurried to the entrance. I could see in my peripheral vision that she hadn't moved. I wanted to look back but kept moving as fast as I could toward the building. It was usually her leaving me behind, but this time, I was the one who pushed her away.

And it broke my heart.

Robbie

I stayed frozen. My hand was on the door handle, but I just couldn't pull it. His words cut me to the bone. I desperately wanted to tell him that I felt the same as he did. That I just came to that realization last night.

He once told me that I only had to say the word, and he was mine.

But I hadn't.

And now it's too late.

He said he wanted space. No, he said he needed space. **From me**.

My heart hurt. But wasn't this a good thing? We were never supposed to get involved. Never. But the electricity between us this summer was so intense and unexpected that it threw me. And now he's finally letting me go.

That's what I wanted all along. Wasn't it?

He was right about one thing, though. We couldn't keep doing this to Shane, Kira, or to ourselves. I couldn't blame him for feeling this way. I don't blame him. The sooner both brothers were rid of me, the better.

Both deserve to be happy.

To be with someone who is honest and who would stay.

Someone who wasn't me.

I pulled the door handle with every ounce of strength I could muster and stepped out. The chill in the air made me shiver, and I zipped my coat up to my neck. I walked toward the school entrance, which felt like it was more than a hundred miles away.

As I crossed the threshold of the main doors, I felt a shift in the air. I had outstayed my welcome in this town. And at the Whitmore's… home. Everything changed for me yesterday in more ways than I had ever anticipated.

I knew my stepdad was a killer, and his motto was "no loose ends."

So that would be my new motto too. It wouldn't be easy with all his resources, but I had to try. For the memory of my mother. For me and my survival this past year.

And that started with letting the Whitmore brothers go.

***

Over the next few weeks, Kirstie stayed busy planning a big, traditional Thanksgiving Dinner at the house. She was so excited to have a family gathering. I, on the other hand, was not. Kirstie had naturally invited Kira to Thanksgiving, since she was technically dating Kyle. They had been together all the time since our "talk" in the car. I tried to stay out of it and not pay attention, but it was hard. I couldn't tell him, of course, that seeing him with her killed me too.

Kirstie also invited this guy named Mateo from her marketing department at work. I guess he was based in the Lisbon office, and they met during the summer. He had just transferred to the NYC office a couple of weeks ago and had no family in the city. Kirstie made sure to extend an invitation so he could be with others during the holidays.

When Kira arrived, she came into the kitchen to help me with some preparations. Shane and Kyle were tasked with expanding the table and retrieving extra chairs. Then, they'd set the table décor exactly how their mom directed. Kirstie had just pulled the turkey out of the oven when the doorbell rang. Both Shane and Kyle rushed over to answer the door. They wanted to meet Mateo and give him the fifth degree.

"All right, all right, you two. Let our guest come in without being accosted," Kirstie teased. Mateo was good-natured and took it in stride. He was a bit younger than Kirstie but acted older and wiser. Not to mention, his accent was sexy. They got along well, and Kirstie was obviously smitten.

Kirstie made the introductions before having us take our seats. She and Mateo sat at the ends of the table while Shane and I sat on one side and Kyle and Kira on the other. That put Kyle across from me, but he never looked over.

During dessert and coffee, the conversation returned to Kirstie and Mateo's jobs at L'Oréal. Shane rested his hand on my shoulder when I felt him tap me.

"I'm sorry, what?" I asked, distracted.

He chuckled. "Mom asked a question."

"Oh, gosh. I'm so sorry. I must have drifted into a turkey coma for a minute. What's up?" I looked over at Kirstie.

"I was wondering if you and Kira wanted to go to my work tomorrow for a couple hours. You girls can sample products." *Oh, ugh.* I barely ever wore makeup, and that was the last thing I wanted to do.

"Yes, that would be great!" I said with too much enthusiasm.

"Wonderful! You girls meet me here at the house at 7:30 a.m. tomorrow morning, and then we can take the bus into the city together." I felt myself stiffen. Not because we were going to the city, where my stepdad was, but because of what happened at the bus station between Kyle and me.

"I can meet you there if you want me to. So, the girls get the full experience," Mateo offered.

"Oh, yes. I— we'd love that," Kirstie's cheeks turned a shade of rose. As they began talking about the details, my mind wandered. Thinking about the night at the bus station with Kyle made my heart race. Even though things between us were tenuous at best lately, he came when I needed him. He always has.

When I stepped off the bus and saw him through my tear-filled eyes, he was like a beacon in a storm, bringing me home. He was the light of my darkness, and I knew at that moment everything would be all right. That I would be alright. Because he's my... home.

My body hummed just thinking of him. As the kiss danced through my mind, a quiet, breathy moan escaped my lips inadvertently. Kyle definitely looked at me now. My face burned when I met his gaze, and his eyes pierced mine.

Shane apparently heard it too because he put his hand on my leg, squeezing my thigh. It diverted my attention with a gasp as Shane let out a soft chuckle. I shifted to look back toward Kyle, but with a disgusted expression, he quickly whispered something to Kira. He then stood up, giving me a little head nod to follow him. I sat there and debated what I should do.

Kira and Kirstie excitedly discussed tomorrow's plans, and Mateo moved next to Kirstie. He lazily draped his arm over the back of her chair and engaged

Shane in a conversation about Lisbon and soccer. I took that moment to excuse myself from the table. Shane reflexively nodded before continuing his discussion with Mateo.

I hastily left the table and ran upstairs. I found Kyle waiting for me just inside the bathroom door. I could feel my pulse quicken, my heart beating faster being alone with him. Near him. I slowly stepped into the bathroom and chose my words carefully.

"I know you said you wanted space… from me, but it seemed like you wanted me to follow you. Or did I misread that?"

"What was that?" he demanded.

"What… was what?" I asked, confused.

"That sound you made at the dinner table. I've heard that moan before, Robin. In case you forgot," he said, upset. Embarrassed, I tried to figure out how to reply to that. Do I tell him it happened while thinking of him touching me? Kissing me? Or should I lie again? Unfortunately, I didn't get a chance to decide. "Look. I accept you're with him. But please, if you have any decency, I'd appreciate it if you didn't fool around with him right in front of me. Because I can avoid looking at the two of you, but I can't avoid hearing you."

"Kyle—"

"That's not even why I asked you to follow me," he said through gritted teeth. "Don't go tomorrow. You can say you're sick or something."

"Why would I do that? I want to see where your mom works. What she does for a living."

"No, you don't. Because I know the real reason why you want to go to the city, Robbie. Please don't do this. He's dangerous and a killer. What you need to do is get the police involved. In fact, I wanted to talk to you about it at the bus station that night, but… we never got around to talking."

I swallowed hard at the memory but stood my ground. "No. No, cops," I said and stormed toward the stairs.

He chased after me and stopped me right at the top step. In desperation, he gently held my arms in place with his hands. "Robbie…"

"NO POLICE!" I yelled.

"What's going on?" Shane asked suspiciously, coming up the stairs. I jumped, and Kyle snatched his hands off me like lightning.

"Nothing," I said, trying to sound convincing.

"It didn't look like nothing," Shane accused. He looked over at Kyle.

"We were having an argument," I said quickly to divert Shane's attention.

"About what? Because I heard you say something involving the police."

I stuttered. "Um… It was … uh… about Mateo."

Kyle

Shane titled his head. "Mateo? What about him?"

"There's something off about him, and when I suggested we should run a background check on him, Robbie said no police," I answered, lying to my brother yet again.

"Well, she's right, dumbass. He's cool, has a good job, and he likes mom. She deserves to be happy. Why would you try to ruin that?" Shane berated me.

"I wasn't trying to ruin that. I—"

"Don't be mad at him, Shane," Robbie interrupted. "He was only trying to protect Kirstie."

"Don't defend him, Robbie." Then, looking pointedly at me, as he growled, "And while I'm at it, I don't like him grabbing you like that."

"Shane, I'm fine. He didn't hurt me," Robbie said, trying to diffuse.

"I don't care," Shane snapped. "I don't want you touching her like that again," he said menacingly.

"Whatever," I sneered. As I started walking away, Shane lunged at me. Robbie stopped him.

"Shane! Don't, please. Come with me. Just let it go, okay? Come on," Robbie pulled his hand toward her room. He reluctantly went with her.

Robin glanced back, but I couldn't bear to look at her. This whole situation and our relationship made me irate, so I went back downstairs.

I helped Mom clean up after Kira and Mateo left. I collapsed on the couch, unable to stomach being near Shane. Knowing they were up in her room together had my blood boiling. Mom sat in the chair by the fireplace, texting away and giggling.

"Who are you texting, all giddy?" I teased, glad for the distraction.

"Oh, um, Mateo," she said shyly.

"Hmm. I like him." I smiled and nodded in approval. She grinned back.

I really was happy for Mom. She does deserve it. Even though it pains me to admit that I agree with Shane about something.

Just thinking about him made me more irritated. Shane demanding that I don't touch Robbie. If he only knew, I smirked to myself.

But I immediately felt guilty the second I thought it. Running fingers through my hair, I scolded myself for being angry at Shane. He was just protecting Robbie, which is exactly what I would have done if she were my... and that's when I heard it. "If she were my..." But she's not.

Shame felt like a weight on my chest as I had exerted so much energy on Shane's girlfriend tonight that I ignored my own. It's a pattern I know all too well now. Unfortunately, even the weight and the guilt were not enough to dissuade me from being involved with her.

And I didn't know how to stop.

CHAPTER 20
How would I…

Robbie

I CALMED DOWN Shane and let him vent. Once he got it out of his system, I reassured him that Kyle was only being protective. I asked him if he wanted to watch a movie to relax; he thought that was code for making out. He hauled me onto his lap on the bed and kissed me hard. When I pulled back breathlessly, he brushed some of my hair out of my face and stared deep into my eyes.

"Can I just say how much you turned me on at dinner tonight? Well, before my douchebag brother almost ruined our evening."

"It really turns you on the amount of food I can eat at Thanksgiving dinner?" I deflected.

He smirked seductively. "It does. But it was also that little moan. I wanted to make out with you right there at the dining room table, and I didn't care who was watching."

I awkwardly smiled at him, knowing that the "little moan" he heard me make was because I thought of his "douchebag brother."

"You are so sexy, Robin. You don't even know it." He kissed me again, this time slowly and deeply. Shane held me close as he raked his tongue along my lips and slipped into my mouth. He moved my legs on either side of him until I straddled his lap.

Still kissing me, his hands slid down my body to my hips as he moved slowly under me. I tried to stay present here with Shane, but earlier thoughts still tugged at the back of my mind. He rocked his hips along with mine as his breathing hitched. We hadn't kissed like this since before he left for the summer. It felt familiar but also very wrong. I cared for him, and he was a great kisser. Yet, something didn't feel the same as it did so many months ago. I wasn't the same. And I couldn't ignore that fact.

When his hands slipped under the back of my shirt, I leapt off him in an instant. First, kissing him like this felt wrong now. Second, he would find my scars. And third… I didn't want to have to explain reasons one or two.

"Whoa, you okay? Was that too fast?" he asked, concerned.

"I'm fine. But yes. It was," I said breathlessly.

"I'm sorry, Robbie. I didn't mean to make you feel uncomfortable."

"I know you didn't. I just think I need a little more time before we… do anything further. I'm… sorry."

"Don't be. It's okay, I can wait. Really, I can," he said candidly. I smiled.

These Whitmore brothers couldn't possibly be real. I've never known men like them who were so considerate and understanding of another person's needs. They both surprise me with their ability to put others first at every turn. I have never had a good male role model in my life. This was jarring to me in the best possible way.

I grabbed my school laptop and pulled up one of his favorite movies. As we watched, he was very aware of my boundaries and respected them all. We snuggled throughout the entire movie and nothing more. He seemed genuinely unfazed that I had rebuffed his advances earlier.

After the show was over, he kissed me on the forehead and told me goodnight. I walked with Shane to the door and leaned against the frame as he slipped into his room. I bit my bottom lip, trying to think and clear my head. I still had to get up early to spend the day in the city with Kirstie. And Kira.

Tomorrow I'd have to feign excitement touring their mom's workplace, but it would be worth being downtown to finish what I started. And I wasn't going to chicken out this time. I still need an excuse to somehow leave Kirstie's workplace without raising any red flags, but I'll figure that out on the ride there. I shut my door and immediately flopped onto the bed to text Kyle.

Im sorry shane misread tonight

• • •

Kyle?

• • •

Please talk to me
Read 1:17 AM

But that was it. He left me on read.

I felt terrible about how everything went down and that I hurt Kyle again. Hurt him, apologize, and repeat. That seems to be my pattern with him, and I'm afraid I can't stop. But am I afraid he'll finally see that I'm not worth it, or am I afraid he won't?

***

When I woke up the next morning, it was Black Friday. The irony was not lost on me as I lay there in the dark. I had slept terribly and felt like crap, but I couldn't squander this opportunity. I had been trying to figure out when to confront my stepdad, and Kirstie offered it up on a silver platter. A trip to New York City.

I groggily lumbered to the bathroom when I saw Shane and Kyle's door open. Popping my head into their room, neither was there. I figured Shane was out running, but where was Kyle? I snapped my head around when I heard Kirstie coming up the stairs.

"Oh, good morning, Robbie. I just made some coffee if you want some. I'll be ready to leave in about twenty minutes."

"Okay. Thanks, Kirstie. I'll be ready," I assured as she returned to her room. I rushed into the bathroom to prep for the trip as quickly as I could.

After I finished, I headed downstairs. That's when I spotted Kyle sound asleep on the living room couch. I stood there for a minute, just watching him. I used to do that over the summer whenever the pain made it impossible for me to rest. Watching his steady breathing had always made me feel relaxed, calm, and safe. I missed that.

I jumped when Kirstie shut her bedroom door upstairs, making me drop my backpack. I quickly grabbed it and bolted to the kitchen to get a cup of coffee for the ride. Kirstie tiptoed in behind me.

"Are you ready?" she whispered.

"Yeah," I whispered back.

"I'll go start the car and meet you out there."

"Okay. I'll be there in a sec."

With gentle footsteps not to wake Kyle, Kristie headed out of the kitchen, through the living room, and out the front door. I finished filling my travel mug and threw one strap of my sunset orange backpack over my shoulder. As I walked out, I paused by the couch again.

I looked at Kyle's handsome face and couldn't resist touching him. Brushing his hair off his forehead, I ran my fingers down his cheek. I hovered over him for a second before leaning in, kissing his lips lightly. I whispered in his ear, "I wish…" But I hesitated.

I wish I could be brave enough to tell him how I felt, but my thoughts were a jumbled mess. So, instead, I said, "I wish I couldn't hurt you anymore. You deserve better than me."

I lingered for a moment longer before slowly walking to the front door. I looked back at him, repeating his words from last night. "Please don't do this," he had pleaded. But I had to, and I wished I could tell him why.

I wish I could tell him the truth.

Kyle

As soon as I heard the front door shut, I snapped my eyes open. I touched my fingers to my lips, still buzzing from her kiss. Every time I was ready to move on and let her go, I was pulled back in. She wished she couldn't hurt me and that I didn't deserve her. But that's where she's wrong. I was just as much to blame for deceiving everyone. While I felt guilty, I was powerless to change it.

I never really thought about the concept of soulmates or if I believed they existed. But that was exactly how this felt between us. Like I would be lost without her, that my future couldn't happen unless she was there. Knowing I would forsake everyone else to make it happen.

I immediately jumped up and grabbed my phone. I needed to get to the city. I couldn't let her confront the man who had tried to kill her and still wanted her dead. I quickly showered and packed for the trip. As I ran out the front door, I crashed right into Shane, who was soaked in sweat from his run.

"What the hell, Kyle?" he asked angrily.

"Sorry… in a rush. Taking the car," I said as I tried running past him. He snatched my arm.

"No way. I need the car."

"For what?" I asked, irritated.

"Not that it's any of your business, but I'm driving into the city to surprise Robbie. I'm taking her to lunch. Mom already knows the plan and is expecting me in a couple of hours."

I panicked.

"I… I was thinking of doing the same thing and surprising Kira."

"Yeah, right. It was my idea, so I get the car."

"Don't be a dick. We can ride together. Let's go," I said impatiently.

"First of all, I need to shower. And second, I didn't say you could come with."

"Are you kidding me? You're still that pissed about last night that you can't ride with me for a measly hour and a half?" I yelled.

"Yes."

"Seriously?" I was exasperated. Shane rolled his eyes.

"Fine. But I still need to shower. Keep your panties on."

"Just hurry," I said, annoyed.

I was frustrated that I had to wait for a ride, but I had to get to the city fast. Unfortunately, that meant playing nicely. All I could do was hope I'd make it to Robbie before she did something rash.

But with my luck recently, that meant I was screwed.

Robbie

I had never seen so much make-up in my life. Who knew there were so many options... and different shades of a few basic colors? I certainly didn't. Kira reveled in every single minute on the floor. I tried to appear interested and excited as we determined the right color palette for our skin tone and... blah, blah, blah. I think I momentarily blacked out while Kirstie talked.

It had to have been hours by now, I thought to myself as I snuck a peek at my phone. I paled at the realization that our time was only half done. I wasn't necessarily paying attention when a rush of footsteps stomped behind me. Someone grabbed me by my shoulders.

"SURPRISE!!" My body tensed as I reared my arm into a low fist. My heartbeat thudded in my ears; my jaw clenched. With a sharp inhale, I realized the person turning me around was Shane. And Kyle. In the city.

Shane kissed me on the lips, and I relaxed as the shock wore off. I glared at Kyle. He tried to avoid my gaze as he rushed over to hug Kira. My head snapped back as Shane excitedly picked me up and spun me. Again, this was the Shane I remembered—thoughtful special trips, and surprises—but I couldn't handle that today. I tried to mask my mix of anger and annoyance.

"What are you doing here?" I questioned Shane with a gritted smile.

"I thought I would surprise you, babe, and take you to lunch."

"Well, I'm surprised!" I replied sarcastically.

"Isn't it the sweetest thing?" Kirstie swooned. "He planned it all out on his own." Kirstie looked at Kyle. "I take it you liked the idea and decided to join?"

"Uh, yeah. It was a great idea. So, I tagged along," Kyle stammered. I glared at him again.

"Well, aren't you two just the sweetest!" their mom gushed. "Aren't they just the best, girls?"

"Definitely the best!" Kira squealed.

"Yeah. They're the sweetest," I mocked.

"So, where are you taking the girls to eat?" Kirstie asked.

"I'm taking Robbie to that little Italian restaurant you rave about, but I have no idea what Kyle planned," Shane mocked.

I interjected, "Oh, I think they should tag along with us, Shane. I mean, you're always saying that we should go on a double date." I smirked, knowing the Whitmore boys too well.

"Wait. No. I meant a double date with someone else. Not my brother. No offense, Kira," Shane said hastily.

"Oh, I think that's a great idea, Robbie. The two brothers and their beautiful dates. It sounds perfect," Kirstie said excitedly.

Shane and Kyle were forced to relent to make their mom happy. And watching their annoyed expressions was the cherry on top. Kira and I laughed, although I was unsure if it was for the same reason. It was the first time I realized that both brothers looked more alike than not as they mirrored each other's expressions.

Once seated at the restaurant, I texted Kyle that I wanted to talk to him. **Alone.** He shook me off, but this only fueled anger through my persistence. How dare he show up unannounced and foil my plans.

I texted him a second message, but he ignored me. Again. Fuming, I finally said, "Shane, why don't you tell Kira about the rodeo you went to in Lisbon? Kira loves animals, especially horses. Kyle and I will get some drinks."

"Yeah, sure. That's a great story!" Shane exclaimed. "So, when I was in Lisbon this summer…."

Kyle appeared miffed as he followed me to the bar. I asked the bartender for four ice waters and told him that we would return soon. I grabbed Kyle's hand and dragged him out the back restaurant door. A haze of smoke and native New Yorkers milled about the alleyway. We weaved through narrow openings within the scattered crowd, searching for a place to talk privately.

"What the hell, Kyle?" I immediately yelled. "You knew my plan, and you came here on purpose?!"

"Blame it on your boyfriend. It was his idea to drive into the city."

"Oh, so you're telling me you weren't coming here after warning me last night?" I accused.

"That's beside the point."

"It's not beside the point. It's the exact point. You're purposely trying to mess up my plans for today."

"And what plans are those?" He shot back.

"You know damn well what they were."

"Right. To confront a killer. On your own. Do you even remember what happened in June? Because I do! And I'm not going to let it happen again."

"It's not up to you, and it's none of your business," I spat back.

"You made it my business!"

"Stop throwing June in my face. I needed your help, and you were there to give it. But I'm better now, and I can take care of myself!" I couldn't believe his audacity. *How dare he.*

"I'm not talking about June."

"Then what?"

"I meant this morning. When you kissed me before leaving with my mom."

I paused, stunned. Anger melted into fear. "You... were awake?"

"Yes."

"Kyle, I didn't mean..."

"Stop. No more lying, Robbie. You feel something for me. I know you do."

"I can't do this now. I need to find him and finish this."

"No, you don't. It's not your job, Robbie. No more putting it off. We're involving the police."

"I am not having this conversation again." Angrily, I pushed through the crowd to get back to the restaurant. My skin prickled as I suddenly heard someone call my name. A name I thought I'd never hear again.

"Wren?" Reflexively, my head spun around to see who spoke it. I didn't even have a moment to hide my reaction from Kyle. When I saw his scruffy, pock-scarred face, I immediately recognized him. He was a low-level sleazebag who did odd errands and small jobs for my stepdad. And... he was not a good guy.

"I'm afraid you're mistaken."

"I don't think so," he growled.

"You have me confused with someone else," I spat, trying to walk away from him. He grabbed my arm. Hard.

"No, I don't," he insisted.

"Let. Me. Go," I seethed through gritted teeth. He didn't.

In a flash, Kyle was there. "Hey. She said let *go*." Kyle threatened.

"What, you her bodyguard?" He dropped my arm, seeing that he was currently out-muscled.

"I don't know who either of you are, so piss off. Both of you!" I quickly turned toward the restaurant door as I heard the sleazebag shout, "He'll be very interested to know that I ran into you, Wren!"

I yanked the restaurant door open, practically running in. I heard Kyle's rushed footsteps approach me from behind when he called out my name. "Robbie." But I kept walking. "Robbie!" He said louder, and more annoyed.

But I didn't look back.

I was almost at the bar to get our drinks when I heard him say it.

"WREN!" It stopped me in my tracks. Shit. Kyle heard the sleazebag say my real name out loud.

How would I lie my way out of this one?

CHAPTER 21

...answer.

Kyle

SHE STOOD THERE, frozen, with her back to me. Slowly, she turned around and looked up at me, pale as a ghost. "That's why you can't go to the police, isn't it? Because you're using an alias."

"Kinda. It's... more complicated than that."

"So? I'm listening," I said expectantly.

"I can't explain it here, Kyle. Shane and Kira are waiting for us," she nodded in their direction.

"Fine. But we're talking about it as soon as we're home tonight. I mean it. I won't take no for an answer."

"Okay. Just, please don't say anything."

"I won't, as long as you keep your end of the bargain." She rolled her eyes at me, but I didn't care.

My world crumbled. She had been pretending for way longer than I had ever imagined. Her name wasn't even Robin. I knew she had secrets, but what else was she lying about? I thought she hid the truth about her past from everyone except me. But that's another lie?

I knew I was in love with her, and I had been convinced she had feelings for me. But now? Well, I didn't know what was real. We grabbed the water and returned to the table. Shane was still going on about his adventures in Europe, and Kira was being way too polite to stop him.

"Sorry that took so long. I had to use the restroom," Robbie said.

"Yeah… uh, me too," I stuttered out. I wasn't that quick on my feet with lies.

"No problem. We were exchanging stories about my time in Lisbon and Montana. Did you know she's been learning how to train her uncle's horses as therapy animals?" Shane asked enthusiastically.

"No, I didn't know that." I was embarrassed Shane knew that about her from one brief conversation. I had been dating Kira for a few months now and didn't retain that about her.

Kira interrupted my thoughts. "His trip to Lisbon sounded amazing! I hope to go to Europe someday because I'd love to travel," Kira said, smiling at Shane.

"I know, right?! I love traveling too!" Shane replied, grinning back at her. Robbie and I looked at each other, surprised at how well they were getting along. I had mistaken Kira's politeness for boredom. But apparently, his stories enthralled her. And he was intent on listening to hers. He bored me to tears when he droned on about Europe, Lisbon, or soccer. So, I assumed the same would happen with Kira. But I was wrong.

After lunch, Shane pulled out his debit card to pay. I was going to offer to help, but Robbie whisked him away before I had the chance. She was doing her usual "avoiding me" technique when she didn't want to confront the pressing cold, hard truth.

As we headed back to Mom's office to get the car, we stopped at Rockefeller Plaza first and do a little Christmas shopping. Kira was thrilled about going, and oddly, Shane was too. They continued busily chatting about their adventures the entire time we were there. Robbie and I hung back like misplaced third wheels on our friends' first date.

The awkward silence and annoyance radiating off us seemed very noticeable. Or I thought it was. But Shane and Kira appeared oblivious. We spent the rest of the day numbly going through the motions of two couples in the city shopping at Christmastime. It was not ideal.

The only positive was that I stopped Robbie from going through with her plan to confront her stepdad. I smiled to myself, happy that I could keep her safe. This time.

***

It was well after 11:00 P.M. when we finally got home after dropping Kira off. Mom wasn't home yet, going out on a dinner date with Mateo in the city. He wanted to thank her for inviting him to Thanksgiving. But we all knew it was more than that.

Thankfully, Shane went straight to bed since he had an early training session in the morning. He had taken today off, so he was anxious to return to his routine. Robbie and I gave excuses to stay up so we could talk. I had made her promise, and I intended to hold her to it. I hoped I could avoid her gravity long enough to get the whole truth this time.

I shook my head. This was getting more complicated than I ever could have thought. We sat on opposite sides of the couch, shifting uncomfortably, waiting to start the conversation between us. We knew we needed to have it, but not exactly how to begin.

"Who was that thug today at the restaurant?" I finally asked.

"One of my stepdad's lackeys."

"How dangerous is he?"

"He's a low-level runner. Not a good guy, but no one to really worry about."

"Will he tell your stepdad that he saw you at the restaurant?"

"Yes." I tried to wrap my head around that statement.

"Robin Fanning is an alias?" I asked.

"Yes." I shook my head in disbelief, but she confirmed what I already knew.

"Robin. Wren. Both types of birds, so I get that. But why Fanning? Is it even close to your real name?"

"No. I just picked it because it's the last name of two of my favorite actresses. Dakota and Elle Fanning." I chuckled. Actresses. Pretending. The irony was not lost on me.

I slid beside her on the couch, taking her hand in mine. "Robbie. We need to get the cops involved. And before you say no again, you need to give me a reason. I mean, a damn good reason not to."

She looked pained by that question, the muscles in my throat tightening as I tried to swallow.

"Okay. So, um… the reason why is… uh… so the reason…" she hesitated.

"Please, Robbie. No more lies. I don't think I can take any more lies right now," I pleaded.

"You're right. No more lies. The reason I can't is because… he is the police."

Robbie

Looking at the shock on his face, I knew I had just gut-punched him with my true reality. He sat there stunned and silent for what felt like forever. "That's why I couldn't... go to the police. Or the hospital. Or keep my phone. Any of it. Because he could find me. He has everyone in his pocket. The cops, judges, thugs... everyone. His reach is deep. He's powerful in both worlds, and I didn't want to put you all in danger."

He raised his brow incredulously as he dropped my hand. "But you did. By lying to us. Lying to me."

I didn't know what else to say because he was right. "I know."

"I don't understand where to begin. This kind of information is important. And now, that guy is going to tell him he saw you. That he saw us."

"That's why I need to get to him first. I—"

"Do you even hear yourself? What are you even going to do, Robbie? Do you honestly think you can kill him?"

"If I have to."

"Robbie, you're not thinking straight. We can't just show up on his doorstep and confront him. We need to be smart about this."

"Kyle, there is no 'we.'"

"Why do you have to be so stubborn all the time?" he huffed.

"I'm not being stubborn. I'm trying to keep you safe. All I wanted to do was get out of this crappy situation. But I kept making bad decisions like dating Shane, trying to get the jewelry, and then getting..."

"Involved with me."

"No. I meant getting hurt in June."

"You meant us," he said adamantly.

"I'm not doing this again." Annoyed, I stood and started to walk away, when he grabbed my hand. He turned me around so I would face him.

"Why can't you admit it? Why can't you just say it?" he asked.

"I don't know what you want me to say, Kyle."

"Yes, you do."

"Okay, I'm sorry. I'm sorry I lied, and that I didn't tell you the truth."

"Robin, you know that's not what I'm talking about."

"It's late, Kyle. I'm tired," I deflected.

"Say it, Robbie."

"I can't!" I yelled.

"Why not?" he asked, his brows furrowed.

"Because if I do, I'll have something to lose," I said honestly. He stepped closer to me. "Don't, Kyle." I tried to push him away, but he held his ground.

"This morning, you wished you could tell me something. What do you wish for, Robbie?"

I looked down at the floor, unsure I could find the words. With a lump in my throat, I finally breathed out the truth. "To tell you everything."

He pulled me to him, tilting my chin up. "I wish for the same thing, Robin. To tell you everything."

"Please, don't do it, Kyle," I begged with misty eyes.

"I love you, Robin. I'm in love with you, and I can't deny it anymore. I won't."

"Kyle…" I whispered.

"I want us to be together. I don't care what your real name is or how you felt it necessary to lie to me too. I don't care about any of it. You don't have to do this alone. You aren't alone anymore."

I couldn't stop myself as I wrapped my arms around his neck and kissed him. He held me tight to his chest, meeting my embrace. I could feel his pulse pounding in his chest, our hearts beating as one. He told me that when I was ready, all I had to do was say the words. That he was mine. I guess the real question is…

Was I ready?

Kyle

As I kissed her, my heart burst. I finally told her I loved her. She didn't say it back, but having her in my arms meant the world. Nothing could bring down this moment. Or that's what I had thought before the subconscious realization that the front door opened. That's when I heard the gasp.

"Mom!" I yelled, stumbling away from Robbie. I felt like a bystander watching a train wreck unfold before me. "It's not what it looks like."

"I think it's exactly what it looks like," Mom accused.

"Let me explain," I pleaded.

"It was my fault, Kirstie. Don't blame Kyle. I was the one who kissed him, and I won't let it happen again," Robbie quickly conceded.

I looked over at Robbie, stung by her words.

"See that it doesn't. Shane doesn't deserve that," Mom scolded. I had never heard her so angry.

"Please don't tell Shane," I begged.

"It's not my place to tell him. That's between you two. Do you understand? Figure out what this is and make it right," she said, disappointed.

"We will," we answered simultaneously.

"You better. I don't want to intervene, but I will if it comes to that." Both of us nodded as she went up the steps. "It's late. I'm going to bed."

We stood as statues for an eternity when Robbie rushed past me toward the stairs. I called out to her. "Robbie." She stopped but wouldn't look at me.

"She's right, Kyle. Shane doesn't deserve this. Any of it." Her sharp tone echoed in the room before Robin rushed upstairs, hiding her face.

My head spun after that devastating moment. My luck absolutely sucked.

***

The next day, I looked over at Shane's empty bed. He had already left for his run, which was a relief. I didn't have to face him yet after everything that went down last night. I walked past Robbie's room, but her door was still shut, so I lumbered down to the kitchen. Mom was already awake, leaning casually against the counter, drinking her orange juice.

"Morning," I greeted cautiously.

"Morning. Want some juice?" she asked.

"Um… sure. Thanks." I sat down at the island as she poured the drink. She handed me the glass, and as soon as I took a sip, she asked a kill-shot question of all questions.

"That wasn't the first time you kissed her, was it?" she asked.

I practically spat out my juice. She held my gaze, and I contemplated whether I should lie or tell her the truth. I decided on the latter.

"No." She let out an exasperated sigh. I felt terrible.

"Does she feel the same way?" She asked, defeated.

"I don't know. I think so, but I'm not completely sure."

"How long has it been going on?"

"Mom…" I begged her not to ask, with the inflection of my voice.

"How long?" she demanded.

"Since the summer."

"Geez, Kyle," she said, irritated.

"I know. I'm sorry."

"Poor Shane. Poor Kira."

"I know," I said, genuinely miserable about disappointing her.

"Is she worth blowing up your entire world? Your brother's world?"

Emphatically and without hesitation, "I love her, Mom." I could barely choke out the words from the pure intensity of my feelings.

"Oh, Kyle." She walked around the island and hugged me. "Love can be messy, hard, and so complicated. But it can also be the most wonderful thing in the world. All at the same time. But that doesn't mean I condone your actions. Or hers." She pulled back from me and looked at me with a severe face. "You need to come clean to everyone. Sooner rather than later, and let the chips fall as they may. Even if you're not sure how she feels. This cannot wait, Kyle. It's been too long already."

"I know. I'll talk to her, and we'll take care of it."

"See that you do." She finished her juice and went up to her room.

I leaned my forehead against the cold countertop and groaned at my predicament. Mom had made it crystal clear that if we didn't make it right, she would. There's no turning back now. I told Robbie I love her. And now I wasn't sure what I hated more, telling Shane and Kira about deceiving them or…

Robbie's answer.

CHAPTER 22
Run.

Robbie

BEING BACK AT school on Monday felt foreign and far removed from everything that had happened over the weekend. In two days, my world was knocked off its axis. I had successfully deceived everyone in this family, leaving no one unscathed. Now, their mom knew precisely the kind of person I really was. A liar and a cheater.

Kirstie gave us an ultimatum to come clean to Shane and Kira, or she would do it for us. I'm sure she was questioning her decision to let me stay with them all those months ago. She had trusted me, and I broke that trust.

"Hellooo? Robbie?" Sarah greeted.

"Oh, sorry. I was lost in thought."

"I saw that," she said sarcastically. "Were you thinking about your dreamy weekend with Shane? I heard you went into the city and got all these free makeup samples. I hope you brought some back for me. You know how I love the new line they've been advertising."

"Um… sure. You can have all the samples that Kirstie gave me. I don't really wear it or need it."

"Are you kidding me? Do you know how lucky you are, and you're just going to give it all away?" she asked, shocked.

"Like I said, it's not really my thing."

"Geez. I guess Kira was right," she said testily. She had my full attention.

"About what?" I asked.

"Nothing."

"No, go on. You brought it up."

"Well, she said you were kind of a stick in the mud the whole time you were in the city," she said almost gleefully.

"She said that?" I hadn't pegged Kira for gossip. But Sarah could bring out the worst in people. I'd seen it. I'd lived it.

"Well, something like that," Sarah said.

"Tell me what she said exactly." I returned sharply.

"Okay. Geez. Don't bite my head off again. She said you seemed distracted and worried the entire day," she said, annoyed.

"She said those words?"

"Or something like that. I don't know. I didn't record our conversation," she snapped. "Why? Did something happen? Did you and Shane fight?"

"Why would you assume that?"

"Well, Kira said she talked to Shane more than you did. And that you looked stressed as hell."

Crap. Kira noticed more than I had hoped. "No. We didn't fight. It was a long day. Plus, the makeup and the city are not my favorite things."

"Oh. My. Gosh. That would have been perfect. Plus, having both Whitmore twins there, well... let's just say that would've been the dream."

I rolled my eyes. "I've got to get back to class. Talk to you later?" I asked, trying to end this nightmare conversation.

"Sure. Maybe I can swing by and get the makeup tonight?"

"Umm..." My gut reaction was to say no, but she would help put a buffer between myself and everyone else in the Whitmore house.

"...Sure. That works. Like around seven?"

Kyle didn't finish hockey until after seven, so this would be the perfect excuse to avoid him.

"Perfect. See you then," she chirped happily. I beamed as she walked away. Not because I was thrilled she was coming over but that I would be able to avoid everyone else.

***

Everything turned out a success. I was even able to secure an invitation to Sarah's house the next night after. I'd do anything to avoid our necessary conversation. Kyle started to notice, Kirstie too, but I knew her patience would only last so long.

I needed a little more time to figure out what to say and what to leave out. I knew my stepdad must have already been informed about me popping up in the city. It felt like it was time to tie up *my* loose ends and say my goodbyes.

The next day, I went through the motions of my schedule. I was distracted as I pushed my tray down the metal slide, indiscriminately picking food items for lunch. When I got to the cashier, I noticed I had chosen an apple, a Jello cup, a cup of mac-n-cheese, and a piece of wheat bread.

I groaned, handing over my ID card to swipe. I couldn't swap my choices now. The policy is, "If you put it on your tray, it's yours." Trying to find a place to sit, I practically dropped my meal after my phone buzzed. Balancing my food, I saw Shane had texted. *It was only one line*, I thought, dismayed.

Meet me in senior hall after lunch
Sent 12:01PM

Crap. I can't tell from his text if meeting him was a good or a bad thing. Anxiety loomed, so I quickly ate my apple and a bite of bread to quell my sour stomach. I threw the rest away and hurried down to senior hall. My pulse hummed in my throat.

When I rounded the corner and saw him waiting, I had a pressing urge to turn and run. But before I could, he motioned me over.

"Where have you been lately? I live with you, and I've barely seen you the last couple of days," he asked, concerned. I hadn't realized Shane noticed too.

"I know, I'm sorry. Sarah kept me busy. She wanted to know about our trip and try the make-up samples I brought back. How to apply them and how to…"

"Okay. Okay. Yikes. Forgiven," he laughed, putting up his hands. "I was wondering if maybe we could get dinner on Saturday. Just the two of us. We haven't done that in a while."

"What's the occasion?"

"No occasion. But I was talking with Mom last night, and there's something I wanted to ask you."

"You were talking to your mom?"

"Yeah. I've been known to do that from time to time," he teased. "So, is that a yes then?"

"To what?"

"To dinner on Saturday."

"Oh, um… yeah, okay," I answered nervously. The class bell rang.

"Oops, gotta go. See ya' later," he pecked my cheek, jogging down the hall.

As I stood there, my sour stomach worked on overdrive from a situation made by my own doing. I could feel my breathing pick up. He talked to his mom, she must have alluded that I had something to tell him. Now I couldn't wait any longer.

But how do I tell him that I had been cheating on him with his own brother? How do I tell him it's been going on since the summer? And how do I tell him that his mother caught us, and that's the only reason I'm confessing now?

My chest heaved, and I felt my throat tighten. My exhalation was loud and raspy. The harder I tried to regulate, the more it occurred. I couldn't slow it down, and now I couldn't breathe. Fuzziness clouded the edges of my vision as I felt my legs wobble. My eyes rolled back.

And everything went… black.

Kyle

I tried to keep my distance when I saw Robbie rushing down the hall. She had avoided me hard this week, and I wanted to give her some space. But I was selfishly glad I didn't have to talk with her either. Last weekend was tumultuous, and we both still reeled from the consequences of our actions.

I turned the corner to the senior hall just as Shane was talking with Robbie. I hung back to listen, but unfortunately, I was too far to hear what they were saying. As the class bell ring, I abandoned my attempt to get involved. I turned to walk away, when I heard what sounded like sobs. I stopped, trying to hear better before realizing it was Robbie. And she wasn't sobbing, she was gasping. For air.

She must have told him about us, and now she was hyperventilating. As I ran across the senior hall, I saw her stagger. I threw down my books, catching her just as she passed out. I scooped her up, carrying her to the nurse's office. The nurse had me place her on one of the sterile, cracked vinyl beds.

"What happened?" Nurse Wilson questioned.

"She was hyperventilating and passed out."

"Why was she hyperventilating?"

"Uuhh…" I stuttered. *Think Kyle. Think.* "The anniversary of her mother's death is coming up. She's been really stressed about it lately. It's only been two years," I answered quickly.

"Oh, the poor dear. Has she done this before?"

"Hyperventilate. Yes. Pass out. No," I furrowed my brows.

"Did she hit her head?"

"No. I caught her before she hit the floor."

"She was very fortunate that you were there," Nurse Wilson said.

Luck had nothing to do with it, I thought.

"Okay. I'll let her rest. I'm sure she'll wake up on her own, but I'll have to call her parents. What's her name?"

I hesitated, thinking of our conversation the night we last kissed. "Robin Fanning. But she lives with me."

"Are you related?"

"Ah... no. Definitely not," I chuckled under my breath. "But my mom's her guardian... well, my mom's her emergency contact. Robin's eighteen."

"I see. Regardless of her age, I'll still need to call your mother. You can head back to class. I'll write you a late pass."

"Is it okay if I stay? She might be scared when she wakes up, and I think it'll help if a familiar face is here to support her."

"Hm... alright. You can stay since I'll be talking with your mom."

I pulled a chair beside where Robin lay, taking her hand in mine. I couldn't believe that she had told him about us. I really didn't think she would.

I smiled. *Maybe this meant...* but I stopped that thought. I didn't want to jinx it. Because it gave me hope. Instead, I lifted her hand to my mouth and held it there, kissing it.

"What the FUCK??!!" a male voice yelled from the door.

I bolted up, seeing my brother standing menacingly. "Shane? What are you doing here?" I asked, surprised.

"What am I doing here? What the hell are you doing kissing her? She's my girlfriend, asshole!" he screamed.

"Whoa, boys! Take it down a notch. Do I need to call the SRO?" Nurse Wilson intervened.

"No!" We yelled at the same time.

"Then you both need to leave this office before I call the principal. I'll take it from here," she demanded. We glared at each other as I stood to meet his challenging stance.

"Now!" Nurse Wilson commanded as she nudged us out of the room and into the hallway.

"What the fuck, Kyle?"

"I was comforting her."

"By kissing her!?"

"I kissed her hand," I replied incredulously.

"What's the fucking difference?"

"A lot, actually. See, the hand is on the end of your arm…" I started sarcastically. He lunged at me, but I sidestepped him. "Geez. Take it easy, bro. Nothing happened. I comforted her till she woke up. How the hell did you even know she was in the nurse's office, anyway?"

"Max saw you carrying her and texted me. What did you do to her?"

"What did I do? What did you do!?" I spat back.

"Me? What are you talking about?" Shane asked furiously.

"She passed out after talking to you in the senior hall!"

"How did you even know we were talking in the senior hall?"

"I saw you."

"Stalk much?" he mocked.

"I happened by."

"Well, now I know that's a lie because your science lab is on the other side of the building!"

"Whatever, Shane. Just tell me what you said to her?" I demanded.

"It's none of your damn business."

"It made her hyperventilate and pass out. She was already falling when I got to her. If I hadn't caught her, she would have cracked her head open. At least I was there. Where the hell were you!?"

"Get over yourself. You've always been jealous of me. My grades. My sports. And *now*, my girlfriend."

"Shut the fuck up!" I yelled, fuming.

"No, you shut the fuck up!" Shane screamed back, pushing my shoulders.

"Well, if I'm so jealous, why did she…" I bit my tongue immediately before I said more. My hand involuntarily curled into a fist.

"Why did she what?" Shane asked angrily.

"Boys! What's going on here?" Principal Harper barked, storming over.

"Nothing," I answered, fuming.

"We were arguing," Shane said.

"Oh, I could hear that. Why don't we take this 'conversation' to my office? Then we can share it with your mother when she picks up Miss Fanning."

Neither of us budged. "My office, both of you! Now!" Mr. Harper demanded.

My bad luck reared its ugly head. Again.

Robbie

My head pounded from the buzzing fluorescent lights above me. I blinked a few times, shifting uncomfortably, trying to figure out where I was when I heard someone speak.

"Hello, dear," said a small, kind voice.

"Where… am I?" I asked groggily. I started to make out the shape of the woman in front of me.

"You're in the nurse's office," said Nurse Wilson

"What happened?"

"You passed out. Your friend brought you here."

"A friend did?"

"Kyle. Kyle Whitmore."

"Oh."

"Your emergency contact, Kirstie, is on her way."

"You called her?" My head snapped over, but I groaned from the sudden movement. Dots flashed in my vision. Maybe I should have eaten more of my lunch. I must be dehydrated.

"Yes. You passed out, sweetie. I needed to call a guardian. I mean, your emergency contact. This is a serious matter."

"She works in the city. She can't just leave and pop over here. Can't I go home? I'm eighteen."

"Sorry, I have to follow school protocol."

I shook my head in embarrassment and frustration. "Where's Kyle now?"

"Well… that's another matter."

"Why?" I slowly blinked, trying to get the dots to stop dancing. "Did something happen? What's going on?"

"He's in the principal's office with his brother."

"Shane?"

"Yes, Shane. They were fighting. First here, then out in the hall. Mr. Harper took them to his office. And since we had to call their mom to get you, the principal will discuss the fight too."

"Shit."

"Language, my dear," she reminded sternly.

"Sorry. But do you know what they were fighting about?"

"You."

Frustrated and embarrassed, I lay there on the tiny bed, staring up at the ceiling tiles. Every time I moved, the paper crinkled under me. This was miserable. Waiting for Kirstie to get here and dealing with the inevitable fallout from the fight… was excruciating.

What was I going to do? Because now they all knew I was a liar and a cheater. The urge to escape the nurse's office was strong, but I was stuck in that curtained cubicle, a middle-aged woman blocking my path. I should take that as a sign and do the right thing. Stay to atone for my actions. But I already knew what I was going to do.

It's what I always did. Run.

CHAPTER 23

...the city.

Kyle

MOM WAS FURIOUS about our fight. She laid into Shane and me hard about our inexcusable behavior. She was already worried sick about Robin. Finding out that we were in the principal's office sent her over the edge. She made it known that our actions were beyond anything she would tolerate.

To her credit, when Mom realized the fight was about Robin, she kept our secret to herself. She didn't reveal she caught me kissing Robin. Thankfully, she convinced Principal Harper to only give us a week of detention and a verbal warning since it was our first offence. We were also grounded for the week to come. Shane had to beg her for to still take his morning run.

When we returned home, Mom wanted to take Robbie to the doctor as the nurse recommended. But Robin worked her magic. She assured Kirstie that she had just been stressed out with midterms and hadn't eaten lunch. That she had gotten a little lightheaded and passed out. I know Mom wasn't completely comfortable with that explanation, but Robin was eighteen. She couldn't drag her in to get checked out.

Obviously, it was a lot more complicated than that. I didn't know the exact reason for her panic attack, but it wasn't because she had confessed to Shane. When I further prompted my brother, he had said they only talked about going to dinner and nothing else. Robin hadn't shared anything either, and I had the feeling that she wasn't going to.

***

The next day dragged on endlessly. Robin wasn't talking to me or Shane. She seemed distant, as if she had already checked out. Emotionally, at least. Shane hasn't talked to me either since our fight and appeared suspicious. I caught him asking Kira if she had noticed anything "unusual" with Robin lately, especially when we were in the city.

My girlfriend mentioned that Robin, and me for that matter, looked really stressed. That didn't go over well with Shane, and I figured he'd confront me about it. But he hasn't. Yet.

"Yo, dude. What's up?" Brody greeted.

"Hey, Brody. Not much. Same ol'. Same ol.'"

"Still have detention after school today?" he asked.

"Yep."

"Still grounded?"

"Yep."

"Still want me to take you to the city and blow off hockey tonight?"

"Yep."

"Okay, I'll be ready."

"Remember, you can't tell anyone," I glanced over my shoulder.

"Dude. Who would I tell?"

"Sarah, for one."

"C'mon, man. I've got your back. Even if you won't tell me why you need to go so badly on a random Thursday night."

"Thanks, man. Appreciate you."

Brody and I headed back to class and would meet in his car after school. I was thankful he didn't push hard for the reason I had to get to the city. He just rolled with it.

Now all I had to do was not get caught.

***

Wanting the day to end made it seem much longer. Detention felt even more eternal. Every tick of the clock's second hand slowed each time it moved. I was desperate to get out of there and could barely sit still. Whenever I changed my gaze from the clock to Shane, he glared. He shot daggers in my direction for the rest of the time. It was hard to ignore him, but I tried.

"Where are we going again?" Brody queried while entering the New York City limits.

"It's a pawnshop."

"And why can't I park in front of the store?"

"Because they have cameras."

"And you don't want to be on any of the cameras because…?" Brody asked, parking down the street.

"Can you trust me on this?"

"Yeah, sure, but if you're buying drugs, man, you gotta tell me."

"I'm not buying drugs."

"I'm not judging if you are…"

"I'm not buying drugs! I'll fill you in after it's done, okay?"

"After 'it's done?' What, are you a hitman now?" Brody teased.

"Geez. Brody. I'll be right back," I replied with annoyance.

"Okay, bro. Chill. Just joking around."

I got out of the car and made sure I avoided looking at any of the cameras. I hadn't known to do that every time I was in the city these last few months, going to pawnshops. But then again, I didn't know "he" was a cop and could find her. Find us.

I stuck close to the buildings, trying to avoid being in sight as much as possible. The store was covered in graffiti, and metal bars were bolted to the windows and door. I almost tripped over a grate on the sidewalk. It was slightly heaved up on one side with a hypodermic needle wedged in between.

I pushed the buzzer next to the bar-lined door, and a raspy voice answered.

"Selling or buying?"

"Uh… buying," I stuttered. As I heard the clicking sound of the lock, I pushed the heavy door open.

"What are you looking for, kid?" he asked, heading over to the counter.

"Some jewelry."

"Okay. Here's what I got." The owner pointed to a glass case directly next to the cash register. "Let me know if anything interests you."

"Um… actually, I'm looking for a locket."

"I only have the one locket." He shifted to hover over the glass, pointing to it. Looking down, I frowned to see a heart-shaped necklace. Robbie had said her mother's locket was an oval.

"Do you have any that are more circular? Or with a bird on it?"

"Look kid, that's all I got—wait, did you say a bird?"

"Yes, why? Do you have one?" I asked hopefully.

"Well, I have a box of broken jewelry that I sell by weight. But I recall seeing something with a bird. Hold on, I'll grab the box." I felt a shift in my body between anxious and hopeful. I had been to so many pawn shops across the city these last few weeks. I almost thought that I'd never find it. "Here's the box. Dig around in there. I'm almost sure I remember seeing something."

As I explored a tangled mess of broken chains, tarnished rings, chipped bracelets, and necklaces, I finally saw it. It was a bird on a dented oval locket. I picked it up and opened it. The inscription said "my little songbird" on the left side of the locket, and on the right side had birthdates just like Robin described. I stared at it.

"Is that it, kid?"

"Yes, sir," I said too excitedly. "How much?"

"Well, I don't have the chain anymore, and the locket is scuffed up, but… I think I can let it go for $200?"

"Yeah. Okay," I said without a second thought.

The man's expression curled into a smile. "Cash or credit?"

"Cash."

I couldn't believe I had found it. I never thought I would after all this time. I guess I should have tried to haggle on price, but I didn't want to risk losing it. I knew he saw my excitement. I was lucky he didn't ask for even more.

I reassured Brody that I hadn't done anything illegal as we headed out of the city. But I told him we needed to return home before anyone noticed I was gone. If we hurried, I could probably catch the tail end of hockey practice, but Coach would be livid. Hopefully, he hadn't called anyone trying to find me. It would suck if he blew my cover.

On the ride home, I repeatedly rubbed the locket in my hand, still stunned that I had finally found it. The anniversary of her mother's death was coming up later this month. I had always hoped I would find it before then. Every few weeks, I snuck into the city to check out another shop. But I was losing hope after all these months.

We pulled into the parking lot of the hockey rink. I thanked Brody for the ride as I sprinted into the building, knowing I had missed most of practice. I rushed into the locker room, hoping the coach would go easy on his punishment, but I knew better. But it didn't matter. It was worth it. I had found her mother's locket. The item she desperately wanted back and had risked her life to get. The locket that forced her to call me for help that night. The night that changed everything.

For me.

Robbie

I still reeled from my embarrassing fainting spell yesterday and desperately needed a distraction. Sarah provided one when she had asked me to help with the Winter Talent Show decorations. I gladly accepted so I could stay after school and not have to go home.

I oversaw students painting giant backdrops for the stage. After a while, the fumes made me lightheaded. Not wanting to faint again, I went out the back gym door for fresh air. As I did, I saw Kyle entering Brody's car and speeding out of the parking lot.

It's Thursday, so I knew Kyle had detention and then hockey practice later. Plus, he was grounded. Kristie had said he could only go to school, detention, and practice. But Brody drove in the opposite direction of our house and the ice rink. So where were they going?

It was late when Sarah and I left school. There was still so much to prep for the talent show, but most of us had midterms, so we needed to get home to study. Sarah asked if I could come by on Saturday to help her decide what song she would sing as her talent. I said "yes" immediately since it was another good excuse to avoid the family again. They had become my weakness. And I need to finalize plans to book it without any distractions.

I walked into the house just as Kirstie was about to climb the stairs.

"Oh, hi Robbie."

"Hi, Kirstie."

"How did the prep go?" She turned to fully face me.

"Good. We got a lot painted."

"That's good."

I nodded awkwardly. "I'm… going to grab a water bottle and head to bed."

"Are you still feeling okay? After yesterday?"

"Yeah, fine. It's just been a long day, and I have a midterm tomorrow. I'm headed up to study, then sleep."

"Okay, then. Goodnight, Robbie."

"Goodnight, Kirstie." I swiped some water from the fridge when Kyle surprised me. He was at the kitchen table studying. We hadn't spoken much this week, and definitely hadn't spoken since the nurse's office yesterday. But I needed to know where he had gone earlier.

"Hey."

"Hey," he said, pulling out an earbud.

"Chemistry midterm?" I asked.

"Um… yeah. Super fun. Were you with Sarah again?"

"Yeah, helping with the Winter Talent Show decorations."

"Oof, that sounds…" he started, making a dying face.

I smiled. "So, how was hockey practice?"

"Um… it was… good. You know, like normal."

"You went to practice then?" I challenged.

"Yeah. Of course, I did. Where else would I go? I'm grounded."

"Right."

"Why do you ask?"

"No reason, really. Making small talk."

"Mm-hmm…" he quirked a brow suspiciously.

"Well, I have a midterm tomorrow too, so I'm heading to bed. Goodnight."

"Goodnight."

I ran upstairs to my room and jumped the moment I entered. There was Shane sitting on my bed studying. I couldn't catch a break from anyone in this family tonight.

"There you are. Mom said you were home," Shane said.

"I was getting water." I lifted my hand as I shook the bottle.

He pulled himself up from the bed and wandered over to me, leaving space between us. "How are you feeling? I didn't get to see you all day to ask."

"I'm good. Um, Sarah roped me into doing decorations for the Winter Talent Show, so I was with her all evening."

"That sounds…" he stuck out his tongue, with a hand on his throat like he was dying. I let out a soft hum of a laugh, comparing the two brothers once again. "Can I ask you something, Robbie?"

"Sure," I replied nervously.

"You'd tell me if something was wrong or stressing you out. Wouldn't you?"

"Of course," I inwardly rolled my eyes.

"Because you know you can talk to me, right? And I would listen. And I would try to be… understanding. Helpful."

"I know. But nothing's wrong. I promise," I lied. "Why are you asking?"

"I was worried about you passing out yesterday. You said it was due to stress, so I wanted to make sure you were okay."

"I'm fine. Don't worry. I do need to get to bed, though. I have a huge midterm tomorrow."

"Right. Yeah, me too. Goodnight, Robbie."

"Goodnight, Shane."

He pecked me on the cheek and went to his room. That was twice in the last two days that he hadn't kissed me on the mouth, making me more tense than I already was. I shut my door and climbed into bed even though I knew I wouldn't sleep a wink tonight.

***

The following day, Shane had already left on his run, and Kyle didn't speak a word on our way to school. He kept fidgeting and genuinely seemed uncomfortable. I think my line of questioning about hockey practice last night bothered him. So where did they go? And why did he lie about it?

"Well, have a good day," Kyle said quickly, sprinting from the car. I watched as he practically ran to the school entrance. Something was definitely up, and I was going to find out what. I was startled when I heard a knock on the car window. It was Sarah and Brody. Brody! That's my chance to corner Kyle.

"Did I scare you? I scared you, didn't I? I saw you jump," Sarah laughed at me while opening my door. *She's a gem,* I thought.

"You sure did," I answered sarcastically, stepping out. I closed the car, making sure to lock the inside handle.

"Where are the twins?"

"Shane's probably working out in the gym, and Kyle... I don't know."

"Oh, bummer," Sarah replied sadly.

"You still got me, babe!" Brody exclaimed hopefully.

"Yeah. Yeah. Yeah." She pecked him on the nose and skipped off toward a group of her friends.

I seized the opportunity. "So, Brody, can I talk to you?"

"I've got to get to class."

"It'll only take a sec.'"

"Um... okay."

"Where did you and Kyle go yesterday after school?" Brody immediately stiffened, blinking twice and licking his lips as he glanced away to answer.

"Uh... what do you mean?"

"I saw Kyle get into your car and leave school headed in the opposite direction of his house."

"Mmm... nope. He didn't get in my car."

"He did. I saw him. He left with you after detention."

"It was just me. You must be thinking of another day."

"So, he went to hockey practice then?" I pressed.

"Uh... yeah. Look, I gotta go. I have a test."

"Okay. Talk to you later."

"Uh... sure... bye," he replied quickly, running toward school.

Oh, he is so lying.

But where did they go that Brody had to cover? And why was Kyle willing to risk the wrath of his mom's grounding and being kicked off the hockey team? Then it hit me. I knew exactly where they went.

To the city.

CHAPTER 24

End...

Kyle

I DIDN'T KNOW why I sprinted from the car this morning. What did it matter if she saw Brody and me leave school yesterday? I found the locket, and I needed to tell her about it. But I wasn't sure if this was the right time to come forward about what I'd been doing. With Mom catching us, having to tell Shane, and then adding the anniversary of her mother's death coming up, it felt like bad timing and self-serving on my part.

I chastised myself. Now I grew a moral compass when it comes to Robbie? It didn't stop me before when I kissed her. Or when I fell for her. Or when I proclaimed my love for her. Why did telling her I found her locket cause me so much anxiety?

"Yo, Kyle. We gotta talk," Brody stressed, pulling me out of my angst as he leaned against the locker.

"What's up?"

"I'm really sorry, bro," he apologized.

"About what?"

"She cornered me, and she was asking me all these questions about you, and I tried to lie the best I could, but I don't think she believed me, and then I tried to get away from her—"

"Okay. Okay. Slow down. Who?" I chuckled.

"Robbie."

"Oh."

"Oh? That's it. Oh?" He ran a hand nervously through his hair.

"What did she ask you?" I asked.

"She saw you get in my car yesterday, and she was asking me all these questions about where we went and if you went to hockey and—"

"It's okay. I'll go talk to her."

"I'm sorry. I tried to convince her."

"It's all right. I shouldn't have put you in the middle. She grilled me about it last night too."

"Dude, what's going on between the two of you?"

"Nothing. There's nothing going on between us. Why would you think that?" I quickly covered.

"Well, it's not just me thinking it."

"Like who?"

"Sarah, for one. She's always wondered. She says you spend a lot of time together, and you both disappear at the same time. Then Kira mentioned that you went off together when in the city. And then yesterday, I overheard Shane asking around if there was anything that seemed odd between the two of you."

"Fuck…"

"So, it's true?" Brody asked, surprised.

"No. Not really. I was… helping her… with something. On the down-low."

"Look, bro. I'm not judging. She's great, and I know a lot of guys who'd go out with her in a heartbeat, but she's with Shane… so no one dared."

"No, it's not what you… never mind. Where is she now?" I asked, flustered.

"She cornered me outside your car, so I guess she went to class?"

"Okay. I'll find her."

"I'm really sorry, dude. I tried."

"This is on me. Just… please don't say anything to anybody. Okay? Especially not to Sarah. You know how she loves gossip."

"Yeah, got it."

I pulled my phone out and shot off a text.

We need to talk
Meet me in the car
Read 7:26AM

As I sat waiting, I reached into my pocket and felt the warmed piece of metal again. I had memorized the shape and dent in the locket within the short time I had it. The door opened, and she got in.

"Why, Kyle?"

"It's not what you think."

"So, you didn't go into the city?" Robbie argued.

"No, I went into the city."

"Why would you do that? Why would you involve Brody? I told you my stepdad is dangerous, and now you've involved another person…"

"I found it, Robbie."

"Found what?"

"The locket. Your mom's locket."

She sat there stunned, her mouth agape. "What? How?"

"At a pawnshop. I've been going to different ones around the city since summer and… I found it. It's not in great shape, but…"

She put her face in her hands and sobbed quietly. I reached for her, rubbing her back as her silky hair draped her face. "Can I see it?"

I pulled it out of my pocket and placed it in her hand. She examined it, turning it over and over. When she opened it, she rubbed her fingers against the etched words and numbers. Suddenly, she looked up, puzzled.

"What?"

"Um… nothing. I can't believe you found it." She tucked her hair behind her ear, turning it again in her hands.

"Yeah. I was beginning to lose hope. And then… there it was."

"Brody knows?"

"No. I didn't tell him anything. I promise. All he knew was that I needed a ride into the city. We planned the trip last week before I got grounded."

"Why didn't you wait 'til after? Why risk pissing off your mom and your hockey coach?"

"You know why," I replied, cocking my head toward her.

"You shouldn't have risked all that. Not for—"

"You?" I quipped.

"Yes."

"Well, it's a bit too late for that." She shook her head, visibly upset. "Brody told me Sarah thinks there might be something going on between us," I said, changing the subject.

"I wouldn't worry. She's always thought that. She basically told me she wanted to date Shane, but that I got to him first. So, she settled for you. But then Kira came along, and well... Sarah lost her mind. She's just mad and speculating. She doesn't know anything."

"Well, either way, we need to—"

"I know," she said, then paused a moment. "Look. I've got to get to class. I've already missed most of it."

"Right, class."

"I can't thank you enough for finding it. This means the world to me. Really," she said dryly.

"You're welcome."

"Goodbye, Kyle."

And without a sideways glance, she left the car and returned to school. I knew she was glad I had found the locket, but the tone in her voice said something different. But what that was?

I wasn't exactly sure.

Robbie

I couldn't believe it. He found my mother's locket. I had resigned myself to the fact that I would never see it again. I didn't know he was even looking, let alone for months. Risking his life, unbeknownst to him, for me. But that's not all. There are three dates on the right side. There should only be two. Her birthdate and mine. Whose was the third? Even more odd, it was in the future.

I was so distracted for the rest of the day that I stayed on autopilot through my midterms. I had no idea what they asked or if I had chosen the correct answers. I went mindlessly through the motions like a zombie. School was the last place I wanted to be, and midterms were the last thing I wanted to be doing. I couldn't sit still; my whole body was irritated and uncomfortable. The end of the day couldn't come soon enough.

***

At dinner that night, the air between us at the kitchen table was heavy. All the secrets and lies weighed on all four of us. Kirstie knew about Kyle and me and kept it from Shane. Shane suspected Kyle and I could be involved. And Kyle was deceiving his brother and his girlfriend.

Then there was me. I was the worst. I had deceived them all. And like a car crash in a snowstorm, I couldn't stop any of it. I watched it happen. The quiet scraping of silverware on plates while eating in an uncomfortable silence drove home that fact. All of us desired to speak, yet remained silent. It was deafening.

I did this to this family. This close and caring family who welcomed me into their home. They were now wrought with secrets and lies. I slipped away to my room after dinner, announcing I wasn't feeling well. After my fainting spell, no one really questioned my excuse. Or better yet, no one stopped me.

I curled up on the bed, lying on my side, and stared at the locket on my nightstand. What the dates could mean consumed me, and I felt stress build again. Instead of fighting it, my heavy eyes closed, and I let the dark in to finally escape the day.

It rained hard. We could barely see out the window. Mom wasn't driving fast, but with slick roads, it felt like we were going a hundred miles per hour. It was a frosty December night, and the rain vacillated between wet and snow.

I always loved the first snowfall. Especially the large flakes that lightly floated down from the sky. But this snow was different. They were small chunks, like hail, and they seemed angry. It was as if the ice wanted to announce its arrival to the world by violently tapping on the car.

Mom was anxious. When she was anxious, she talked. Like, non-stop. I knew it was best to just let her be when she was like that, and I would listen. She kept going on about how life throws curveballs, and sometimes, you can see them coming. And then other times, you couldn't. As we drove out of the city that stormy, wintry night, she told me how much I meant to her and that she would do anything to protect me.

Mom reminisced about her favorite memory of us together at the pier by the ocean when I was a child. She rambled about how the ocean is majestic and beautiful, but it can also be dark and dangerous. How sometimes, when you're looking across the water, it could appear peaceful and calm. But under the surface, a shark could lurk. And to fight off a shark, you had to hit back. You had to hit back hard.

The metaphor wasn't lost on me. I was only sixteen, but I knew she was talking about my stepdad. She kept asking if I remembered going to the pier when I was little. I did. She gushed that it was her favorite tradition. We would go ice skating on the night of the first snow and rent skates and lockers there. Then, after ice skating, we would head to the red and white striped lobby and get a cup of hot cocoa.

She kept reiterating how nice the lockers were there and that she would rent one when we went skating. I thought it odd that she focused so much on that part of her memory, but she was rambling after all.

As she continued talking, I closed my eyes and let the memories wash over me. I could almost smell the hot cocoa and feel the cold snow on my face as I spun around and around on the very smooth ice...

Suddenly, I felt dizzy. I snapped my eyes open, and I could hear my mother screaming. The car spun out of control. Her foot pumped the brakes, but nothing was happening. Even the emergency brake didn't work.

She reached across to me and held me against the seat with all her might. Right before we hit the abutment, she looked at me with wild eyes and said, "The locket," and then my vision blurred.

As I focused on a shrieking wail, I realized I was screaming. I sobbed at the top of my lungs. "Mom! Mom! Mom!" When the light turned on in my room, I saw Kyle and Shane in the doorway. I tried with all my might to call out to Shane. To run to Shane. But instead, I croaked out, "K-Kyle..."

He ran to me as I jumped out of bed, holding me tight. I wasn't sure where he ended or where I began. I cried into his shoulder, "She's dead... the pier... all the ice... she's dead, Kyle... and she's never coming back..." I said, sobbing. He held me tighter.

When I finally picked up my head, I looked over Kyle's shoulder and saw Shane. The pain in his eyes shattered me. He turned and pushed past his mom, who was now also in the doorway. She glared at me before rushing down the hall after her son.

I pulled back from Kyle. He reached up and brushed my tear-soaked hair away from my face. "He saw it all," I whimpered.

"I know."

"We need to talk to him," I said, my voice cracking.

"Absolutely not. He's pissed and needs time to cool off. Trust me."

"Your mom looked at me with such..."

"I'll handle her. Don't worry."

"Don't worry? I destroyed your whole family."

"No, you didn't."

"I did. And if you think otherwise, then you're deluding yourself."

"Robbie, it's gonna be—"

"No! Don't say it. It's not okay. This is over. All of it."

"We'll work through this. I promise."

"Stop making promises, Kyle. In what world will Shane, or even your mother for that matter, ever be okay with how this all went down?"

"You never thought she'd let you live here, but she did."

"And look how that turned out? All the lies and secrets just poisoned this family, and it's because of me, and you know it."

"Robbie, that's not true. They love you. I love you."

"But I don't, Kyle. That's why I couldn't say it back, and I should have been brave enough to tell you that a long time ago."

"C'mon, you don't mean that."

"I do mean it, and you need to believe it this time! We're done, Kyle. It's over! Get out of my room."

"Robbie…"

"GET OUT, KYLE. I MEAN IT. GET OUT!!"

He begrudgingly left my room, and I slammed the door. I stood there in fury, fists shaking while my body stood paralyzed. I lied to him again. I hurt him again. My lungs felt heavy.

I tilted my head and took some deep breaths to stave off another panic attack. My heart broke into a million pieces, but I need to stay strong now more than ever. My dream gave me clarity, and I knew what was next. And it meant waking up Sarah.

It was a little before dawn and still dark outside, but I needed a ride to her house. We had planned to get together today anyway to prep for the talent show, but she wouldn't be happy that it's so early. I didn't care.

While I waited for Sarah, I thought through the dream. My mom left me clues the night of the accident. And if I'm right, she gave me the last piece of the puzzle. I needed to finish what she had started.

I decided that when I got to Sarah's, I would purchase a bus ticket to leave later tonight. But to do that successfully, I needed to sever all ties to this town. My relationship with this family was ruined, and Sarah was next. And I knew exactly how to end our friendship.

The Whitmore Twins.

Kyle

I debated if I should go into my room where Mom and Shane were talking. I could hear him yelling about how it was all a lie, and that he couldn't believe his own brother had screwed him over like that. He wasn't wrong, and I should have walked away… but against my better judgment, I entered our room.

"Not now, Kyle!" Mom strongly warned.

"You better listen to Mom, man. I'm in no mood for more of your lies!" Shane yelled.

"I just want to—" I tried to explain.

"You've done enough, Kyle! I told you to take care of this a long time ago," Mom said furiously.

"Wait? You knew, and you didn't tell me?" Shane directed his anger toward Mom now.

"Shane, calm down. It wasn't my place to tell you. I told them to handle it," Mom explained.

"Oh, that's just great, Mom. Take his side. You should have told me! Now I look like an idiot!" Shane raged.

"Shane! I wasn't taking anyone's side," Mom pleaded.

"I don't want to talk to either of you. Get out of my way!" Shane shouted. He grabbed his hoodie and threw on sneakers. He rushed past Mom toward the hallway. I tried to step out of the way, Shane shoving me as he stormed past.

"Where are you going?" Mom asked.

"Out!" Shane bellowed as he bounded down the stairs.

"Shane, please. It's barely daybreak," Mom yelled, running after him. I followed her, watching Shane grab his jacket, heading out to the car.

Mom spun around. "I told you to tell him!"

"He would have reacted the same way."

"But at least he wouldn't have been blindsided. I am so furious with the two of you. I should go up there and give her a piece of my mind!"

I gently blocked her way to the stairs. "She knows, Mom. Trust me. She feels terrible about it."

"Does she? Well, thank goodness for small miracles. I hope this was all worth it for the two of you to be together."

"She broke up with me too."

"Finally, some common sense. Both of you boys will be better off without her. We'd all be better off without her."

"You don't mean that."

"Oh, but I do, Kyle!" She thundered back upstairs to her room and slammed her door. *That went well,* I thought sarcastically.

I flopped down on the couch. I needed everyone to cool down so we could have a rational conversation. I felt terrible about how Shane found out, but he needed to know. I despised going behind his back all these months, but what I felt for Robbie was more powerful than I could ever have imagined.

I didn't set out to fall in love with Robin, and I certainly didn't mean to hurt my brother, but sometimes the universe has other plans. Mom would come around eventually. She always did. Then there was Robbie. That would be far trickier to navigate.

Her first reaction to everything was flight rather than fight. She hadn't had a family to fight for in so long that she didn't understand that this wouldn't break us. It may take time, but we would be stronger when we came out on the other side. I needed to convince her of that because losing her wasn't an option.

I sat up straight on the couch when I heard Robbie bolt down the stairs. She had her hoodie, shoes, and backpack on.

"Where are you going?" I asked.

"Sarah's. We made plans."

"You don't have to lie."

"I'm not lying. She'll be here in a minute."

"You planned to go to her house at six-thirty in the morning on a Saturday?" I mocked.

"No, but I thought it was best for all of us if I wasn't here when Shane got home from wherever he was going."

"Robbie, about what happened…"

"It's over and done with, Kyle. There's nothing more to talk about; please drop it."

"Robbie…" I started when a car horn started blaring.

"There's Sarah. I gotta go."

And Robin flew out the front door without looking back. My little songbird taking flight instead of fighting.

Again.

Robbie

I couldn't get out of the house fast enough. I had never been so thankful for Sarah. Or to even see Sarah. She blared her car horn.

"Hey," I said, leaping into her car.

"I still can't believe you woke me up. On a Saturday, no less, to come get your ass this early in the morning. This emergency better be good."

"It is."

"Well?" she said expectantly.

"Can we go first? I need to leave. Like now."

"Fine," she said, annoyed, backing out of the driveway. She waited a whole minute before she asked me again. That's a record.

"So?"

"Can I tell you at your house? You're driving, and it's kind of shocking."

"You can't dangle that in front of me and not tell me. So, tell me right now!"

"I think Shane and I broke up." She screeched the car to a halt, and I had to catch myself on the dashboard despite having my seatbelt on.

"What? Are you serious?"

"I wouldn't joke about that."

"Holy shit! I can't believe it!" she said, overly excited. I wasn't sure if she was pumped for a juicy story, or the fact Shane could be available. I rolled my eyes. It's the latter.

"What happened?" she asked.

"Let's grab breakfast first and then head back to your house. I'll tell you everything. I promise."

"Fine, but I want every single detail," she demanded, taking her foot off the brake. I told her I had started seeing someone behind his back and that he had found out. She didn't like that at all, demanded to know how I could hurt him on purpose. And second, asked why I would hog him while still seeing someone else. She called me selfish and deceitful. She wasn't wrong, so I let her lecture me for a while.

As I sat there listening to her admonish me, I felt a sense of sorrow. After tonight, this was the last time we would be together. It struck me that no matter how strained and complicated our relationship had been, she was the closest thing I had to a real friend.

Even if she never openly admitted it, I knew she was lonely. Whenever her mom missed a special event, or parent night, or pictures for homecoming, it affected Sarah. Her attitude was a mask, and I knew that mask technique well, so I felt for her.

After her sermon, we picked up breakfast and went back to her house. It gave me a moment to book a bus ticket leaving later tonight. Forlorn, I still had to follow through. Drop the Kyle news at the right moment, so she wouldn't try to stop me from leaving or tell anyone I left.

***

As night fell, I knew it was time. I asked Sarah to come over and sit on the bed. I told her I was ready to divulge who I cheated with. She gleefully skipped over. Waiting expectantly, she looked like a kid in a candy shop.

"Sarah—" I began as the doorbell rang, interrupting me. *Who the hell is here?* I thought, frustrated.

"Hold that thought." She jumped up to answer the front door. I stayed in her bedroom, waiting for her to come back. I hoped whoever was at the door wouldn't take long.

Sarah returned, looking perturbed. "It's for you."

"For me? Who is it?"

"A Whitmore twin," she said flippantly.

"Shane?"

"No. The other one."

Why was he here? I thought. "Okay. I'll be right back." I rushed to the front door, and there was Kyle waiting on the porch. "What do you want?"

"Shane hasn't come home, and Mom is a little worried. I told her he's probably at Max's house, but he won't text either of us back."

"What do you want me to do?"

"I… uh… was thinking we could go over there together and explain to him what happened between us. That we never meant to hurt him, but we can't help how we feel about each other."

"No. I told you it's over. With both of you."

"Robin, c'mon. You didn't mean that."

"I do. I do mean it." I hissed.

"Robin, I love you. And I know you love me too."

"Well, you're wrong. I already told you I don't."

"You're just being stubborn." He groaned.

"I'm not. Stubborn. It's how I feel. You have to accept it, Kyle."

"Well, I don't. Because I know you. You're scared. But we can talk to him together and explain everything. You need to stay and fight for us, Robbie."

"I have to go back inside, and you need to leave." I tried to look him directly in the eyes to get my point across.

"I'm not giving up on you. I will fight for us."

"Then you're wasting your time." I turned in a huff and went into the house. I shut the door and leaned against it, trying to stop the tears falling from my eyes. I waited until I heard his footsteps descend the porch steps, and then his car pulling away.

I can't stop now. I'm in too deep. I wiped the tears from my cheeks before I returned to Sarah's room. She was sitting on her bed with a massive scowl.

"You heard?" I asked.

"Yep," she growled.

"Sarah…"

"Both brothers? Really, Robbie? You are unbelievable. Tell me how long it's been going on and be honest for once."

"Since the summer."

She fumed. "Wow. You're despicable and an excellent liar. Get out of my room before I do something I regret!" she demanded angrily.

I had never seen Sarah so pissed. "Let me explain…"

"Oh, I know what happened. You are a selfish, selfish person, Robbie. You had a chance to have the Whitmore brothers all to yourself, so you took it. You even weaseled your way into living with them and pretending to be this doe-eyed, innocent damsel in distress. And the whole time, you played them both. Played all of us! I bet it was your plan the moment you transferred here and laid your eyes on them to move in. Made it more convenient to have them both," she screamed.

And there it was. My out. The end of our friendship.

"You're absolutely right, Sarah. That was my plan the whole time. And it worked perfectly. I could have either of them, whenever I wanted," I said, my words dripping with venom.

"Get out!!" she spat.

I picked up my bag as I walked out of her bedroom. I turned to look at her. "For what it's worth, Sarah…"

And with fury in her eyes, she slammed the door in my face.

As I walked out her front door, I stood silently on the porch. I took a deep breath of cold air, and right as I did, Sarah turned off the light. She left me standing in the cold, dark night. I thought to myself, *how fitting*. I had been playing a role this whole time, and now that role was over.

Fade to black.

End scene.

CHAPTER 25

In the...

Kyle

ROBIN PERFORMED THE usual avoidance nonsense. You would think by now that she'd get that it wouldn't work on me. I wouldn't let her push me away. I'm not giving up on her. While she cooled down, I headed to Brody's. I asked if I could stay the night, but I didn't tell him why. I knew if Shane came home and I was there; all hell would break loose. Mom was already upset; I didn't need to pile it on.

I grabbed my bag and jogged up the front path of Brody's house. Suddenly, he burst out of the door.

"Dude? What the hell's going on?" Brody snapped.

"What are you talking about?"

"Sarah just called. You lied to me. You've been seeing Robbie this whole time," he accused.

Fricking Sarah. "I didn't really lie per se…" I said regretfully.

"The hell you didn't. You said you were helping her with something. Not sneaking around with her behind our backs. Shane had to be pissed!" *Oh, now Brody remembers what I said to him. Word for word.*

"Can we go inside and talk? It's freezing."

"Sarah said I shouldn't talk to you."

"Are you serious? It's me, Brody. I'm still your best friend."

"Yeah, but she's my girlfriend. Oh, and just a heads up… Sarah said she was going to call Kira too."

"Like now?" I asked, exasperated.

"Yeah. As soon as we hung up."

"Shit." I took off back down the path to my car.

"Where are you going?" Brody shouted out.

"Kira's."

This whole thing is such a mess. What was I going to say to her? I didn't want to hurt her any more than I already had. I didn't even know how she'd ever forgive me.

I pulled up to her house and debated whether I should knock on the door or text her. I decided to text.

Im so sorry can we talk
Im out front in my car

• • •

Please kira
Read 7:49PM

I'll be right down
Stay in the car

I breathed out, relieved she was coming to talk to me, but also nervous. She knew what I had done, and there was no going back now. I needed to take responsibility for my role in this mess, and it killed me that I hurt her.

She got in the car without saying a word, staring out of the front windshield. Minutes went by before I dared to say something.

"I'm sorry, Kira. I really am. I never wanted to hurt you, and I never meant for you to find out this way."

"You mean find out at all," she snapped.

"I was going to tell you. I was."

"I don't believe you."

"You have every right to be mad."

"Yes, I do. You lied to me, Kyle! The entire time we were together. I defended you. Every single time Sarah had any suspicion. To find out she was right? Do you even know how that makes me feel?" Kira let out a sob.

"All I can say is that I'm sorry. I never meant for any of this to happen. Or to make you feel bad. I wanted to make it work with you. To forget about her."

"So, I was the consolation prize for you to forget about Robbie? How dare you be so disrespectful toward me and my feelings!" I cringed. Kira's words mirrored the ones I had said to Robbie a few weeks ago when I accused her of doing the same thing with Shane.

"That's not what I meant… I'm not saying the right things."

"No, you're not," she hissed. The heat of her anger could fog the windshield. I remained silent. "When did you start seeing her? And remember, Sarah word-vomited every painstaking detail when she called me earlier, so I already know the truth."

"The end of summer."

She shook her head in disgust. "So, you were with her at the mixer?"

"Yes."

"And that day, we picked her up on the side of the road? The very same day you kissed me for the first time?"

I hesitated. "Yes."

"Was the kiss you trying to forget about her?"

"No. I meant the kiss."

"Don't lie to me!"

"I'm not." I tried to meet her gaze.

"And homecoming? You were with her then, too?"

Damn, this sucked. "Yes."

"New York?"

"Kira…"

"I'm such a fool. You made me look like a fool this whole time."

"Let me explain."

"Don't even bother, Kyle. It makes me sick to my stomach. Remembering all those times you would leave me behind on dates or at dances so you could be with her."

"Kira, please…"

She snapped. "Is the truth too much for you, Kyle?"

I stared out of the windshield. It was harder than I thought. That was the problem. I didn't think about my actions or how they would affect those around me. All I thought about was myself.

"Yes, it's too much." I finally answered. "I never took anyone's feelings into account. Especially yours. And Shane's. I've hurt the two people closest to me, and I'm ashamed. I have no excuse, and I deserve everything you throw my way. I was selfish. I'm so sorry. I truly am!" I tried to bite back everything I was feeling, gripping into the fabric of my jeans.

She was so quiet I could practically hear her heartbeat.

"Do you love her?" she croaked. I turned to her; my breathing laced with guilt. She looked at me with tears streaming. It broke my heart that I did this to her, but I had to answer her. Honestly.

"Yes," I whispered. She looked away from me, wiping her tears. We sat in silence again, letting that truth seep into our pain.

"I need some time, Kyle. To process. I really need you to try very hard to give me space. Do you think you can do that?" The irony of her words hit straight through the core of my heart.

"Of course. Whatever you need."

"It's what I need. Then maybe… someday… we can be friends again."

"I'd like that. Very much," I answered honestly. Without another word, she opened the door, exiting the car.

And she walked out of my life.

Robbie

I've seen her mad before, but this was a new level of pissed, even for Sarah. But it's exactly what I wanted, right? To cut all ties with the people here so I could keep them safe. At this moment, I had successfully alienated everyone from myself. I knew this day would come, but I didn't realize it would hurt this much.

I kept walking, almost jogging to the bus station. The cold air knew how to bite, a sign that the year's first snow was coming soon. I closed my eyes, trying not to mourn that thought.

At the station, I boarded the bus to Midtown. Not as many people as I thought would be on a bus to the city on a Saturday night. It was nice that I didn't have to sit next to anyone. I pulled out my phone and searched for "cheap" hotels I could crash at for the night. I rolled my eyes at that daunting task. I had brought all the cash I had earned this fall, working concession stands at sporting events, tutoring, and doing odd jobs for the sweet older lady across the street.

I knew I would arrive late in the city late tonight, so Chelsea Piers wouldn't be open. I needed to find a hotel as close as possible to the bus station to rest up. It had been one hell of a day, and I need to start fresh tomorrow. I had to find out if the clues my mom left me in the locket and in my dream weren't just my imagination running wild.

I laid my head against the window of the bus and watched the lights of the cars and streetlights flickering past. I rubbed the locket over and over in my pocket, remembering the day Officer Markham gave it to my stepdad. I was still in the hospital after the accident, and she had come there to check on me.

Officer Markham had kind, dark brown eyes and a very thick New York accent. She told me how brave I was through this terrible ordeal and that the entire police department was pulling for me to get better soon. She showed sympathy for the loss of my mom. Told me that if there was anything she could do for me, I could always reach out to her. Day or night. Anytime. Here and now, or in the future.

As she left, she handed me a bag with my mom's locket. My mom was wearing it the night we crashed. As I reached to take it, my stepdad came into the room and snatched it away. He said it would be safer at home, and he'd give it to me when I was discharged. Officer Markham awkwardly smiled and hugged me goodbye.

As she turned, my stepdad hugged her unexpectedly. She seemed caught off guard as they were never close. But she returned the hug anyway and gave her condolences before she left.

I asked if I could see the necklace. He held up the bag but wouldn't let me touch it. He said it wasn't safe to keep valuables in the hospital, so he took it home. I didn't question him then because I still thought he was a good guy. Little did I know.

Shocked awake by loud pistons, I realized the bus had stopped. Apparently, I had dozed off. As I looked out the window, I saw we were in the city. When we got to the central station terminal, I only had to walk a couple of blocks west to get to my hotel.

The place only had one room available for the next few days. It was the cheapest I could find, close to the bus station and Chelsea Piers. The room looked cute but small and was a bit funky from the pictures I saw online. It would be perfect for me to rest and plan my next steps.

If I were right, Mom tried to remind me about Chelsea Piers the night she died. I thought it odd she would bring it up since we hadn't been there in years. With my mother being manic at times, I had assumed it had to do with her mental state. I guess it wasn't.

When the locket had an extra date engraved inside, it threw me at first. Then I remembered Mom mentioning us skating and renting skates and… lockers there. Then it all made sense. She knew exactly what she meant that night and was leaving me clues. The extra date in the locket wasn't a date at all. It was a combination.

So, if I was right, and there was a locker my mom rented at the pier…

What was in there?

Kyle

It was late when I made it back to Brody's house. He finally relented and let me stay the night, like we had planned before Sarah tried to interfere. I had no doubt she had been on the phone with the whole school all night. By Monday morning, everyone would know. But I can't worry about that right now. I was physically and emotionally exhausted from the day that started well before sunrise. I collapsed onto the blow-up mattress on Brody's bedroom floor, and I don't remember my head hitting the pillow.

In the morning I went home. I didn't really want to go, but it was time I faced my family and took responsibility for my actions, like with Kira.

"Hey, Mom. How are you?" I cautiously asked.

"Okay. I guess. Had time to process. I'm still unhappy with how everything unfolded, but I am sorry I snapped at you."

"I deserved it. It was on me to make things right, and I didn't. That's why I'm here. I want to make things right. I already spoke to Kira, but I still need to talk to Shane. Is he home? I didn't see the car."

"No, but he did finally text me last night. He's staying at Max's to cool down. I think that's the best thing for him to do right now."

"Okay. It's good he let you know where he was. He didn't respond to any of mine. I wanted to talk to him. You know, apologize."

"Give him a little more time. That's what he needs. Time and space."

"I wanted to talk to you too. I'm really sorry about how everything went down. We were going to tell him, but everything kept getting in the way. Her panic attack, and then the fight at school. It got away from us."

"I know. But can you see how quickly things can spin out of control?"

Unfortunately, I understood all too well. "I do, actually," I answered truthfully and with experience.

"Have you talked to Robbie? She hasn't been home yet either," Mom asked with concern.

"She's at Sarah's. I'm going over there now because she still won't return my texts. Can I keep your car?"

"Sure. And good luck."

I smiled wryly. *I'm going to need it.*

I felt anxious when I walked up Sarah's porch stairs. First, I knew that I was walking into the lion's den. I knew she would come at me strong. Second, seeing Robbie. I pushed the doorbell, and Sarah was already there to open it.

"What are you doing here?" Sarah spat.

"Can I talk to Robbie?"

"She's not here."

"Where did she go?"

"I don't know. It's not my job to keep track of a cheating little liar," she growled angrily.

"C'mon, Sarah. Cut her some slack. It wasn't just her. I was involved too."

"Oh, I know. And you're not off the hook either. Plus, I'm so pissed at Brody for caving and letting you stay last night. What you did to Shane—"

"I know. I get it. And I promise I'll let you lecture me as long as you want. But right now, I need to talk to Robbie. What time did she leave this morning?"

"This morning? I kicked her out last night after I found out about the two of you," she answered, annoyed.

"What do you mean you kicked her out?"

"She pissed me off, so I kicked her out."

"Last night? Where did she go?" I asked, concerned.

"I don't know. She's not my problem."

"Sarah… she didn't come home last night. Where is she?"

"I don't know," Sarah said unfazed.

"Fuck," I said under my breath.

"Why? What's wrong now?" she asked, agitated.

"I can't get a hold of either of them. Shane or Robbie. And they won't return my texts."

"Maybe they ran off together instead," she said smugly.

"Shut up, Sarah."

"Don't tell me to shut up. This is my house, and I don't have to put up with this!" She slammed the door in my face.

As I jogged to my car, I racked my brain as to where Robin could have gone. There's no one else she would crash overnight with except for Kira, and I know she's not there. Maybe Sarah's right and Robbie was with Shane. Maybe she went to Max's to talk to him after all. No, that wasn't like her. She would rather run than confront the problem head-on.

Suddenly, a memory flashed across my mind. I remembered that when she came down the stairs yesterday morning, she had her backpack with her, and it looked extremely full. I had thought it was odd, but didn't give it a second thought. Till now. I knew exactly where she was.

In the city.

CHAPTER 26

...the plan.

Robbie

LAST NIGHT, THE hot hotel shower helped calm my nerves and recenter me. I actually slept all night, which hadn't happened for a very long time. I took that as a good omen that I was on the right path and that everything would work out. I packed my backpack with what I needed and bundled up. Winter in New York brought a chill. I grabbed a quick bagel in the lobby and headed out onto the busy city streets.

Losing myself in thoughts of my mother, I picked up the pace. The bitter air stung my face and hands, making my nose drip. Finally, I could smell the brine and taste salt on my lips. The closer I got to the water, the more I longed for all the moments I had spent here with my mom.

My poor mother. Who put her trust in the wrong man and paid the ultimate price. I paid for it too, losing her. It made my blood boil just thinking about him and how he got away with murder. Even if it were the last thing I did, I would finish this. Make him regret ever thinking we were easy targets.

As I continued down the city streets, the old familiar sounds bombarded my senses. I pulled my hood up over my head. The bustling life of NYC created a stark contrast to the sleepy little town I had been staying in for almost a year.

For all the faults and craze of the streets, the nicest part was nobody paid attention to you. Everyone was too busy with their own lives to worry about a single random teenager roaming. I was one of hundreds of people walking on the sidewalk to their destinations. It was nice to be invisible again.

I saw the signs for the Chelsea Piers and Sky Rink, quickening my pace. I stopped outside the building, trying to find the courage to head inside. I knew the memories would overwhelm me, so I looked out over the ocean and took one last deep, cold breath. I turned, facing the fear before me, and confidently trailed a group of people entering. They carried hockey bags, and I hoped to blend into their group and stay unnoticed.

Once in the building, I saw the old, familiar red and white striped walls along the lobby. They brought back good memories from my childhood, a slight quirk of a smile gracing my lips. Checking the ice rinks, I spotted the little blue lockers with their orange keys. But these weren't the ones I was looking for. I turned my attention to the family changing rooms next.

I continued trailing the family into the large dressing rooms and was immediately bombarded with the number of lockers present. Now what? I needed to figure out where to start my search. I scanned the room, trying to decide which locker to try first. My eyes landed on number 22. That was always my mom's favorite number.

I rushed over, but nothing was inside as I peered through the metal cage. I stepped back, turning my view and trying to get inspiration from anything that could help me figure it out. My brain stayed blank, and I couldn't try them all. People would notice that I didn't belong.

Frustrated, I returned to the main lobby. As I stepped out, I saw a few hockey team members exiting a smaller room closer to the rink. I waited by the blue metal door for a few minutes, trying to see if anyone else was heading in or out. When the coast seemed clear, I turned the knob and entered through the heavy, creaky door.

The changing room for the players was a stark contrast to the formal locker room I had just searched. The accommodation was functional at best and desperately needed a paint job. Chipped blue benches stood out in the middle from the tall burgundy metal lockers like they were an afterthought. Above each one were the players' numbers and their last names.

I scanned the room and suddenly spotted something. A locker plate that said: "22 Ronan." I inwardly chuckled at my mom's subtle nod of combining my grandparents' names, Ron and Nancy. I couldn't believe this was becoming real. My mom had left me clues everywhere to follow when the time was right. She knew I'd dig into this and wouldn't stop until I figured it out.

I quickly glanced at the Master combination lock hanging off the door. I shook my head in disbelief, knowing I had been right. I had the code, and it was in the locket. As I pulled out the trinket, my hands shook. I took a deep, calming breath, spun the dial a few times, and then I entered the newly engraved numbers from the locket, 11-9-22. I pulled the lock, and... it opened. I sharply inhaled.

I removed the padlock, setting it aside as I slowly opened the metal door. I tilted my head, raising a brow. There was only a hockey bag and a couple of sticks. Why lead me here for this? Paranoid, I stepped back, checking behind me, but still no one had entered the room.

I pulled out the bag, setting it on the blue bench. Slowly unzipping the oversized black mystery, the only things inside were a jersey, kneepads, a bunch of other hockey gear, and skates. My heart sank. *This can't be where the trail ends*, I thought. I had to keep digging.

Underneath all the junk was an old, stained towel wrapped around an object. I rechecked the door before carefully unwrapping the rag to reveal a hard-sided case. It was about the size of a small briefcase and held another combo lock. A three-digit code. Another roadblock.

I sat down, the briefcase in my lap, as I sorted through my mind. There were no other numbers engraved on the locket. I knew Mom wouldn't bring me this far to have it be a dead end. Right? I had to know the three-digit number somehow.

I closed my eyes, trying to force a number into my head. I focused on my mom, her spirit, and everything I loved about her. Mom was obsessed with numbers, so I had to have something stored in my brain. She had always believed it was fate that she was born on a special day.

Her birthdate was April 22nd, making her Angel number 422, the most powerful number in numerology. Mom said it meant protection. That when you faced a threat, your guardian angel would be with you, always guiding you to safety. Tears fell from my eyes. Mom was with me. I had always brushed off her belief in the spiritual as some sort of hocus-pocus nonsense. But she was guiding and protecting me from him, in life and now in death.

I wiped my eyes on the back of my sleeve, clearing my throat. I steadied my resolve, keying in 422 on the case. The lock popped right open. I couldn't help myself from grinning. I excitedly opened the lid, freezing as I saw what was inside. It was full of drugs, money, documents, a thumb drive, and… a gun.

Holy shit. I slammed the case shut and relocked it. Whatever this was, it was dangerous to have. This was either my mom trying to run away or why she lost her life. I panicked, whipping my head to look at the door again as I tried to jam the box into my backpack. No luck. It wouldn't fit. I'd have to take the whole hockey bag with me to get out of the building without stirring attention.

As I shoved the case back inside, the locker room door opened. Startled, I knocked the hockey bag onto the floor. My chest tightened in horror as part of the briefcase, and a lot of the contents spilled out.

"Oh, sorry. I didn't know anyone was in here." It was a younger, college-aged adult, dressed in goalie gear. He must have stayed longer on the rink to practice.

"Uh… no problem. I was just leaving. It's all yours," I sputtered, trying to pick everything up while nonchalantly pushing the case back inside. I zipped up the hefty bag and threw it over my shoulder, letting out a huge grunt as the weight almost toppled me over. Now, all I had to do was reach for my backpack. God, this thing was heavy.

"You got all that?" the guy asked, chuckling.

"Oh yeah. I'm used to carrying this. I play all the time," I puffed out my chest as the words stumbled.

"Really? I've never seen you before. What team do you play for?"

"Um… the uh… Sorry, I've gotta go." I bolted out of the locker room. That was my worst lie yet. I practically burst into the hall, hearing someone yell behind me. I didn't dare turn around, knowing I had to get the hell out of there.

As I approached the main foyer, someone grabbed my arm. I let out a surprised shriek. "Whoa, sorry. I didn't mean to scare you, but you left your hockey sticks behind," the goalie guy said, out of breath.

"Oh, right. My sticks for hockey… that I play. Sorry about that," I rambled.

"Yeah, I yelled 'Ronan' the whole time. You must have not heard your name."

"Uh… thanks." I grabbed the sticks from him, jogging away as fast as possible without looking back.

I rushed down the pier to the streets, heading back to the hotel. I was paranoid and out of breath, making a zig-zag path. I had to make sure no one could follow me. I knew that I was being overly cautious, but I was carrying a lot of… well, let's just say, "sensitive material."

I stuck out like a sore thumb, lugging a giant bag, sticks, and my backpack down the streets of New York City. My bag kept hitting people in the crowd as I rushed past them. I was terrified I'd pick a fight or drop something; the case spilling its secrets.

When I saw my hotel, I hurried through the lobby to the elevators. My shoulders ached, and I was freezing. The duffle was so heavy that I had to stop multiple times to rest. It took forever to get back to the hotel. To safety. Or what I hoped was safe.

Once in the room, I bolted my door and sighed in relief. My muscles had spasmed during the long walk back. Now that I was in my room, the adrenaline was wearing off. I checked my phone, which had blown up with messages, but ignored them as I placed it on the nightstand.

I picked up the hockey bag and laid it on the bed so I could spread out next to it. I closed my eyes as I held my hand to my heart. I whispered to the empty air around me, "Thank you, Mom, for protecting and guiding me. Thank you for being my guardian angel."

I immediately succumbed to my exhaustion.

Kyle

I drove into the city without knowing where to even begin looking for her. Her phone went straight to voicemail, and I had no way to track her. I knew she was going after him and thought she needed to do that alone. But she's wrong. We made each other stronger. The two of us. Together.

She worked hard to push us all away because she thought it was the right thing to do. And now she was rushing into danger without any way for me to stop her. I felt helpless as the realization settled in.

I figured Robin, I mean Wren, took the bus into the city since it was cheaper than an Uber. So that's where I started. I headed straight for the Midtown Bus Terminal. I tried to get any information I could on arrivals from last night, but of course, they couldn't give out any names or specifics because of their policies.

Frustrated, I started walking out of the terminal when a man approached me.

"Hey, kid. I overheard you were looking for your girlfriend."

"Yes, I am. Did you see her?" I pulled up a picture of her on my phone. It was from the end of the summer, the two of us grinning as we sat on the porch. Robin ate an ice cream cone, and me? I was trying to snatch a bite.

"Yeah, I saw her. She was on my bus last night. I noticed her because I was worried. She only had a hoodie on, and it was freezing yesterday. It looked like she was on a mission or something but struggled to breathe. I tried to ask if she was all right, but she ran out."

"That sounds like her," I said with a mix of relief and worry. "Would you be able to tell me where she went?"

"Well… um…" he hesitated.

"I'm not stalking her, I promise. Truth be told, I'm in love with her. And I know she loves me. Alright, that… sounds even more stalkerish." I cleared my throat. "She has this misguided idea that she needs to face something difficult alone. That I would be better off without her. I need to find her and tell her she's wrong. I swear that's the truth and that I'm being completely honest with you." Oh man, this guy had to know something.

"I believe ya, kid." He did? "I've always been a sucker for a good love story. Well… I don't know exactly where she was going, but I do know she headed west when she left the bus station. Unfortunately, that's all I know. I'm sorry I can't be more helpful than that."

"No, that's super helpful. I really appreciate it. But can I ask you one more question? Where are 'the' piers?"

"You mean Chelsea Piers?" he asked.

"Um… yeah."

"So, you head a few blocks west till you reach Eleventh Street, then take it south. You'll run right into it."

"I can't thank you enough for all your help."

"Sure, kid. Good luck with your happily ever after!" he answered jovially. I shook his hand before heading west out of the station. As my body slammed into the cold air, I lamented the fact that she could be literally anywhere. I would need as much luck possible to find her. My heart sank through my core, knowing my fortune had always sucked.

The task felt daunting, and I knew I had to be systematic in my search. If she went west late at night, where could she have gone? I searched for businesses in the area: banks, bars, and a hotel. She had to be at the hotel, but it was already noon. She must've checked out by now. I had to try Chelsea Piers first. I left my car at the station and started walking. I wouldn't find parking in the city, anyway.

As I walked, I hoped I was going the right direction. As the bus driver said, I wanted my happily ever after. But I needed to find her first. When she had her nightmare the other night, she kept mentioning "the piers" and ice as she cried.

It reminded me of a story she had shared during the summer. It was about going to the piers in the city to ice skate with her mom as a child. She mentioned it was one of her favorite memories. And although she never specifically said "Chelsea Piers," I hoped it was the place.

I walked briskly through the harsh wind, feeling an icy burn nip the edges of my face. If she was only wearing a hoodie, she had to have been freezing out here. By the time I got to the rink, my face and hands were numb. I went into the red and white striped lobby, looking around. There were skate rentals, an ice rink, and… they served hot chocolate. This must be the place. I remember her saying she would drink hot cocoa where the walls were like candy canes.

I scanned the lobby and concession stand but didn't see her anywhere. As I walked over to the locker area, I saw several police officers chatting. My heart jumped, fearing one of them might be her stepdad. I turned away, slowly backing out, and was about to leave when I overheard what they said.

They were talking to a hockey player, probably in his college years, who said he saw a girl in the locker room. He thought she may have stolen equipment. He said she was leaving as he came in and seemed… nervous. After she left, he had a bad feeling about her, so he called the cops.

They asked him what she looked like, and the man described Robin perfectly. He said he didn't get a good look at her but that she was wearing a gray hoodie, faded jeans, and sneakers. She had been carrying a black hockey bag, sticks, and had an orange backpack. *For not getting a good look, he sure remembered a lot about her*, I thought, unable to stop an edge of jealousy.

I carefully left without being seen and went back out onto the docks. I had to be about an hour or two behind her, but I had no idea where she would go after. As far as I knew, she could be headed to meet her stepdad and walking straight into danger.

I shook my head, knowing I had been so close to finding her. My stomach twisted into knots, knowing I was right back where I started. Only this time, I had more questions. Why did she have to stop for a duffle bag? What was in it?

I wandered the freezing streets of the city, not sure where I was going, when eventually I found myself almost back at the bus station. I looked up and realized there was the hotel I had passed earlier on my way to the pier.

It was getting late, so it wouldn't hurt to check it out just in case. It was a long shot, but what did I have to lose? The desk clerk was busy. But when it was my turn, he reached for a pen and asked me if I had a reservation.

"No, I don't. But I need to contact a guest," I said with trepidation.

"What's their name?"

I hesitated at first. "Robin Fanning. Please tell her… Kyle's in the lobby."

The desk clerk looked up her name and dialed the phone. I was shocked that I found her, and it had been that easy. The desk clerk relayed the message before hanging up.

"What did she say?" I asked impatiently.

"She said, 'Thank you.'"

"That's it?" I asked, perplexed by her reaction.

"Yes, sir." I audibly groaned. "Is there anything else I can help you with?"

"No," I replied disgruntledly. I dragged my feet over to the front lobby seating area. *UGH!! She is so hardheaded*, my thoughts screamed. I pulled out my phone to text her a piece of my mind when the phone dinged.

Youre not gonna leave r u

No im not
Read 8:47PM

And u call me stubborn
Be right down

My heart skipped knowing I would see her soon. I texted Mom that Robin had run off after the whole Shane debacle but that I found her. I mentioned that we were fine but wouldn't be home tonight. I promised to explain everything as soon as I could and to please trust me.

I also told her that we were both safe and to try not to be too mad at us. I was going to be grounded forever. I shut off my phone, knowing Mom would try to call as soon as she read the message.

The elevator doors opened, and there she was. Robin Fanning. Wren. My songbird. I had never been so relieved in my life. I went to hug her, but she put her hand on my chest and pushed me back.

"What are you doing here?" She asked, annoyed.

"You know why I'm here."

"You need to go home, Kyle… I'm sure Kirstie is worried sick."

"I'm not leaving."

"Well, I'm not going back," she replied defiantly.

"I know."

She sighed, "Kyle, I made it very clear that there is no us."

"And I made it very clear that there is. I guess we'll have to agree to disagree."

"You are so infuriating."

"And you're stubborn." We stood there momentarily, trying to stare the other down. To make the other one relent. But it ended up being this weird silence that made us both chuckle.

Robin shook her head, clearly frustrated. She took my hand, pulling me into the elevator and didn't let go once we were inside. When we got to her floor, she pulled me down the hall and only released it once she fished the key card out of her pocket. Robin pushed the door open with her shoulder, nodding for me to step inside.

I entered a funky-looking, tiny hotel room. There were hockey sticks in the closet to my left, along with her backpack. On the bed to the right was the hockey bag. Papers were spread across every open counter surface. I looked at her as so many questions swarmed my mind. I pointed at the bag.

"Would you believe me if I told you I started playing hockey and I'll be on your team now?" She smiled her traffic-stopping smile.

"Oh. Is that right? And no, I wouldn't believe you." We both chuckled. "So, what's really in the bag?" She turned serious, letting out an audible breath.

"The final phase of the plan."

CHAPTER 27
Officer...

Robbie

I WENT OVER to the hockey bag and patted the bed for Kyle to sit down beside me. He complied, sitting quietly and looking between the hockey bag and me.

"I was right. My mother left me clues. In the locket and in my dream."

"Clues? What do you mean?"

"When you gave me the locket, there were three dates in it. There should've only been two. The third date threw me off until I had that nightmare. I had a flashback of the car accident. I was in the car with my mom. She kept going on and on about Chelsea Piers and how she loved going ice skating. I assumed she was having a manic episode, but I think she was planting seeds in case something happened to her."

"She knew he was trying to kill her?"

"No. I think she did something to make him so mad that we were on the run. But then she died before she could finish what she started."

"What did she do?"

"This!" I pulled out the case and opened it.

"Holy shit? Are those **drugs**?"

"And money, documents," she pointed to the papers across the room and still in the case, "and this flash drive. I think she found out about his little side hustle as a dirty cop and was trying to take him down. But he got to her first. There's also a life insurance policy in there for her. And me."

"Apparently, he took them out a long time ago. He must have been planning to kill us and take the money. I guess she figured it out, and we tried to escape. I don't think she realized he would sabotage the car when we left that night. But then… I survived. Messing up his plans since the insurance money went to me. It's in a trust until I turn twenty-one."

"Shit."

"Yeah. Shit."

"What are we going to do?" he asked.

"I don't know. I can't just stroll into a police station. He's got people everywhere. I'm sure he knows that I'm in town by now and has people looking for me."

"Oh, crap. That reminds me," he said, alarmed. "When I was at Chelsea Piers earlier, police were talking to this guy. He described you perfectly and said you stole some hockey equipment from a locker room."

"Are you sure?"

"Yeah. He apparently got a very good look at you and described you to a tee. He said you were wearing a gray hoodie and had a giant black hockey bag, sticks, and an orange backpack. It was definitely you."

"You were at the pier today?" I asked, surprised.

"Yeah. Looking for you."

"How would you know to look there?"

"I pay attention to everything you say. And everything you don't say." He looked into my eyes intently, my heart beating faster. He reached for my hand, staring into my eyes as he tucked a strand of hair behind my ear. "I would do anything for you."

"I know you would. That's why I was… trying to let you go," I answered weakly, my voice wavering.

"And now?" he questioned. *That was the question*, I thought, trepidation impeding my answer. "I love you, Robbie. I will always fight for you. For us. Because we're stronger together. I'm not going anywhere. You can say it now."

I inhaled sharply as he took both my hands and squeezed them gently. And that was it. I wasn't afraid anymore, and I finally had the courage to say what I felt in my heart for so very long. The truth.

"I love you too, Kyle. I do. I was scared. I've never been able to count on anyone or trust anyone before. But I can now because you're right. We are stronger together."

He smiled. "Say it again."

"We are stronger—"

"No! Not that part," he smirked.

I giggled. "I love you, Kyle Whitmore!"

After months of pent-up emotions that overwhelmed our senses, he pulled me to him and kissed me. I could feel my body on fire. Fire, full of passion. I wanted to tell him that I loved him for so long. All my reservations melted away in his embrace.

He parted my lips with his tongue, and the taste of him lingered in my mouth. He kissed me slowly and sensually, my body reacting in ways it never had before. I placed my knee on the bed, leaning into him, when I realized the dumb hockey bag was in my way. I tried pushing it off the bed without breaking or interrupting our kiss.

He pulled back from me, realizing what I was trying to do. With one swipe of his hand, he sent it flying off the bed. I breathily laughed, expression cracking into a smile as he returned the look with dark, lustful eyes.

I got up and stood in front of where he was sitting. I timidly stepped between his legs as he looked up at me, biting his bottom lip. He placed his hands on my hips and tugged me close to him. I leaned down and kissed him hard. I needed the air he breathed in my lungs.

Kyle moaned, slipping his hands into the pockets of my jeans. I blushed, memories of the bus station parking lot flashing through my mind. He squeezed, holding my body close to his. I let out another soft laugh, grinning as I felt his excitement at how close we were. It was like a jolt of electricity coursed through my veins, and I wanted more. More of him. All of him.

Our kiss grew deep and desperate. I held onto his shoulders, moving to straddle his lap. He wrapped his arms around my waist, keeping our bodies close. We moved together as one, and I tilted my head back, letting out an unashamed moan. He placed a hand behind the back of my neck and pulled me in, muffling the sound with a needy kiss. My legs trembled with blissful fatigue, and I let my body weight settle onto his hips.

We broke the kiss, breathless from the all-consuming love emanating between us. I reached for the hem of his shirt, pulling it up. He lifted his arms, allowing me to shift the fabric over his head. I tossed it onto the floor on top of that silly hockey bag.

I took a deep breath, slowly lifting my arms for him to do the same, but he froze. I shot him a small, crooked smile. I let my limbs fall, taking his hands and helping him slide off my shirt. I hadn't been this vulnerable around him since that fateful night in June, but I wasn't scared. I was right where I wanted to be.

He rubbed my arms up and down as I held his face in my hands. I kissed him on his forehead, his nose, his cheeks, his mouth. He hummed when I licked his lips, parting his mouth. Our tongues tangled together in a feverish kiss. Wild and blissful. I rocked forward on his hips, and he responded in kind. I could feel how much he wanted me, and my heart burst.

He reached around to my back, sliding his fingertips over my scars. I didn't flinch when he traced them, which surprised me at first, but he knew every part of me inside and out. It felt right. Everything about him felt right.

"Beautiful," he whispered. I glanced away with a blush, pushing off his hips to stand near the side of the bed. I shimmied out of my jeans, kicking them aside. He stood up hesitantly, knowing he was next. My eyes flitted between his eyes, his lips, and the button of his jeans.

I stepped closer, unbuttoning his pants. His eyes never left mine as he slowly slid them off his body. I explored his chest, tracing my hands across his abs. He let out a heavy breath, and I could see how much he wanted me. I felt the same. His chest rose up and down, breath uneven, as he allowed his eyes to drink in every inch of my body. I couldn't stop a shiver shaking through me.

As we moved toward the bed, I knew I never wanted to be apart from him. He was the one. And I trusted him with my mind, heart... and my body. Being this close and vulnerable with someone seemed impossible. I never allowed myself to look forward because I was always running from my troubled past. But I could now.

Because he was my future.

Kyle

The ecstasy I felt lying here with her in my arms was overwhelming. I had surrendered my mind, body, and soul to her last night, and she had done the same. The love we shared was nothing I had ever felt before. We fit perfectly together, and sometimes, it felt like my heart would burst out of my chest because of how much I loved her.

As I lay in pure rapture, I could hear her deep, resting breaths while she slept. I smiled, unable to remember the last time we laid in bed like this. The last time she had truly slept. Peacefully.

I saw light peeking in through the blinds, and it pulled my thoughts back to our unfortunate reality. The dire situation we faced today loomed over us while we lay here happy in this bed, in this hotel, in this city.

We knew the case was something he would kill for. What would he do when he found out we had it? He was a cop with a lot of resources at his disposal. But for us, this case was all we had. And each other.

Still basking in the glow, I felt her stretch and yawn as she woke. She looked up at me and smiled. Her traffic-stopping smile that I adored so dearly. I bent down, kissing the tip of her nose as she had done to me the night before.

"Good morning," I said lovingly.

"Good morning!" She rolled toward me and kissed me. Her hand rubbed down my chest, over my abs. I bit back a sound behind my tongue, narrowing my gaze on her. The rumble at the back of my throat was audible.

"So easily encouraged," she mocked.

"Then don't be so damn sexy." I leaned down, kissing her again, full on the mouth. First, it was slow, but our bodies rolled together as the kiss took on a life of its own. She responded fervently and with an urgency that took my breath away. My heart swelled as we became one.

We finally peeled ourselves away from the bed and ordered breakfast to the room. As she was dressing, I could feel myself grinning at her, and she called me out for it too.

"What are you smiling at?" she smirked.

"You."

"Why?"

"I've never been this happy before," I answered honestly.

"Never?"

"No. Never. And you?" I asked her coyly.

"Umm… I'm okay, I guess."

"Okay, I guess…" I mocked her as I grabbed and tickled her. She giggled hard.

We held each other tight, knowing we needed to return to reality, but neither one of us was willing to move. The whole situation weighed heavily on us, but we didn't want to spoil our brief moment of happiness.

***

After breakfast, we finally turned our phones back on to deal with the barrage of messages we knew we would have. Especially from Mom. I'm sure she'd be pissed that I left a vague note before turning off my phone. I could see another lecture in my future.

Our phones had blown up while they were off. There were dozens of messages. Most were from my mom, but I had some from Brody, and even Sarah had left me some, which was unusual. A feeling of dread crawled through my body, grasping at my chest.

I started listening to my messages when I looked over at Robin listening to hers. She was as pale as a ghost. I could see her hand shaking while holding the phone to her ear. I mouthed to her, asking what was wrong. That's when horror flashed in her eyes, tears streaming down her cheeks. Then her gasping started.

She struggled for air as she dropped her phone on the floor. I had never seen her in this much distress before. Not at the mixer, in the senior hall, or even in the bus terminal. Something horrible had happened, and I wasn't sure if I was ready to hear what that was.

"Robin? Are you all right?" I asked, alarmed. She couldn't speak.

I ran over to help her breathe. She folded over, her hands on her knees as she gasped loudly. I rubbed her back, trying to help her slow her breathing with my own. Eventually, she was able to calm herself but still appeared terrified.

"Robin, what happened?"

"It's Shane," she said between gasps.

Blood drained from my face. "What about Shane?"

"He has him! My stepdad has him!"

"How do you know?"

"He left me a message using Shane's phone. I could hear Shane in the background!" She sobbed.

"What did he say?" I asked, trying to stay calm.

"He… he said that if I don't call him back by noon, he'd hurt Shane worse than he already has."

"FUCK!" I screamed. Couldn't we just have one small moment to enjoy being normal teenagers without everything going to shit?

I grabbed my phone and looked at the time. It was almost 10:00 A.M. I started listening to my voicemails. Mom was freaking out. She left message after message about how someone took Shane.

She told me Max had called her, freaking out that someone had kidnapped Shane. Max said my brother was pulling out of the driveway to go home earlier this morning when a black car pulled up behind him and blocked him in. As Shane got out to confront the guy, the man walked up and punched him.

The stranger dragged Shane to the back of the black car and threw him into the trunk. Max said he ran after Shane, but the guy pulled a gun on him, so he had to back off. Max immediately called 911, and then my mom.

Brody also left messages asking where I was because my mom was freaking out about Shane and was frantically looking for me and Robin. Even Sarah's voicemails mimicked her concern. I looked over at Robbie, who now paced the floor as she mumbled to herself.

"No, no, no. This was what I was afraid of. This is what I didn't want to happen!" she cried. I went over to Robbie, trying to hold her, but she pushed me away angrily. "He's going to hurt him, Kyle! If anything happens to him, I'll never forgive myself."

"Okay. Just let me think," I held up my hands, running them through my hair as I racked my brain.

"We don't have time, Kyle. I need to call him now! I know him," she gasped.

"Okay. Shh… shh… shh. Look at me. Look at me," I said, holding her face. "We're stronger together, remember? We need to think first before we react. Let's be smart about what we do next. So, breathe, Robbie. Breathe." She rapidly sucked in air, her eyes wild. "Okay. There you go. Keep breathing. Slower. You got this." While I reassured her, my heart still pounded out of my chest. "Where would he take him?" I asked.

"I'm not sure. Our old house, maybe?"

"Okay. Do you think he knows you have the briefcase?" I asked her.

"Probably. I'm sure his buddies told him about the girl stealing a big bag of stuff at the rink. And he knows I'm in the city… so, yeah. I think he's smart enough to figure it all out," she said, alarmed.

"There's got to be someone who can help us. Is there anyone you can think of that wouldn't be on his bankroll?"

"I mean, it's been a couple of years, but there was an officer. She was a friend of mine and my mom's, who always helped us out. She visited me once at the hospital after my accident."

"Would she tip off your stepdad if you contacted her?"

"I don't think so. There was no love lost between them. I can try. I heard she retired from the force and is now doing consultant work for the FBI. I'm not sure where she's living, but I know she's still definitely in the city. I think I can get a hold of her."

"What's her name?" I asked.

"Officer Markham."

CHAPTER 28

...loose ends.

Robbie

KYLE WAS CALM and being so levelheaded. He had always been able to talk me down when I panicked. Then, he'd look at a problem pragmatically. I blame my panic attacks on always having to put out the next fire in my life. I could never see the forest through the trees, so to speak.

I lost Officer Tanya Markham's number when I destroyed my phone several months ago. Unfortunately, I didn't remember her cell on my own. I had to rely on the power of the internet. I searched for her name, receiving several hits immediately. There were articles about her retirement, an award, and her new position doing consultant work for law enforcement agencies on an as-needed basis. The white pages mentioned she was in her late 40s, listing several possible addresses and phone numbers for her. It was her all right.

Searching for her brought back glimpses of memories. Tanya lived a couple of blocks down and had been a beacon of light to Mom and me when my stepdad lost his temper. She'd let us hang out whenever he was on a rampage, giving him space so he could cool down. That's when Mom and Tanya started becoming friends. Their friendship was like oil and water, but sometimes opposites attract—even with friends.

Tanya was a warm, kind, and caring person at home and as an officer. A stark contrast to my stepdad. It's not that Officer Markham's life was easy. It wasn't. She had her own set of problems to handle. It was tough being a cop in NYC. She always had to work harder to prove herself to move up the ranks. Not only as a woman, but as a woman of color too.

She had to work harder at home as well. She got divorced several years ago, raising three kids on her own. Before my mom died, Tanya had to take some time off to care for her sick mother. Eventually, her mother became too ill to live on her own, moving in with Tanya. Then, around the same time, Tanya's son moved back home after graduating college. He wanted to save up money, trying to find a job. Meanwhile, her two daughters were freshmen in college.

Despite it all, Tanya always remained upbeat, even when dealing with adversity at work and at home. Although challenging, she stayed on the right side of the law even though so many others didn't. Like my stepdad. For all the excitement, opportunities, and wonder of the big city, it also had its negative underbelly that would rise to the surface no matter how hard you tried to avoid it. Apparently, that undercurrent of greed and easy money was too tempting to pass up for my stepdad and his band of shady cops and thugs.

"I think I found her number. It looks familiar," I called out excitedly.

"Do you think she's still one of the good guys?"

"Yes, I do," confidence filled my tone.

"Okay. Call her. She'll have a better idea of what to do next and how to take this bastard down for good!"

"We have to do this fast, Kyle. My stepdad has Shane, and he doesn't make threats. He makes promises. And if he said he'll hurt him, he'll hurt him."

"I know. Call her."

***

"Wren? Oh gosh. I haven't heard from you in years. How are you? What have you been up to? I can't believe it's really you," Tanya greeted, shocked.

"Tanya… unfortunately, this isn't a social call. I'm in trouble, and I need your help. Urgently."

"Okay. Anything. You know that."

I filled Tanya in on the current situation and that time was of the essence. Although surprised to hear from me, she wasn't shocked my stepdad had illegal dealings. She never liked him, and he harassed Tanya about her friendship with my mother after she died. He'd badger her about what my mom told her or pestered her to know if she was conspiring with her. Really paranoid stuff.

Tanya apologized profusely for not reaching out after her visit to the hospital following the accident. She'd been overwhelmed by work, raising kids, and then her mother fell ill. It was all-consuming for her.

She mentioned having a lot of influential contacts and could assemble a team quickly. Officer Markham had retired after more than twenty years in police service and later took on work with the FBI and Internal Affairs. She preferred consulting. The pay was good, and it gave her flexibility to care for her family. It also allowed her to move to a nicer area in the city, closer to her mother's specialists. She hadn't heard anything about my stepdad since retiring, until now.

"And you're sure he killed your mother?" Tanya asked again, shocked.

"Yes. He told me himself in June. When he… assaulted me," I said, swallowing hard.

"Wren, I had no idea he'd stoop that low. I really didn't know. I swear it."

"None of us knew what he was capable of. I have a sealed bag of my torn and bloodied clothes from that night. It should have his blood, maybe skin samples, and his… saliva on them. I tried to preserve as much as I could."

"Wren…"

'I'm ok. He beat me up, but I stopped him before anything worse."

"I'm so sorry, Wren, that I wasn't there for you."

"You're here now, and I want to take him down. I need your expertise to do that. So, what are our next steps?"

"You said his demand was to call him by noon, or he would hurt the boy. And the briefcase has drugs, money, classified documents, and a mystery flash drive. Is that correct?"

"Yes," I replied nervously.

"Okay. This is what you're going to do. At noon, call him and try to get him to agree to a neutral place. Tell him the case contains all the items your mom stole, and that you're willing to do an even swap. Let him pick a neutral spot so it doesn't raise any red flags. Now, I need to see what's on that flash drive. Where are you?"

"I'm at a hotel in Midtown. I'll send the address."

"Let me do my thing and make calls to my contacts. I'll be there as fast as I can, Wren. I'll text you when I'm in the lobby."

"What if he won't agree to a neutral spot?" I asked anxiously.

"He will. Turning to kidnapping means he's desperate for the case. He needed leverage to force your hand, but he also knows he has to limit the fallout. You can do this, Wren. You're smart and savvy, just like your mom. Take deep breaths and keep as calm as possible. I believe in you."

"I'll do my best," I said, far less confident than Tanya had sounded.

"Record everything. Put Steven on speakerphone and have your boyfriend record your conversation. Also, turn off location services if you haven't already. Just hang tight, Wren. I'm coming." Then she hung up.

Kyle wrapped his arms around me from behind as I gathered the courage to call. I took a deep, slow breath. I closed my eyes, wishing I knew how to be brave. Brave enough to talk to my stepdad. Brave enough to confront and deceive him. Brave enough to keep Shane safe. Oh, Shane… he was in this mess all because of me. I had to do this for him. For all of us.

As if Kyle could read my mind, he spoke up. "You are the bravest person I know, Robbie. And Tanya's right. You've got this."

***

Minutes before noon, I turned on the speaker and dialed Shane's phone number. Kyle started recording. My throat tightened. It had been a while since I heard his low, gravelly voice.

"Hello, Wren! Right on time. I guess you believed I'd really hurt him if you were late."

"I believed you…" my voice trembled.

"Did you? Because he has you to thank for all our fun and games earlier. He put up quite a struggle when he finally came to. He's a tough kid. Really hung in there. But I've got to tell you, Wren. It was a real rookie move to have him pay with his own debit card at the restaurant. You made it way too easy," my stepfather gloated.

Hearing that he hurt Shane, I stifled my tears. I steadied my voice as I spoke. "You're vile. Let me speak to him right now or no case, Steven. I mean it."

"You have three seconds."

"Shane? Are you okay?" my distress clear.

"I'm okay. Banged up a bit, but I'll live. What the hell is going on?" Shane groaned, confused.

"Okay, that's it. You've got your proof of life. Bring the case to the house, Wren," Steven growled.

"No way. Pick somewhere neutral."

"Do you think I'm playing, little girl?" he threatened.

"I know you're not, Steven. You proved that to me in June. That's why I'm not walking into your trap again."

"You know you had it coming, you bitch. You always did. Both you and your mother couldn't keep your noses out of my business."

"You mean drugs, kidnapping, murder? You're not very good at that last one since I survived your murder attempt twice. Now you have to deal with me."

"Oh, I plan on it." He paused to think, "Meet me at the storage facility where we kept all the stuff your mother had when she moved in with me. That neutral enough for you?"

"When?" I pressed.

"Staff leaves at three-thirty, be there at four. Come alone. I'll know if you double-cross me, so don't even think about it."

"Who would help me? Everyone I know either works for you or they're dead," I mocked.

"I mean it, Wren. I'll hurt him worse. You know I don't make threats. Four o'clock. Don't be late." I ended the call and could already hear my gasps. Kyle enveloped me and held me close.

"You did great. He didn't suspect a thing. This is going to work."

I wanted to share Kyle's enthusiasm. I really did. But all I could think about was, *how do I keep Shane alive*? Because the cold, hard truth remained. I may have survived Steven killing me twice before, but could I survive a third try? Because I knew how he operated.

No loose ends.

CHAPTER 29
Dread...

Kyle

I HELD HER only a moment when she pulled away, distracted. She approached the case, placing it on the bed before unlocking the front. The lid popped up, Robin retrieving a flash drive. She stared at it, letting off a soft hum as she turned it over between her fingers.

"You, okay?" I asked.

"Why does he need this so badly that he'd kill for it?" she wondered aloud.

"I don't know." Setting the drive aside, she continued her earlier rifling through the paper documents within the case.

There were folders and scattered pages of classified police evidence lists, confessions, and surveillance documents for many criminals in New York City. Then there were two life insurance policies he took out on Robin and her mother. I wasn't sure if her mom knew that he'd kill for what she had taken, or what it really was. Robin's phone dinged.

"She's here," Robbie exclaimed, rushing out the door. "I'll be right back." She shortly returned with Officer Markham.

"Kyle, this is Tanya Markham. Tanya, this is my boyfriend, Kyle."

I smiled, surprised that she used that word to describe me. It made me feel like she had considered sticking around this time. Sticking with me. "It's very nice to meet you," I formally greeted.

"Likewise." She turned to Robbie hurriedly. "Okay, Wren. We only have a few hours before we must get on the road. I called in all my favors, and I have a team assembling as we speak, with a judge signing warrants. Let's get a look at that flash drive."

She pulled out a high-tech laptop and began tapping on the keys. She plugged the thumb drive in on the side, starting the download. There were so many files. Her mother had secretly recorded his conversations from both his police and thug life for months. She had uncovered his ties to the mob and how he stole police funds to pay his deals on the street. He traded guns, drugs, money, and information about police evidence, witnesses, and raids.

"I had no idea he was in this deep. Your mother shook the hornet's nest. Steven is more dangerous than I'd imagined. No wonder he wanted this so badly. The info on the drive will put him away for life."

"I also found policies for my mom and me at the bottom of the case. Apparently, he planned on getting rid of us, but I survived." Robbie handed the life insurance papers to Tanya.

"Unbelievable," Tanya filed through them in dismay.

"So… how do we make this deal?" Robbie asked.

"Well, that's the tricky part. We'll need warrants since she recorded him without his knowledge, but I'm handling that. I'll follow up on all the red tape on my end. Then, I'll make sure the team is ready and in place when you meet him at the storage facility. Unfortunately, we can't send you in with a bug. He knows what to look for and will probably check. But you will have eyes and ears on you the whole time."

"She's going in alone? No way. That's not happening," I answered as I stepped forward, shocked and angry.

"It'll spook him if you tag along," Tanya objected.

"She's my girlfriend, and he's my brother! I've seen what this man can do. He didn't hesitate to beat her mercilessly and force himself on her. There's no way in hell I'm letting her go in there alone."

Tanya's deep frown flashed at the reminder of Steven's depth of depravity, but she calmly reiterated her stance. "Kyle. I get it. He's a monster, and what he did was heinous. But he has your brother, and we need to retrieve him unharmed. To do that, we need her. He's expecting her to come alone. Anything else, and he *will* do something rash. We can't afford any surprises. We need to get Wren in and out as cleanly as possible."

I felt my nerves teetering on the edge, my voice shaking with pain as I processed her words. "I love them. I can't lose them."

Robbie pulled me to her and held me tightly. "I can do this, Kyle. I'm stronger because of you. I'll keep Shane safe. I promise."

"Us… together, Robbie. We're stronger together." While my words echoed clearly in the strange, small hotel room, my thoughts raced differently. The gravity of everything unnerved me. My entire whole world, everything important to me, was in jeopardy.

She looked up at me, holding my face in her hands. "We *are* together. Even when we aren't. I can do this," she repeated confidently. She kissed me quickly yet tenderly on my lips. The sharp edges of my fear slightly softened.

"Okay. Are we set now?" Tanya asked me directly.

"On one condition," I demanded.

"Which is…?" Tanya asked, annoyed.

"I want to be there. With the team of eyes and ears."

"That is a terrible idea. *If* I bring you along, you need to be quiet, calm, and do everything I say. That's **my** condition," Tanya relented.

"I will."

"Everything I say, Kyle," Tanya said sternly.

"Okay. Got it."

"I'm going to make a few phone calls and secure things on my end. Remember, Wren, keep it simple. Make the exchange and get out of there. We need to move quickly, or he'll suspect something's wrong."

"I'll do my best," Robbie said.

"I know you will," Tanya smiled affectionately. "You're strong. Just like your mother. She was so proud of you, Wren. And she loved you so very much." Tanya's voice cracked. It was the first time since she got here that I saw a crack in her armor. "You and Kyle, take some time together and regroup. But not too long. We need to leave soon." Tanya directed, her armor whole once more.

Tanya left the room, and we were alone. I looked at Robin as she was packing up the case. She seemed different. She even looked different.

"You ready?" I asked.

"It's almost over, Kyle. I'm going to get Shane back, and Steven is going to get what he deserves. I believe it now. I'm not afraid of him anymore. He may have taken everything from my past, but I won't let him take my future too. This is my life, and I'm taking it back!" She glowed with newfound confidence and determination. It was… mesmerizing.

"I always believed in you. I knew you were strong and a fighter from that first night in June. You're passionate, stubborn, and you'll do anything to protect the ones you love. But know this… I'll do the same. I will never stop fighting for you. Ever." We embraced in a passionate kiss that made my whole body want to vibrate. We heard a knock on the door, indicating Tanya and her team were ready. Robin and I stared at each other as I walked out of the hotel room. Our eyes said it all.

***

Tanya and I left first with the team first so we could get into place. Robin would get an Uber and leave within the hour. In the elevator, my stomach and heart ached. Tanya seemed on top of everything, and I felt confident… somewhat but anything could go sideways. I couldn't help but feel worried. It doesn't sit well with me that a madman could hurt them both on a whim. And when that reality set in, I was uneasy.

Tanya settled her squad around the corner from the storage facility. It was already getting dark, and that made me sweat. Would we be able to see and hear them the whole time? We seemed so far away. But the team assured me that we could.

Tanya reminded me that I was to be seen and not heard before I was relegated to the back corner of the van. I could see the storage units on the monitor, but all I could hear was white noise. I hoped that would change when they started talking.

The waiting was torture. I fidgeted with the zipper on my sweatshirt when I saw a man appear on the monitor. His black car pulled up and parked, a lone man stepping out of the driver's seat. He didn't look how I pictured him. In my mind, he appeared like a monster in human form. I was taken aback when he looked "normal." A random guy you'd see on New York City streets.

He walked to the back door and opened it. With a pistol in hand, he signaled for my brother to get out of the car. Shane's hands were bound behind him, and he had what looked like a gag in his mouth. Shane stepped out of the vehicle on his own but was limping. Then, in the bottom corner of the screen, I saw Robin come into view. And she pointed a gun in his direction.

"What the **hell** is she doing? Where did she get a gun!?" Tanya screeched in my direction.

"I don't know. I had no idea she had a gun. I swear!" I held my hands up defensively. This was the first time I knew of Robin ever having a weapon.

"Turn the audio up, now!" Tanya ordered her team.

"Well, well, well. The little brat is learning to come prepared," Steven laughed. His words oozed with sarcasm.

"I'm a quick study. You made sure of that. Guess you regret showing me how to use a gun now, don't you? I would keep that in mind," she barked. She looked past Steven. "Shane, you okay?" He nodded, his eyes wide.

"As you can see, I held up my end of the bargain. So, where's the damn case, Wren?" Steven snarled. That's when I noticed there was no case. *What the hell is she doing?* I thought. The sense of my alarm quickly turned to dread. I knew exactly what she was planning. She was going to kill him herself. I knew she had looked different in the hotel room earlier, but I thought she was getting her confidence back. What I really saw was... revenge.

"This is between you and me. Let him go. Then I'll take you to the case," Robbie demanded.

"That's not part of the deal. I told you I'd hurt him." He elbowed Shane in the gut, my brother groaning and doubling over.

"It's not a trick. You can check me for bugs, but you will let him go first, or you'll never get the case. And if you think you can just kill me and take it, think again. In one hour, scheduled emails about that case and flash drive will be uploaded to every television station and internet provider in the city. So, I repeat. LET. HIM. GO."

Tanya turned to me with fury in her eyes. "What did you two do?"

"Nothing. I have no idea what she's talking about. I'm telling the truth," I replied, completely shocked.

"Team Two. Team two, be ready. On my word, move in," Tanya ordered.

"What? No! She could get killed," I objected.

"She's working on that all by herself. Shut up and let me do my job!" The audio crackled, and we all stopped to look at the screen again.

Steven pushed Shane ahead of him. "Fine. But if you double-cross me, Wren..." When Shane was close enough to Robbie, she pulled his gag.

"What's going on, Robbie? Who the hell is Wren?" Shane questioned.

Steven started laughing. "You mean he doesn't even know what your real name is? Classic. No wonder he seemed confused when I snatched him."

"Your real name is Wren?" Shane asked.

"Get behind me. I'll tell you everything later," Robbie pleaded.

"Yeah, boy, you better listen to her," Steven mocked.

"Shut your mouth, you bastard," Shane fumed.

"Just get this over with," Robbie commanded, stepping closer to Steven, still pointing the gun at his chest.

Steven reached into the open back door, pulling out a device. Never taking his eyes off them, he headed back over to Robbie. He waved the wand all over her body, looking for bugs. Then, he followed up with his hand on her body, keeping his gun trained on her with the other. "Mmm…" Steven sneered, lingering his touch. It took everything I had in my soul not to run out of the van and murder him myself.

"Get your fucking hands off her," Shane ordered, lurching toward him. Steven easily knocked him back.

"Tsk. Tsk. Tsk. You do not want to do that. Does he, Wren?" he grinned.

"Satisfied?" Robbie asked dully.

"Not really… Oh, you meant about you being wired. Yeah. I'm satisfied," Steven sneered cockily.

"You're disgusting," Robbie spewed.

"Now, the case. Where the fuck is it?" Steven growled.

"It's close by."

"It better be, Wren," Steven threatened.

"Like I said before, just you and me. Shane can leave."

"No!" Shane said, shocked.

"Aww. The noble boyfriend comes to the aid of his damsel in distress," Steven mocked.

"I've got this, Shane. You need to go," Robbie repeated, keeping her eyes trained on Steven.

"I'm not leaving you," Shane protested.

"I said go!" Robbie yelled, pointing the gun at Steven.

"No!" Shane yelled back.

"You really can't take a hint, can you? Now or even when it comes to your brother. I'm only here to clean up my mess. That's it. I'm with your brother now because I. Don't. Want. You. I never did. Leave so I can finish this! Get out of here while you can!" Robbie snarled.

The pain on Shane's face devastated me. It cut me to the bone knowing I was the reason for his pain. Robin's words were said to save him, but the implications of their meaning reverberated. Shane stared for a long moment, stepping back slowly as he looked between Steven and Robbie. He limped as he reluctantly left. When he turned the corner, he was out of view on the surveillance monitors.

Officer Markham shouted orders, "Team two. Team Two. Stand by. When he's at the entrance, take him. Report status when complete." I sharply exhaled, not realizing I had been holding it in this whole time. Shane would be safe, and I was relieved. I couldn't wait to see him. But after what Robbie said, I'd be lucky if he ever wanted to see me again. Would he forgive me?

Will I forgive myself?

Robbie

Once Shane was out of sight, I knew he'd be safe. I did it. I got him out without Steven hurting him any worse. I felt a boost of confidence that I could really do this. End everything, once and for all.

"Wow. That was harsh. You're a stone-cold bitch. Maybe I should have recruited you into the family business," Steven teased.

"You're unbelievable. The shit in that case opened my eyes to just how despicable you are."

"Did it now. And what was that exactly?" he taunted.

"That you're worse than the criminals you lock away. That you swore an oath to serve and protect, but instead you're a hypocrite. You play both sides, benefiting from all of it, doing anything to get your way. You hurt people for fun, Steven. All the while hiding behind your badge. Intimidation, assault, murder. And now? Kidnapping an innocent teenager. It's all loathsome, and you have no redeeming qualities."

"And your point?" he sneered.

"Enough! I'm here to get answers."

"Answers to what? That I'm the bad guy? That I was mean to you and your mommy? Well, boo hoo. Now take me to the damn case!"

"All my mother gets is your sarcasm? She loved you, and you deceived her!" I screamed, holding my aim steady.

"Well, isn't that the same thing you just did with that poor sap and his brother?" he chided.

"I didn't murder anyone! And how dare you make this about me? I lost everything because of you. My home. My mother. I need to know why. Why us? Was she an easy mark because she was a single mom with a kid? Was she too trusting? Too clueless?"

"Till she wasn't," he snapped.

"So, that's it then. That's where you screwed up. You underestimated her. And now you've underestimated me. I keep coming back no matter how many times you try to kill me."

"Well, that ends now. Take me to the case, or I will…" he fumed, training the gun on my face.

"Will what? Hit me again? Kick me again? Grope me again? Or will you skip all that and just shoot me this time?" I seethed.

"So mouthy now. Lark would have—"

"You do *not* get to say my mother's name," I screamed, and through a blind fury, I hauled off and hit him across the side of his head with my gun, stunning him. He stumbled back, blood pouring down his face.

"Oh, you're dead!" he spat, lifting the gun toward me again, trying to see.

I stood my ground and pointed my gun back at him. "I wouldn't do that if you ever want the flash drive. I mean it, Steven! Tick tock. The emails will go out soon."

"You're lying," he said, wiping blood dripping down his forehead.

"Try me," I challenged.

He hesitated, contemplating whether I was lying or not. "Take me to the case. I'm done playing these games."

Kyle

I was glued to the monitor and Robbie, who dug herself in deeper with every moment that passed. Staying in the van felt far too difficult of an order. I jumped when one of Tanya's security team tapped me on the shoulder.

"What's happening?" I asked, concerned.

"Your brother's outside and wants to talk to you."

"Oh, thanks."

I reluctantly stepped out. I felt conflicted between leaving the monitor and seeing my brother. I was thankful Shane was safe, but worried that Robin was not. The parallel of his injuries to Robin's was strikingly similar, and all because of that same man. It sent a chill through me.

Shane held ice to his eye, looking pretty banged up. He had a black eye forming with a cut above his brow. His mouth and nose looked swollen and bloody, and he was limping. But overall, I guess he was okay. For just having been kidnapped.

I stood there trying to get words out. Any word. There was so much to say. To apologize for but I wasn't quite sure where or how to begin.

"Hey," Shane said.

"Hey. You okay?" I asked.

"Yeah. Sore, but okay."

"I saw you limping. How are your knees?" Soccer meant everything to Shane. It's been his dream for as long as I can remember.

"A little banged up, but I think they're good."

I nodded my head.

The long, awkward pause between us spoke volumes.

"So… Tanya's team filled me in on everything. You should have told me, Kyle. You should've told me that he hurt her this summer. That she was in danger and needed help. That our family was in danger. I could have done something. We could have done something together.

"But instead, you lied to me about everything. The assault, her alias, and about… the two of you. I could've handled it, but you didn't give me a chance. And then this dude shows up demanding answers about Wren? Roughing me up when I couldn't answer? All because I had absolutely no idea who the hell he was talking about," Shane's voice strained.

"I know. I'm sorry, Shane. For all of it. I should've told you everything. And I'm so sorry he hurt you. I never thought he'd go after you. Neither of us did. And I'm sorry I hurt you too. That we hurt you. Honestly, it just happened. The two of us. Everything was so chaotic at the beginning of summer, and when it finally settled… she's like a force I've never known before. And by the time I realized what was happening—"

"It was too late," Shane said wistfully.

"Yeah. It was," I said, surprised, because that's exactly what happened. "I really tried to forget about her, Shane. To move on with Kira, but…"

"There's something about Robbie that draws you to her. It's hard to describe, and it's hard to let go of," Shane answered pensively. It was like I was looking at Shane for the first time. Despite our closeness in age, we never really "got" each other until now, and it was because of her.

I knew what he meant because I had felt it this summer. Her gravity pulls you in, and it won't let you go. The attraction of her life force is so powerful—

Suddenly, I heard Tanya barking orders from the van, and I swung around to see what was happening. "Move in. Move in. Neutralize. I repeat. Neutralize," Tanya conveyed to her team. The look on Shane's face mirrored my own.

Panic.

Robbie

Steven and I walked around the corner of the storage units to a garbage tote rack behind the building. I knew we'd had to have been out of view of Tanya and her team, and I had to act quickly. Everything was going exactly as planned, for the most part. A sense of euphoria took over, knowing that I would finally be able to avenge my mother's death and make him pay.

I lifted the garbage tote lid, and he pulled the case out. He sat it on the lid and tried to open the case. Frustrated that he couldn't, he swung it around for me to open. As soon as I did, he snatched the briefcase back and started digging around inside, distracted by the case's contents.

"Where is it?" Steven scowled as he continued digging.

"Oh, you mean this?" I showed Steven the flash drive taped to the butt of my gun. He looked down to grab his gun, and that's when he saw I had grabbed his in that moment of distraction. The look of shock on his face was priceless.

"You look surprised, Steven. Karma's a bitch, isn't it?" I boasted.

"I should have killed you in June," he spat.

"Yes. You should have."

"So, what now? You're going to kill me?" he asked icily.

"It's what you deserve."

"Go ahead then. Pull the trigger, little girl," he goaded. And I tried.

I tried so hard to squeeze that trigger. But I couldn't. No matter how hard I willed myself, I just couldn't do it. I cursed myself for being a coward as he laughed in my face.

Unexpectantly, the sound of Tanya's team approaching in the distance diverted my attention for a split second. Steven launched the case at me, and it knocked me off balance. He crashed into me, and we fell to the ground. He banged his head and blindly grabbed for a gun when I kicked him.

I crawled away, trying to stand, but he gripped my legs and flopped me onto my back. He pulled himself up my body. I tried to shove him off, but he was too heavy, and I couldn't move. He smacked me, my face wincing in pain. In that moment, he rolled off me and grabbed his gun from my hand.

We both raised our guns and aimed.

Kyle

As Shane and I strained to hear what Tanya was yelling, we heard a gun go off in the distance. The sound made the blood drain from my face. I sprinted toward the storage facility's entrance when the security team stopped me. They pulled me back to the van.

"Please, Tanya. I need to get to her. I need to see if she's okay. Please!!" I begged for my life. For her life.

"The best thing you can do right now is to stay put and let us handle the situation. We are trained for this. Let us do our job," Tanya ordered.

"I'm begging you, please!" I could feel the burn of tears pricking my eyes, the lump in my throat, and the ache in my heart.

"Keep him here," Tanya demanded. I stood there in shock with the not knowing killing me. Tanya said neutralize. That couldn't be good. It could mean she was shot or worse. A shiver ran through my entire body when I felt a hand on my shoulder. I spun toward my brother.

"Shane," I choked out. I didn't have to say anything more. He knew and pulled me into a hug.

"It's going to be okay. She's going to be okay. She's strong. Stronger than I've ever seen before. She was... incredible," Shane reassured.

"I know she is," I confirmed.

Shane pulled back and stared at me intently. "Let's get you into that storage facility. Call for a medic."

"What?" I asked, confused. Shane fell to the ground, groaning and flinching like he was in agonizing pain. He looked at me and nodded his head toward the security team.

"I... uh... I need a help. Something's wrong with my brother!" I yelled. Emergency personnel swarmed, and I was able to slip by Tanya's distracted team at the entrance. Once inside, I sprinted as if my life depended on it. Because it did.

As I turned the corner, I stopped dead in my tracks. I saw a dozen security team members, all with their guns drawn, yelling, "Drop the weapon." I couldn't see what was happening. I quietly made my way closer, staying tight against the storage units. I squeezed against a nearby group of garbage totes and tried to get as close to them as possible.

The agents were still making demands when I saw Steven sitting on the ground, bleeding from his head but still very much alive. My heart sank. The shot I heard wasn't her gun going off. It was his. He furiously pointed his gun at the team.

As I inched forward, an iron laden smell wafted past my nose. That's when I realized he wasn't pointing it at the agents; he was pointing his gun at Robbie. Her body lay on the ground while a medic gave CPR. I felt sick and stumbled back, almost losing my balance.

I knew I had only a small opportunity. I lunged to get to her when I was grabbed by more of Tanya's team. They dragged me away from the scene. From her. I fought with all my might to break free, but it wasn't enough. The agents picked up their pace and quickly removed me from the area.

As we went past a few rows of storage units, I heard another gunshot. Hurried chatter on their walkies called for backup and more medical support. The agents continued moving me toward the facility's exit when I heard another transmission over the walkie. To send in a coroner.

I felt my body go limp in the agents' arms. "It can't be her. It can't be her," I repeated, shock setting in.

Dread overtook me as I felt my future slipping away.

CHAPTER 30
I didn't have to...

Robbie

AS MY EYES fluttered open, I felt every nerve in my body. And they were all on fire. Every single muscle ached, and it hurt to move. I glanced around groggily and couldn't focus on my surroundings.

That's when I heard a familiar snore. I slowly turned my head, seeing Kyle slouched in a chair asleep next to my bed. I tried to speak, but nothing came out. That's when I noticed all the wires and the beeping machines.

A nurse entered the room.

"Well, hello there. You're finally awake. Let's get some vitals," the woman said with an upbeat, singsong voice. I turned to look at Kyle again. "He's been right there for the last two days, practically growing roots. He refused to leave your side. Even for a minute. The rest of your family's here too, but they're in the waiting room. I'll let them know you're awake when we're done."

"Thank you," I squeaked out through my scratchy throat. When the nurse left, I heard Kyle shift in his chair. When I looked over at him, he was grinning from ear to ear.

"Hey there," he said, sitting up.

"Hey back," I replied, smiling.

"Boy, you definitely know how to make a scene, don't you? And here I thought you were only dramatic at school. You just had to prove me wrong." He chuckled, leaning over to kiss me gently on the lips.

"What happened?" I asked.

"Well, the bastard shot you. Hit you square in the shoulder, above your heart. You lost a lot of blood and stopped breathing, but they got you back. You needed surgery, and you've been out cold for two days."

"And Steven?"

"He's um… well, he's dead."

"I killed him?" I asked, surprised.

"No. But you did shoot him. You clipped him, but it was enough that he couldn't get away before the security team moved in. They held him at gunpoint, trying to get him to drop the gun and surrender. I guess deep down, he knew his life was over either way. Especially since you looked dead. So, he put the gun to his head and… died there on the scene. You really don't remember any of it?"

"No. Not really. I mean, I remember aiming and the gun going off, but that's it." I said, processing all the information he shared.

"You okay?" he asked.

"Yeah. I just didn't expect to feel… nothing. I thought at least I'd be happy or relieved that he was gone, but instead I feel nothing."

He held my hand. "Well, I'll feel glad for both of us. Because when I saw you lying on the ground, I felt my soul leave my body. I thought I lost you, Robbie. It was the worst, most horrible moment of my life."

"I'm sorry that I scared you. But you're stuck with me. Apparently, I don't die easily," I joked.

"Don't even joke. I only want boring days in our future. I think I've had enough danger and drama to last me a lifetime."

I giggled. "How mad was Tanya?" I asked nervously.

"Oh, man. She was furious. I mean, it was a good thing you were already shot because I think she would've done it herself."

"Oof," I said.

"Yeah. That's putting it mildly. Once she knew you'd survive, she made it known that you were coming in for a very long debriefing. Something to look forward to when you get out of the hospital." I grimaced, and he mirrored the expression back. "Robbie, can I ask a question? It's something that's been weighing on my mind."

"Sure."

"Where'd you get the gun?"

"Oh, I... it was in the case. My mother had it in there. It must have belonged to Steven."

"And you didn't tell me about it in the hotel room, why?" he chided.

"Because of how you're looking at me right now. I knew you would have stopped me."

"Damn straight, I would have. That was reckless, Robbie. What were you thinking?" he scolded.

"That I needed to finish this; the gun was my only insurance. I fell into his trap in June and was practically killed. I was unprepared then, and I wouldn't let that happen again. He was never going to let us live, Kyle. Never. I needed to throw him off his game just enough to keep the upper hand so I could save Shane. And myself, hopefully."

"It was dangerous," he rebuked.

"It worked."

"You got lucky," Kyle admonished.

"I know. I'm sorry. I really am," I said sincerely.

Kyle took a cleansing breath. "Robbie, I love you, with everything I am. And I know it all worked in the end, although it was messy as hell. But we can't have secrets or lies between us anymore. About anything. You have to promise me."

"Okay. I promise, Kyle. Only the truth moving forward. And in the spirit of truth, I have one more to share."

"Now what?" he questioned nervously.

"I love you, with everything that I am, too."

He smiled and shook his head. "You definitely like to make my heart race."

"Yes, I do," I grinned.

He grinned back as he leaned down and gently kissed my lips, my heart fluttering. This kiss was filled with so much love, trust, and truth. It was perfect. The heart rate monitor beeped as Kristie burst into the room.

"Oh gosh, Robbie! Thank goodness you're okay. We've been worried sick," she exclaimed breathlessly. She hugged me, and I groaned from the bullet wound. "I am so sorry. I forgot," Kirstie apologized. She left to chat with the nurse, who had entered with them, as Shane approached my bedside.

"Hey there," Shane greeted.

"Hey. How are you?"

"I'm okay. Just banged up a bit. You're the one that took a bullet, which is pretty badass if you ask me," he joked.

"Thanks. It feels pretty badass too, but not in a good way," I grumbled before pausing a moment. Unsure how to begin. So much happened that an apology wasn't enough. I needed to beg him for forgiveness and hope that someday he would find it in his heart to do so.

"Shane, I wanted to…"

"I know. We don't have to talk about it now. We need time to process. All of us. But I want to say thank you for literally putting your life on the line for mine. You were brave, and I've never seen you so strong before. It made me see the real you, Robbie. The type of person who's selfless, determined, and smart. Who would risk everything, including their own life, for someone else? It reminded me of why I fell for you. And why Kyle did too."

"Shane…" I barely choked out.

"It's okay. We'll be okay. I know there are conversations that need to be had, but we don't have to do them now. I want you to know that I'm so happy you're okay. I really mean it."

"Shane. I can't tell you how much that means to me. I'm glad you're okay too. That's all I wanted," I said honestly.

"Thanks for saving me."

"Anytime," I teased.

Kirstie abruptly interjected, wiping tears from her eyes, "Nope. Nope. Nope. All of you are out of the danger business. I mean it! My heart can't take it. And since you all live under my roof, you must follow my rules. And from now on, my number one rule is: no more danger!"

"You're still letting me live with you?" I gasped.

"Of course," Kirstie replied, surprised. "I know it'll be hard. There'll be some awkwardness and tough times ahead, but you're a part of this family, Robbie. And that means you take the good and the bad. The highs and the lows. Because we fight for family. And if what you did doesn't prove that, then I don't know what will."

Kyle squeezed my hand and smiled. I blinked, trying to stop the tears from falling, but it was useless. I looked around the room at all of them. Kirstie. Shane. Kyle. They were my family now. My future. It's what I've always wanted. Kirstie was right. Family was worth fighting for, and I would fight for this family. I knew my mother would approve, looking down on me and smiling. The best part of my future?

I didn't have to pretend anymore.

Continue the story with...

Misdirect

The companion book to my debut novel
<u>Pretend</u>

Follow Shane Whitmore as he embarks on his rise (and fall) in the world of soccer.

Will he push everyone away? Or will he accept help and find solace?

Available NOW!

About the Author

I'm a dreamer and love all types of storytelling: books, movies, TV, and music. Over the years, I have made many stories, but they've only lived in my head. With raising a family and teaching full-time, I was always too "busy" to follow my dreams. I had always hoped to write a book and publish it one day. So finally, I did. Although it's super scary to share the stories in my head, I knew in my heart it was time. I'm a published author. Dream achieved!

Now, a few acknowledgments: Thank you to my team at Tempered Ink for all their hard work with editing, cover art, and website design. I literally could not have done it without you!! Thank you to my family for encouraging this literary journey... once they knew about it. ☺ Thank you to my beta readers: Debbie, Nancy, Dianne, and Julie. I appreciate all the feedback to make it a better story.

Jennifer Conklin, a former special education teacher, turned full-time author. She resides in New York with her husband, their younger son (recent college grad), and their two sweet pups. Their older son, his wife and their infant daughter live nearby, making her a VERY happy mom and grandma!

Check out my other books:
Fine Line Series (YA Novel Series)
**MISDIRECT- Book 2*
The Adventure Above Series (Children's Book Series)
**SHE WHO WALKS ABOVE THE TREES- Book 1*
**SHE WHO SWIMS ABOVE THE SEAS- Book 2*
**SHE WHO FLOATS ABOVE THE BREEZE- Book 3*
Visit me at:
www.jenniferconklinauthor.com
or www.happydetours.com
Facebook & Instagram: @jenniferconklinauthor